Crappily Ever After

By Louise Burness

For the real life Ramseys, including the ones who now watch over us.
You give me no end of stories to tell. Thank you for your never-ending humour, love and support.

Chapter One

Have you ever wondered what sets the precedent for a lifetime of choices? Perhaps it is the earliest memories that will determine your choice of friends, career path and partners? For me, it was probably my male influences who set the tone for my future failures – and believe me when I say some of those failings were quite spectacular. Don't get me wrong, the women in my life were wonderful people; but being female myself, they didn't hold the same mystique. The men surrounding me then set a high ideal that now seems impossible for any man to live up to. OK, they weren't infallible, but they were certainly way over my innocent expectations. Maybe it's the memory of being pulled onto my Granddad's knee for a hug when he came home from work, having the honour of choosing the scores for his pools coupon and discussing what we'd do with the money when he won?

Could it be the various adoring uncles who looked on fondly as I made my first attempts to apply make-up to my five-year-old face and then told me, without laughing, how beautiful I was, despite looking like I belonged more in a circus than a beauty pageant? Or perhaps it was the early trauma in my life that created an air of mystery surrounding the male species? I'm not sure, but I know it exists for me. Do I assume that all men will be as wonderful as my first experiences of the opposite sex? I guess so, otherwise why would I have ended up with some of the biggest losers without meaning to? Yet time and time again have the expectation that they will be fabulous – the perfect man. I mean, by your mid-thirties you should at least have some degree of cynicism, instead of the hopelessly idealistic anticipation of a child, combined with a puppy's need to please and the memory of a goldfish, to forget those failings, and blunder blindly from relationship to relationship. What a mess. But I'm complicating things. Let me start at the beginning.

My first memory of romantic disillusionment began, aged nine, in my Grandmother's living room. My younger sister, Mary, and I were snuggled under a blanket, fresh in from making a slush man in the Scottish December. It was two days before Christmas and the fairy lights on the tree twinkled brightly. It was 6pm and already dark outside, with patterns of frost on the window panes. The perfect seasonal ambience. We had worked ourselves into a state of exhaustion with the excitement of the forthcoming days. Gran walked into the living room and smiled tenderly at us. She put down two steaming mugs and walked over to the electric fire. Having switched on an extra bar, she pulled the fleece blanket tighter around my sleepy, thumb-sucking sister.

'Mary can have her hot chocolate if she doesn't fall asleep. It's still a bit hot, leave it a minute or so.' Gran switched on the old black and white TV with the folding doors which, when guests happen by, disguised the fact that we're anti-social enough to have a television. Luckily, the movie that was playing – It's a Wonderful Life – was in black and white, so for once we didn't feel poor compared to our friends with colour sets.

I was later given the movie in 'Glorious Technicolor' by my sister, and though the -It's no longer the '70s, we should not be deprived-sentiment was well meant, it just wasn't the same. 'I love this movie, Lucy, you will too. Mary will be old enough to appreciate it next year.' Gran smiled nostalgically and stroked back my over-grown fringe.

She was right. I did love it; I liked George, he had dreams. Me too, I had just completed my Brownies First Aid badge and I wanted to be a nurse when I grew up. George was funny, kind and saved an orphanage kid from being poisoned, as well as his little brother Harry from the ice. So there we were, Lucy and Mary Ramsey, having been encouraged into a rite of passage movie classic. Except Mary had fallen asleep, her hot chocolate now cold. I thought about drinking hers too, but it had that horrible skin on top that I hate. Like swallowing a slug. I sat agog as George stormed out of his home on Christmas Eve. Why would anyone want to leave the festive atmosphere? What could possibly be so important that you would forget the wreath for the front door? This normally fun-loving person, a wonderful father and husband. Something must be terribly wrong. This was the moment I decided that, I too, would marry the perfect man and be as strong and loyal as Donna Reid's character. Once I had found my soul mate and had my four children (yes, one named Zuzu), I would live happily ever after in a cosy world of Christmas-time, where *every* angel gets his wings.

The movie ended and my eyelids grew heavy. I snuggled into Mary. Gran nodded over to Granddad. He scooped up my sister and carried her upstairs, returning to pick me up and tuck me into the double bed that Mary and I shared. He reached down and switched off the electric blanket and kissed us in turn on the forehead. I inhaled his scent of Brylcreem and Old Spice, before drifting into a deep, warm sleep. At 8am Mum crawled in beside us. Back from nightshift. Chilly from the winter air and smelling of early morning wood smoke from the chimneys. Mary and I instinctively flung an arm each around her neck. It's Christmas Eve, I realised, with a small, excited squeak, and squeezed closed my eyes in a vain attempt to drift off again.

Fast-forward twenty-six years. In the London suburb of Islington, a Vodka-fuelled session has culminated in a screaming match at my portable TV.

'Loada shite!' yells Becky, good friend and flatmate from

Dublin. 'Absolutely no feckin' men out there like George Bailey!'

'I don't know,' I shrug. 'I've known a few suicidal Mummy's Boys who couldn't wipe their own arses in my lifetime.'

'Whatever,' dismisses Becky, 'I'm off to bed; it's Saturday tomorrow, only three sleeps 'til Christmas – so many men, so few morals. I have to look my best. And no, before you say it, I know I can't lose half a stone overnight! So I'll just have to go with reduced eye bags and take it from there.'

Becky pauses and gazes sadly at our dilapidated Christmas tree. It's been ten months since she broke up with Bob, her partner of three years. It had come as a huge shock to Becky, who had been deliriously happy and had assumed Bob was the same. He had begun to act nervous and distant in the weeks running up to Becky's birthday. She had called me at work and declared that he was most definitely about to propose. Becky was then on a mission. She dragged me into every jeweller we passed to fuss over rings. She held each one up to catch the light and told the saleswoman that her boyfriend had already asked her to marry him, and had sent her out to find a ring. In reality, she simply wanted to have found the perfect one when he finally asked her, but without the pitying glance of a sales person thinking she was deluding herself. God forbid Bob would choose one himself. Many a discussion we had on how to get around this. I was to chat to him about it discreetly; I never got the chance. Bob had 'the talk' – as it was now referred to – with Becky one week later. It turned out he was nervous and distant because he had been sleeping with a girl from work. He had tried to wait until after Becky's birthday, but couldn't stand the guilt any longer. He told her about his fling and promptly dumped her. For her own good, of course, according to him. She didn't deserve him and should be with someone who adored her and wouldn't even look at anyone else. Too true, but she was devastated.

I nursed Becky through almost two months of despair; bringing her soup in bed and agreeing that, yes, all men *are* bastards. Demanding she get showered and dressed on weekends, before finally flipping out on week seven. I informed her that I'd had enough of the moping. I did understand – I truly did – but enough already. I told her I was off on a night out on the pull and had bought a new top and she could get her own soup that night. A flicker of interest illuminated her eyes. I attempted to decipher the flicker. Soup? No, surely not. Going out on the pull? Possibly, but doubtful.

'Can I see your new top?' Becky asked tentatively. She was on the road to recovery.

But that night, three days before Christmas, Becky was obviously caught in a moment of feeling haunted by the ghosts of boyfriends past. I decided I was too exhausted to deal with the inevitable tears and hysterics that would no doubt ensue, and vowed to be a much better friend in the morning. I would only be too truthful about what I thought of him right now; she would be defensive and we'd end up falling out. Sometimes it's what you don't say that speaks volumes, I reasoned.

Allow me to digress slightly. I have discussed my own personal issues about men – in depth – with family and friends. Responses vary from:

'You're far too bloody fussy!' and 'stop trying so hard' to my Mum's contribution,

'You have the Cinderella complex. Stop looking for a Prince and settle for a nice frog.' Helpful? Well no, actually. Not when your Prince is George Bailey and not even Jimmy Stewart himself could have lived up to that. I wouldn't actually mind a nice frog, but the ones I seem to attract are, in fact, toads. Besides, my life *is* a fairytale. Let's see: there was Grumpy, Dopey, Psycho, Stalker, Liar, Idiot and Thief. Gullible and the Seven Tossers!

Saturday dawns – far too early for my liking – with our over-enthusiastic housemate vacuuming outside my room. I swing open the door and give him a glare worthy of Medusa. What could possibly possess someone to clean at nine o'clock on a Saturday morning? Mind you, Ian is a bit of a goody-two-shoes and in bed ridiculously early, even at weekends. I'm suspicious of teetotallers, unless it's for health or religious reasons. His are neither. Why would you choose not to drink? Nothing puts Mr. Bluebird on my shoulder faster than a large glass of Pinot Grigio.

Ian smiles sweetly at me and informs me that there is fresh coffee in the pot. Oblivious to the mascara- encrusted, 'styled by having fallen in a hedge' mad woman who doesn't look best pleased to see him. I shove past, grabbing one of a selection of our chipped mugs. Choice of today is 'Do I *look* like a people person?' Pretty apt for how I feel.

I pour a strong black coffee and pluck a cigarette from the spare morning pack I keep in my dressing gown pocket. Well, if Ian can ignore the 'No Housework before lunchtime' house rule, I can ignore the 'No Smoking in Shared Areas' one.

I carefully flick my dog end into next door's garden. The old bat next door is mad as a box of frogs. She raged at me last week, for forgetting my keys and shouting up to Becky to let me in. I'd only just got back from work, it was hardly the middle of the night.

I pad along the freezing hallway to the shower. The bathroom window rattles in the frame as I turn on the water. I look at the cubicle in disgust. Time for yet another note for the hairy Italian man who shares my landing.

'Do not use my soap! I will send it for DNA-testing if

necessary, but I am pretty sure that these are your pubes!'
He is truly disgusting. My last note, a week ago read:
'Peeing whilst showering is *not* good time management!'
As was his excuse last time I complained about this.
I know it's him, there are only three of us who use the bathroom; Ian is obsessive about scrubbing out the shower once he's used it and it certainly wasn't me.
There was no mistaking the yellow puddle. I finish my shower and decide to see if Becky is awake. Maybe a little pre-Christmas lunch out would be the order of the day.

Sitting in our local pub, the Frog and Bucket, two and a half hours later, we are well into a third bottle of wine. I reflect on the fact that I had informed Becky that I was going home by six o'clock. I'm on an early train home to Scotland tomorrow and do not relish six and a half hours on a train, with a hangover. She had sniggered knowingly and raised her eyebrows in disbelief. And, true to form, by six o'clock I was back at the bar, shouting my order to the barman for two cocktails. On my somewhat wobbly return to the table, Becky dissolved into uncontrollable giggles. It bothers me that she knows me so well, and how little encouragement I need to be led astray.

By seven we're staggering around our local Supermarket. Trying desperately – and failing – to not find it funny that we are so blatantly hammered. So far our basket consists of: one chicken tikka masala, one lamb bhuna, poppadoms, a multi-pack of crisps, a family sized bar of chocolate and two bottles of Pinot Grigio. Added to this by the time we leave the shop are two packs of cigarettes; this is due to the fact that I always completely over-estimate how much I will actually smoke and drink, when drunk.
'Will you take a look at that? A heart attack in a carrier bag,' I

announce, peering into our selection of shopping.

We get off at the stop after our usual one, having missed it due to dulled reactions. We walk back towards home, arguing over the importance of whose curry should be heated first. Becky wins, based on the fact it's her microwave from the old flat, and if I had to oven cook mine it'd take forty minutes as opposed to the six minutes it will take to wait until she cooks hers. We lean into each other for support as we walk and cackle at the earlier amorous attempts of one of the bartenders who so obviously fancies Becky, but who is so 'under her league', as she puts it.

By nine we decide that it's best to open our presents for each other, from under the tree. It saves taking them all the way home to Ireland and Scotland to open them and then bring them back. Ten o'clock and we're dancing to one of Becky's gifts from me – titled something along the lines of, '*Cheesiest Christmas Songs Ever, Volume Two*' – and wearing the suitable attire of one of my gifts from Becky; Stripy socks, one each; matching gloves, one each; and, to complete the set, a bobble hat, taking it in turns to wear – at the moment it's mine. We really did wish it would be Christmas every day. The walls reverberate as Ian and crazy lady next door take it turns to hammer on them.

'Bah bloody humbug,' shouts Becky. She turns the volume up further and hammers on the walls back at them. I don't quite remember anything after that, other than the horror of looking at the clock and noticing it had turned midnight. So much for good intentions.

I stir blearily at eight o'clock the following morning, raising my spinning head to take in a stripy-socked leg draped over me. The bobble hat has slipped over Becky's eyes and all I can see is the tip of her nose and a wide snoring mouth.

Sitting bolt upright, I ponder my situation.

'Late! … Work? … Shit, *train!*' I frantically put together the pieces of today's planned events. I have one hour to get to King's Cross; luckily, Becky has three hours to get to City Airport. Shoving her off me, I make the dash to the shower. Gagging at the exfoliant effect of hairy soap grazing my body. I bolt back to the bedroom and throw my wet towel onto Becky, with the aim of hiding her eyes from the sight of my bare backside. I'm pretty sure it's the last thing she needs to see this morning.

'What's up?' her muffled voice queries from under the towel.

'Get up! We have flights and trains to catch. We have to go.'

Becky shoots out of bed as if she's been electrocuted and sprints upstairs to her bathroom. Luckily, she has a separate one from me, shared by clean and sweet-smelling girls. How unfair. I was living there first. Luckily for her, Stu the serial shagger had been evicted two weeks after she moved in; his presence was why I hadn't taken her room over mine when the last idiot who inhabited her room left – and she moved in. Sharing a bathroom with Ian and the elusive, hairy Italian who left more skid marks down the toilet than you'd see at Brands Hatch had seemed, at the time, infinitely more appealing than constant sleep disruption from the squeaking springs emanating from Stu's room as he entertained his latest conquest.

Fifteen minutes and two hastily packed cases later and we're standing at the bus stop, squinting in our hungover states through the low winter sun in the direction our buses will arrive. My wet hair drips uncomfortably down the back of my neck as Becky licks a tissue and wipes the mascara from under my panda eyes. The Number 27 lumbers up the hill, Becky gives my arm a squeeze.

'Here's mine. Merry Christmas Luce, sweetie,' and she was off. Jammy bugger, I thought. Some of us landed on our feet in life. Some – and I was one of them – were arse-landers. She, who had infinitely longer than me to get to where she was going, was on her way first.

By some grace of God, I make it. Rushing through the doors of King's Cross Station, dodging tourists, business people, suitcases and buggies. I skip the queue as I know fine well that waiting at point A, B or C will only result in being directed to the platform that I can find instinctively by now. Another veteran 'Scot going home for Christmas' pulls up in position beside me. He hasn't booked a seat either – I just know it. I have learned a lot since the first pre-Christmas train I had taken from London, when I had to spend almost seven hours sitting on my rucksack. Obviously, I hadn't learned enough since then to make sure that I actually book a seat. Each year I had done the manic-eyed dash through the train to find the Unreserved Seats – until, that is, they introduced the Holy Grail for disorganised passengers. The Unreserved Carriage! Platform announced, fellow Scot and I make our way as swiftly as we can in a nonchalant 'I'm not in a hurry' kind of way. Eyeballing each other occasionally. Less seasoned travellers dwindle metres behind. If getting to the Flying Scotsman's Unreserved Carriage was ever made an Olympic sport, I would be a five times-over Gold Medallist.
'Which is the unreserved carriage?' fellow Scot bellows at the guard.
'There isn't one. It's Christmas!' He rolls his eyes, baffled by the stupidity of non-booking travellers. This bought me precious seconds. I wasn't involved in the niceties of conversation so, with a most unladylike snort and a smug look at fellow Scot, I make my way to the train like a bat out of hell.

Sitting contentedly in my seat, I had watched through my

eyelashes as he attempted to shove his bag into the storage compartment, before making his way down the aisle looking for any vacant seat without a ticket on the top. I was pretty sure I had the only one in the carriage. I couldn't help but mumble:

'Messing with the big girls now, huh?'

'Sorry?' he said, throwing me an attitude-laden glance.

'Oh nothing,' I soothed. 'Just saying what a pain it is to find a seat when you haven't booked. That's all.'

'You know for an extra £20 you can upgrade to First Class,' fellow Scot ventured. 'How about we go find out, crack open a bottle of wine and make our journey less traumatic?'

'OK, I'm up for First Class but after last night, you can hold the wine,' I shudder.

We make our way towards First Class with our upgrades. The carriage is practically empty. All these people standing in the corridors, yet all these seats sitting vacant. Mike introduces himself and buys us two coffees. We settle down in our luxurious seats.

'Heavy night last night?' Mike enquires.

'God, yes. I'm off home to see my family today, my sister has a rare night off from being the responsible adult and I just know she will want to party. I best get some recovery time in before I begin again.'

'Hey, isn't it strange to be talking to someone you don't know again. It's a very Northern thing,' Mike laughs.

'Yes, I know what you mean, just asking for the time in London has a person body-swerving you like you're about to mug them,' I laugh.

Mike explains he is an Advertising Consultant for a Victoria-based company. He's been in west London, living just off Chiswick High Road, for six years and originally from Aberdeen. He lives with his fiancée of two years, a beauty therapist, who has gone off to Hampshire to spend time with her own family. For some unknown reason, Mike has never been invited to spend Christmas with them.

'Sam would sort those eyebrows right out for you,' Mike offers generously. I frown and stroke a protective finger over a sadly neglected brow.

I tell Mike about my job in Highbury Fields, caring for three children, aged two, five and fourteen-years- old.

'I'm so over being a nanny,' I moan. 'Look up dysfunctional in the dictionary and you would find their family portrait.'

I explain how the two-year-old boy, Georgie, throws the most spectacular tantrums you have ever seen and regularly called me 'Mama'. This seemed to mainly coincide with the exact moment that the cutest guy I had seen that day walked by.

'No. Not Mama. Lucy,' I'd say every time, with great deliberation. Throwing a 'he's not mine, please ask me out' kind of look in the direction of aforementioned man.

'The five-year-old girl hasn't been able to stand me since the second day of my employment. On the walk to school – and in an attempt to break the ice and bond – I spotted a patch of oil mixed with rain on the road. In mock horror I turned to her and wailed:

'Oh no! A dead rainbow! It must have fallen from the sky and...'

Cue fifteen minutes of tears and a shamefaced new nanny explaining to Miss Smith that, 'Katie tripped on the way in and...'

'No... she... she said,' sobbed a hyperventilating Katie.' I sigh dramatically, noticing Mike covering his mouth to stifle a smile.

'That's the problem with five-year-olds. They have far too much damn vocabulary.

I have since discovered that the no-go areas – and their potential demises – with five-year-old girls include: ponies, kittens, puppies, fairies, butterflies and, of course, rainbows.

The safe list includes: snails, slugs, spiders, *boys*! (I nodded a bit too agreeably at that one) and Daddy when he's grumpy – and Daddy is not grumpy when?' Mike now openly laughs at my tale of woe.

'My third child and problem,' I complain, 'is fourteen-year-old Henry, who also hates me. Well, most of the time. After a particularly virulent week of acne, I enquired if he was attempting to grow another head – or perhaps it was an undeveloped conjoined twin seeking revenge? Jeez! Fourteen-year-olds really have no concept of humour. I actually would prefer it if he hated me full-time. It would keep him out of my way. Let's face it, he doesn't need a nanny apart from to make his meals and wash his clothes (I don't even want to know what those stains are). What can he possibly need? The downside is that he goes through these phases of fancying the pants off me. Snapping away on his crap excuse for a camera phone whenever I load the dishwasher and finding any excuse to brush past or touch me in some way. It's like looking after the reincarnate of Benny Hill,' I observe with a frown.

'Hmm,' muses Mike, in a mock 'get the hell away from children, Social Worker-type manner.' 'So quit then. What's your real love?'

'To go back to college, train to be a chef and eventually open my own restaurant,' I reply. 'However, my financial situation won't allow it; until I find a rich husband, I'll just have to carry on wiping arses, noses and tending to the needs of those spoilt brats.'

I tell Mike about the previous week at work and how I am becoming increasingly frustrated with my job.

'Funny how an entire week of my input and good work can be undone in just two days of the children being with their parents. Gone is 'please' and 'thank you' and in their place is 'I want!' and an angry snatch whenever they receive something. All in the space of a weekend.'

Mike nods sympathetically.

'Things reached boiling point two Friday mornings ago. Georgie threw the most horrendous tantrum in Sainsbury's over a toy he wanted, but I wouldn't buy. I had struggled to get him back in the buggy, but the harness is broken and, despite many requests by me, it hasn't been replaced. I guess it doesn't matter when you're so used to going everywhere by jeep. Why do so many London families feel it necessary to have 4 x 4s? I mean, just how much off-roading do they expect to be doing in Notting Hill or Putney? Of course, this means they also have to have the standard uniform of Barbour jacket and wellies combo for the school run.'

Mike laughs heartily and taps his plastic cup against mine in agreement.

'I know what you mean. There are some things I will never get about London. So, you find the perfect partner to either marry or cohabit with. Great! So far, so normal. Then, certain rules seem to apply: Buy a house: get a cleaner. Have a kid: get a nanny. Adopt a dog: get a dog walker.' Mike warms to his subject. 'I mean, when did people become so lazy that they could no longer take a dog out for a pee?'

'I know, and what grates so much on every nanny that I know is that dog walkers and cleaners get the same hourly rate as us. Can you believe it? I mean, put it in the perspective of responsibility here .I wrote this down once to present to my boss. She said she would read it and I found it on the top of the bin the next day.' Mike grabs a pen from his pocket and a napkin from the table. He poises his pen officiously and awaits my list.

Cleaners:
Aim: To clean house without breaking anything.
Objective: To leave the home shining like a new pin.
Main responsibilities: To not mix cleaning solutions together (can cause chlorine fumes which can kill). Do not use the same

cloth you used for the toilet on the kitchen surfaces.

Dog walkers:
Aim: To promote exercise
Objective: To allow dog to let off steam and having done its business.
Main responsibilities: Clean up said business accordingly. Return animal intact and without having mauled the leg of a toddler.

Nannies:
Aim: To nurture and keep safe.
Objective: To cater to all physical, intellectual, emotional and social needs. Organise activities and outings with the skill and expertise of Sir Edmund Hillary embarking on a climb up Everest (and with a similar amount of equipment). Educate within the constraints of the National Curriculum. Possess the ability to change a nappy, tackle a pile of ironing containing miniature items, put on a load of washing, discipline, tackle homework that you didn't understand first time around, provide fun activities without the use of television, praise, reward, sort out fights, arrange play dates for the next week, make up bottles, put a plaster on a knee, take phone messages for employer and collect dry cleaning. All while making an organic pot roast.
Main responsibilities: Spend ten hours a day averting danger from the combination of small people and trains, buses, cars, swings, climbing frames, plug sockets, kettles, cookers and each other. Ensure that they are fed, watered, sweet smelling, pyjama'd and in a good mood for when mummy and daddy return, crack open a bottle of Chablis and tell you how crap their day has been. While you slobber like one of Pavlov's dogs at the sound of a cork popping.

Mike finishes writing and glances up with a wry smile.

'Do you see what I mean? It's not that I begrudge cleaners

and dog walkers the money they get. Just like us, they provide a necessary service to the middle and upper classes. Nor do I think they should get less money for what they do. It's just that nannies should get more. People think it's a design flaw that so many career nannies remain childless and/or single. It's not. Equate it to a frustrated housewife who has spent 20 years raising a family and putting up with the mood swings of a husband who thinks you are beneath him because you don't have a 'proper job'. Then, imagine the liberation when the kids all leave home and you boot out said husband. Who would want to recreate that 24/7 scenario? Nobody.'

Mike nods sagely,

'Nanny burn-out. You've spent too long raising other people's families and you don't want to do it for yourself. You lack the energy, incentive and motivation.'

'Exactly!' I enthuse, 'Men resisting commitment should get themselves a nanny girlfriend; there are so many of us just as happy to avoid the marriage/baby route as you guys are. Preferring, instead, to commit to Caribbean holidays, a nice apartment in the city, spa treatments and spending all the money we've earned over the years and been too busy and knackered to spend. So many children are so very entitled these days too, it really doesn't help matters.'

I recount how last week Katie came out of school wailing that she hadn't been invited to the latest birthday party of a class member.

'You don't even *like* Sasha,' I'd protested. 'Last week she was a poo-poo head I seem to remember. How can you expect her to invite you?'

'That's not the point!' shouted Katie. 'This week I gave her a lolly.'

'Only because you knew the invites were going out on Thursday.' I'd raised my eyebrows at her. I had her on that one. I watched as her young mind tried to think of a suitable retort. She failed, and resorted to scuffing the toes of her shoes all the way home.

We returned to find a sulky Henry watching the Hard Rock channel on cable.

'How was your day, Henry?' I tried to arrange my features into something resembling an interested smile – and ended up with a half grimace, half escaped mental patient look.

'Hmmph.'

'Lovely,' I'd grinned sardonically.

Teatime had been traumatic. Georgie had tipped his bowl upside down onto his head and smiled at the other two through spaghetti hair. Hysterical laughter alerted me while I was loading the tumble drier. Katie's laughter, that is. I'm not sure Henry snorting and grunting through five octaves counts. I cleaned up without a word and spoon-fed Georgie the second batch of Spaghetti Bolognese.

'Eat up please, Katie.'

'Don't like 'sgetti.'

'You said last week it was your favourite. I made it with meatballs.'

'Actually, I think you'll find that I don't like Bolognese.'

'You obviously don't like ice cream either, then. Since you're not having any unless you have at least three more spoonfuls.'

Katie had reluctantly licked her fork and continued, holding her nose dramatically.

Bath time had arrived at last. One hour until the official start of the weekend.

'I'm not having a bath with *that*,' Katie had informed me disdainfully, head held high and indicating at a food-covered Georgie.

'Katie, you're fine, it's only food. He doesn't mind that he's running the risk of nits, worms and other school child afflictions.'

'Would you like to have a bath with a doubly incontinent,

slobbering mess?' Henry asked me, pointedly. I chewed my lip and thought frantically of a suitable response. An image of my Great Aunt in her rest home sprang to mind. He had a point.

Two separate baths later and I heard the tinkling tones of Sylvia, my female boss.

'How are my babies?'

'Mummy!' screamed the two youngest, thundering down the hallway.

Two hugs and one 'don't touch me' later, Sylvia opened a bottle of wine and poured herself a large glass.

'What a day, Lucy,' she sighed. 'You don't know how lucky you are being here all day. Oh, you do remember you're babysitting tonight, don't you?'

I'd looked up sharply. Never! There is no way I'd agree to a Friday night's babysitting – or any night for that matter – unless I was really, and I mean *really*, broke.

'Oh, Lucy,' she'd said exasperatedly. 'We arranged it weeks ago. It's on the calendar.' She'd waggled a finger knowingly at me.

I walked to the calendar. "Friday 16th of December. Lucy babysitting," feeling smugness emanate from behind me, I had swung around to look at her.

'See?' she'd smiled, triumphantly.

I ran my finger over "Lucy babysitting," It smudged.

'Oh my God! You just *wrote* that.' I'd whispered in disbelief.

'Oh Lucy, please,' Sylvia had pleaded. 'I totally forgot we have a dinner party with Simon's boss and he'll kill me if I've forgotten to book a babysitter.'

'I'm sorry, but I can't help. I have plans for this evening.' I put on my coat without looking at her, shouted goodbye to the kids, and left. By now, Mike has tears of laughter running down his face.

'Seriously, we need to change the subject before I actually piss myself. Please!'

We turn the conversation to what Mike wants from life. He confesses that he's always wanted to work overseas in his own bar. Preferably Greece or Spain. I emphatically agree and we decide that once I have done a cookery course we will open a place together: Mike on the bar, me in the kitchen, Sam giving massages on the beach and with my rich husband-to-be funding the whole thing. The journey flies by. Before we know it we are heading across the Tay Bridge towards Dundee station. We swap numbers for a New Year catch-up and so that Sam can fix my Denis Healey's, as my eyebrows are now referred to. I do the obligatory call home, so Mum can have a glass of wine poured and tea in the microwave. I wish Mike a happy and relatively painless time at home and brace myself for the biting North Sea air.

Chapter Two

I battle with my case and backpack up one flight of stairs and down the second set at Arbroath station. I spot my sister leaning against her car, smoking a roll-up and observing my struggle with an amused expression. Seemingly oblivious to the fact that all hell has been let loose in the back seat of her car, as her young daughter and son scream at each other over a packet of sweets.

'Hi sis, are they all right in there?' I envelope her in a nicotine-clouded hug, plucking the roll-up from her fingers, and inhaling several lungfuls before she snatches it back.

'Good to see you, doll. Don't worry about them. We've been at Mum's all day, wrapping and hiding *your* presents,' she accuses. 'Mum doesn't trust you after you opened and rewrapped them all last year. The kids are on a Haribo high, it should pass in an hour or so. I'm dropping them at home to their Dad now, so we can party.'

Mary is one year younger than me, but has always been the more mature one. She always seemed to know where she was going in life while I, in comparison, seemed to be the only one with no direction and no clue. We are also a complete contrast to each other; physically, Mary takes after our Mum's side of the family, while I take after Dad's. She has gorgeous red curls that everyone admires, but she hates them. God invented hair straighteners just for her, she claims. Mary had married young. Too young, she now says. Bill had been her first love and they were completely smitten with each other. Walking round High School holding hands and not caring who laughed. Neither had any aspirations to go to Uni. Bill started an apprenticeship as an electrician for the same company his Dad worked for; Mary took a job in our town's one and only department store, later changing to a different in-store shop when she got bored. They married two years later.

'I wish I'd held off until I had a bit of dress sense – and they had invented straighteners,' she later told me, putting down her wedding picture with a wistful sigh. A mass of red curls and a huge puffball dress was not, in her opinion, such a good look. We suggested she get married again in a blessing ceremony when the kids were born, with her new updated look.

'Do you really think I'd be stupid enough to marry him twice?' was her incredulous reply.

They did, however, hold off having kids until they were both thirty. Before they decided to start a family they took off for a late gap year around Australia and Asia; Mary came back already pregnant and, shocked beyond belief, tearfully asking me what the hell you do for nine months with no fags and booze? It was beyond me. She's the only person I know who had pre-natal depression.

It wasn't until Mary had Josh and Jess that things really started to sour with Bill. He did nothing. Absolutely nothing. Well, unless you count the fact that he gambled, drank too much and ignored her requests that he smoke outside away from her babies. Mary decided to discuss it with her mother-in-law, Joan.

'He's just like his bloody father,' snapped Joan, bitterly. 'If I haven't been able to do anything with Bill senior in thirty-five years, then I don't rate your chances with Bill junior.' They gripped their coffee cups with clenched fists and stared into space. Identical pained expressions on their faces.

We drop off the now sleeping children with their very reluctant father.

'Unbelievable that just fifteen minutes before they were screaming like banshees,' I observe.

Mary had informed me that she might have to stay at home as it could be a two-man job. Bill claimed he couldn't cope with them awake. So, we had driven around for an extra twenty minutes to send them off to sleep. We each struggle up the garden path, littered with roller skates, bikes and a football, under the heavy weight of a soundly sleeping child. Bill watches us mutely from the door with a can of lager in one hand and a fag in the other, looking as unattractive as ever in greying socks and boxer shorts. A fetching curry stain on his once white T-shirt. Mary informs Bill that he can stop looking at her with that combination of shock and disgust. She couldn't drink for the best part of two years while she carried Josh and Jess; one night of sobriety and being the responsible adult was not going to kill him. That said, we head down to Mum's. On arrival, Mum gives me a big hug and tells me I'm getting far too skinny, as she does every time I see her, despite my almost eleven-stone bulk. She places a huge plateful of sausage, mash and gravy in front of me – heart disease is one of the main hazards of having a Scottish mother. 'I know it's a lot, but it's the Taurean need-to-feed. It's out of my control,' she explains.

We have a lovely evening of festive TV. Normally, we would never dream of watching a church service but, as ex-choir girls, Mum and I love it. Despite thinking she could give Celine Dion a run for her money, Mary's singing – bless her – conjures up images involving a bag of cats, bricks and a river. There is something warm and comforting about a carol concert. We screech out hymns as if we still had fresh, non-nicotine addicted lungs. Within hours, the evening spirals downward into debauchery with a hilarious game of *Cataroo*. Think of the childhood game, *Buckaroo*, but on a live, sleeping cat. Mary goes first with a carefully placed gift tag. Poopsy, so named due to her aversion for the litter tray, snoozes on oblivious. I go next with a candy stick plucked off the tree. Mum tuts and fusses, declaring the game cruel and unnecessary, then wanders over with a bauble, also from the tree. By this stage we are all convulsed with silent laughter, apart from the odd snort or whimper. Two minutes later Poopsy has the addition of a Twiglet, a pickled onion, a mobile phone, one of my nephew's Power Rangers and then, the *piece de resistance* from Mary, the TV remote is heading Poopsy's way.

With an expectant 'Oooh' from Mum and me, Mary gently places the remote on Poopsy's rump. It's too much. The cat stands, shakes and strops off, much to the amusement of Mum and I. Mary rants that our gasp had disturbed the cat and therefore cost her the game. We end the evening with a ready-prepared buffet that, courtesy of Mum, appears from the never-ending fridge, and one more drink. The kind of house measure that'd see Geoff Capes off.

I come round briefly an hour later to the mutterings of my sister manoeuvring me into bed, *sans* boots, socks and anything I could inhale or choke on through the night in my inebriated state. My mother takes her role as a Health and Safety Officer very seriously.

'If she pisses the bed, don't expect me to sort it,' declares Mary. 'I do it at least twice a week as it is. And then there's the kids too.'

'Oh no, has Bill done it again?' Mum wearily enquires.

Just to add to his charms, Mary's wayward husband suffers from alcohol-induced enuresis. Actually, to be honest, Bill has enuresis – it's Mary who suffers from it. At least it's generally reserved for the hall cupboard and, luckily, has only ever been 'number ones.' Mary was on her third hoover purchase this year. Mum had informed her under no circumstances to plug it in. Mary did once and it stank of wee, but it didn't blow up like Mum had said it would.

Unbeknown to my sister, she had a new hoover from Mum as a Christmas present; something I had tried to talk her out of, whilst trying to hide from Mary in the Electrical Department, when I was last home in August.

'Who wants a Christmas present of a new hoover just in case your husband pisses on the current one in the next year?' My mother shot me the death stare for swearing in public. 'Mu-uum! It's right up there with a Lily of the Valley gift set,' I attempted to explain, to no avail. Ever practical, Mum won with a steely glare at me for my trouble and I stood there for another twenty minutes while she argued with herself whether an upright (kinder on the back) was better than a pull-along jobby (better for stairs). Eventually, I headed to the hardware department to buy Mary a padlock for the cupboard as a reinforcement – and to make sure that she never gets a hoover again for Christmas. Mum gives me a suspicious look, as if I am trying to out-do her gift with a £3.99 lock. They manage to get me into bed and I hear Mum ask Mary if I've mentioned a boyfriend?

'Nah. Luce by name, loose by nature,' my sister cackles. I briefly stir from my coma to hear a slap and an 'Oww' – Mum is a perfect shot. Reactions of a cat. I make a mental note to add a slap to that one tomorrow for Mary being a cow about me. But I forget by morning.

Christmas Day arrives. Brighter than any day I remember. I groan and attempt to roll over and disappear into the darkness of the duvet. A heavy weight on my chest stops me and I open my eyes to see Poopsy staring intently at me with yellow eyes. This Taurean need-to-feed of my mother's is most apparent in the cat – the one who lives there 24/7. Obviously, this is Poopsy's attempt at *Humanaroo*. I chuckle at my own joke and stroke her soft, white head. She begins to purr. I remove her gently and get up to walk to the bathroom in my underwear. At some point in the night I have shed the rest of my clothing. I meet Mum in the hall carrying an artery-clogging full Scottish breakfast.

'Merry Christmas poppet,' she kisses me on the cheek. 'Hungry?' I am actually, I observe. 'Merry Christmas Ma. I am, thanks. Feeling a tad rough though. I'll just go remove this badger's arse from my mouth and I'll be right back.'

'Can't say I'm surprised, darling,' she replies with only a touch of disapproval (it is Christmas after all).

'You always tell me that the liver is a very forgiving organ,' I remind her.

'Yes lass, but your liver would require the forgiveness of Mother Teresa.' I smile at Mum's joke and head off to de-badger.

By lunchtime, I am surrounded by discarded paper with Poopsy somewhere underneath the lot, torpedoing out occasionally. I marvel at how Mum can always get it so right. Every present thoughtfully considered and with the individuality of the recipient taken into account. It doesn't stop her from staring at me like Paddington Bear as every piece of sellotape is removed.

'You don't like it,' she informs me. 'That's fine, I'd rather know, I have the receipts for everything.'

'Mum, I love it,' I announce, chuckling at her worried expression, which increases now that I'm laughing. 'I'm only finding it funny because you're looking at me like that. If I didn't like it, I would say. I wouldn't waste your money that way.'

She visibly relaxes. I'm talking money, so I must mean it. I do genuinely love it – all of it – but I also know that mentioning money when I'm broke is the best way to get that across to her.

'Not the same without Scratcher this year is it?' reminisces Mum.

'Ahh no, it's not. He was a poorly puss though.'

Scratcher, so named for his love of soft furnishings, had died in the summer. Mum and Poops still missed him lots. 'Do you remember last year when I was writing Christmas cards by candlelight?' I giggled nervously, not sure I was forgiven yet. 'Scratcher flicked his tail through the candle and it set alight.'

'It brought a whole new meaning to putting the cat out,' Mum replied, and we both laugh.

'You don't think maybe that caused..?'

'No!' replied Mum firmly.

As I reflect guiltily on the incident, Mum begins clearing away the wrapping paper, finding an astonished looking Poopsy underneath the deepest pile.

I watch as Mum re-arranges the piece of tinsel around Dad's photograph. She smiles fondly at him and strokes a finger down his face. Dad was sitting on Gran's sofa with a can of lager in his hand and a pink party hat from a cracker sat lopsided on his head. Poor Mum found Christmas quite difficult to cope with. The photograph on the TV was the last Christmas she had with Dad. I was only a baby and Mum was pregnant with Mary when the news arrived. On 23rd December, a year after the picture was taken, a frantic call came from Dad's boss, asking if Mum had heard from Dad. He was a long distance lorry driver and had been taking a delivery to Glasgow. It was his last drop-off before Christmas and Mum and Dad were both looking forward to two weeks off together. There had been an accident on the M8 and Dave, Dad's boss, had put a call out on the CB to all his staff expected to be around that area, letting them know to divert to another route. Dad hadn't responded to the call. Mum immediately switched on the radio to hear the travel news. Gran tried to stop her and insisted she shouldn't listen. The crackling voice spoke of breaking news, of a jack-knifed lorry on the M8. Two other vehicles were involved. Mum just knew it was Dad. She and Gran sat quietly and waited for the police. Dave came round and joined the vigil. Head bowed, hands hanging loosely between his knees and a cold cup of untouched tea on the floor next to his cap. There was a knock at the door. They were here.

It turned out two young guys and their passengers were racing along the motorway. One had cut off the other several miles back and a chase ensued. Eye-witnesses said that Dad had desperately tried to miss them, swerving left and right, until he hit the central reservation. You didn't have to wear seatbelts in those days, hardly anyone did. The boys were fine – just cuts and bruises. Dad was killed instantly after smashing through the windscreen. Christmas was a non-event that year. Despite me being far too young to remember, Mum had felt horrendously guilty that I had a bad first Christmas and has tried to make up for it ever since. Mum puts Dad's picture down gently and walks through the living room. She stopped briefly to kiss me on the top of my head.
'You are so like him, Lucy,' she smiles sadly.

Later that afternoon we all congregate at my mum's sister's house, my Auntie Betty. We arrive to a cacophony of sound. A light-hearted argument over who was the funniest member of the family was the current topic. After doing the whole rounds of Merry Christmas wishes, I join in wholeheartedly and add my contribution – my sister, Mary. After all these years, she still cracks me up. 'Remember how she always used to make up her own words to songs rather than learn them?' I ask, smugly proud. Due to the fact that I had collected every issue of *Smash Hits*, I had the monopoly on knowing every word to every song from the 80s. Add to that the fact that I gained sound knowledge on trivia, such as what type of pants Ben from Curiosity Killed the Cat preferred, and George Michael's shoe size.

'I'll never forget the time I caught her singing along to *Tesla Girls* by OMD.' I double over with laughter. 'Testicles! Testicles!'

Everyone laughs and admits that this definitely puts her in the running.

'No, no, there's a better one,' I announce. 'How about, *Tonight, I Sellotape my Glove to You* by Peabo Bryson and Roberta Flack?' The room explodes into laughter. Mary, even though she hasn't arrived yet and is oblivious, is the favourite in the running.

The subject turns to the most unsuccessful family member. Bloody hell, are they planning to start a family yearbook I think defensively, knowing full well that this is my *forte*. The attention immediately turns to me. Silence. I wait for the tumbleweed to sweep through the family room. It's not that they don't know what to say, that's never a problem in my family. It's more that they don't know where to start. My Auntie Betty goes first. She smiles affectionately and says: 'Well, not too many people start their career in a 99p shop, pal.'

'I was fresh out of college and had yet to put my stamp on the world,' I state indignantly, but secretly enjoying a family title of some sort. Albeit a derogatory one.

'And besides, I think you'll find I was the Assistant Manager of a 99p shop,' I smile sarcastically. This does not carry the desired respect I crave. Laughter, yes.

'Oh, but her love life!' announces my Uncle Robert. 'Now that is where your lack of success really lies.'

This divides into sub-conversations throughout the family like a game of Chinese Whispers. With the aim of the game – whispering – somewhat wasted on them.

'James, now he was one of the worst!'

'Nah, Sean definitely, my own personal favourite.'

'How about Paul though? Remember that time he…'

Mary arrives. Husband and kids trailing behind.

'Who are we talking about?' she enquires.

'Lucy and her crap boyfriends,' my Aunt Sarah supplies helpfully.

'Oh, Alfie. Now he was undoubtedly the worst ever!' Mary smiles knowingly at me. The room nods as one.

'To my niece,' my Uncle Robert raises his glass and holds it in my direction. The others follow suit, 'The Fairy Tale Princess destined to live crappily ever after' I look around the room as a ripple of applause begins. I think I'd better explain.

Chapter Three

The Wonder Years... as in, I wonder what I was thinking? Despite the good intentions of my younger self, I have in total wasted 18 years – over half my life – on the biggest losers known to womankind. I have also lost a good few years of the 1980s to horrendously bad style. A fashion casualty, if you like. It's also the time I took a wrong career direction; childcare – too stressful and low paid – in my opinion now. It's also around this time I started smoking. Eighteen: you think you have it sussed, but for me, when I reflect on it now, it was the point when I made all my worst choices. Looking back, I am amazed I ever managed to even find someone who wanted to date me. These were the dodgy perm years. We all had them in the 80s. I was not alone on this. I had all mine done by a family friend's daughter, who was a trainee. She charged £3.50 – £2.50 for the solution and £1 for her time. I grudged every penny.

I'd tried to keep my emotions intact, having looked in the mirror for the first time after the deed. Being a trainee in a salon specialising in blue rinses hadn't helped Marianne's case at all. She had blow-dried me within an inch of my life. I stared at the elderly bouffant that looked super-imposed on my teenage face. It was strangely amusing and horrific, all at the same time. If it had been on someone else, I would have laughed my ass off. But, visualising having to take shares out in Insette on a college grant of £32 per week did not help. The industrial strength 1980s hairspray was a godsend to many a teenage girl and I must certainly put up my hand to a contribution to the hole in the ozone layer, along with my childhood budgie's fatal asthma attack. Having done the walk of shame across the street, I am greeted by Gran at the front door, buttoning her coat on her way out.

'It's lovely, dear,' she says. 'The ladies at the Stroke Club will love it. You should pop by for a cuppa.'

I head straight to the shower attachment over the bath and immediately soak my hair through. I wipe the steam from the mirror and stare, long and hard. I have been warned by Marianne to only comb it with an Afro comb. Otherwise, the curl will be damaged. Good, I think – and grab a paddle brush belonging to my aunt. Half an hour later, I am still confronted with a mass of curls. Mortified, I decide to peek round the door of the bathroom, where I encounter Robert in the hallway, red-faced and speechless with mirth, pointing silently at me. A minute passes as he runs to fetch Mary and Betty. I loiter self-consciously, may as well get it over with in one go. Apparently, I am so amusing that tears are now streaming down their faces. Eventually, Robert finds the words he is searching for:
'Pube head!'
Profound. The others collapse against him, nodding frantically through their laughter. It is my new name for the next two months. Actually, it's a blessed release from 'pancakes' – my previous name, due to my undeveloped chest.

Anyway, back to the disaster that is my love life. The first, being Sean, with whom I lived with for almost three years. I was at college studying to be a Nursery Nurse. Oh, if only I could now talk to my seventeen-year-old self in so many ways. I was at college only fourteen miles away and therefore still lived at home. I met Sean in a student bar in Dundee. He was standing at the end of the bar smoking a rolly and leaning lasciviously towards the barmaid. A peroxide blond with a top on that left nothing to the imagination. Tight, short and what appeared to be the arse of a Sumo wrestler protruding out of the top. Yes, the early warning signs do seem to be the most correct. Something I will take years yet to learn. If instinct makes your feet want to move in the opposite direction, do please listen. I whisper to my friend, Holly, with whom I have bunked off for an afternoon of snakebite (no blackcurrant, it's common) that I like the cutie by the bar.

'Join an orderly queue,' sighs Holly, tossing a glossy red lock over her shoulder and raising her eyes to the ceiling. 'That's Sean Taylor. Studying music, he's the lead singer in a band – The Magic Mushrooms. Everyone and their dog fancies him. He even has a huge gay following,' she states in a 'the subject is now closed' voice.

'Are you saying I have no chance?' I question.

'Well, of course you do.' She examines a spot on my chin closely. 'I just think it's a disaster waiting to happen. Cut out the middle man and just go spending the next three months from now bawling your eyes out and listening to your heartbreak tape whilst eating your way through an entire tin of Quality Street.'

Holly is three months older than me and therefore thinks she is much more worldly. I sulk and light up a Regal Small. I hate smoking. Again, if I could talk to me then… I do it because it gets me in with the rough mob at college. Always handy to have them on side, even if they did practically wet themselves on day two outside our college building. The ringleader, Jan, pointed at me, just in case there was any doubt about who she was humiliating, and spluttered:

'*You* smoke?'

'Have done since I was twelve,' I lied, trying to hold in a cough.

Ignoring Holly, I take a large slug of snakebite, lean forward and shake my 32A bosom further up in its training bra and saunter casually towards the bar.

'ID!' barks peroxide Sumo tits.

'Aww c'mon,' laughs Sean. 'Leave her alone Charmaine, she's far too small and cute to pick on.'

'ID,' smiles Charmaine smugly.

'No, that's fine,' I say. 'I actually take it as a compliment looking young for my eighteen years. Means that I won't look like a crack whore when I'm in my twenties.'

Sean explodes with laughter. Charmaine plucks my student card disdainfully from my hand and examines it. Even though I have checked it in various lighting since I doctored it with tippex and biro, it's still a tense moment. Those were the days; laminated paper ID. Thanks to a friend's ultra-cool mum who worked in an office and actively encouraged under-age drinking. Our reasoning being that she hoped other girls would get knocked-up aged 14 and have as crap a life as her. My ID was freshly laminated.

'Fine,' states Charmaine sarcastically, tossing it in a puddle of beer on the bar and reluctantly pouring up two snakeys.

'Are you in College?' asks Sean. 'You look fresh out of Primary School.'

'Yep, but I have a boyfriend. Don't get too interested,' I say over my shoulder as I walk away.

'Treat 'em mean,' my Gran always said. She had great success with men until she muddled up two letters to the RAF guys she was trying to decide between – and was dumped by both. I remember her telling me this as she glanced at my Granddad cutting his toenails in a basin of water, emitting a loud fart with the exertion of it all, and chuckling quietly to himself.

'God works in mysterious ways,' she sighed.

I arrive back at the table and Holly informs me Sean is looking over at me. I sneak a glance. He is indeed, incredibly. 'Oooh, he's coming over,' she laughs behind her hand. I look the opposite way.

'Fancy a game of pool?' Sean slimes up to me, tossing his Andrew Ridgeley-style locks.

'Only if you can handle having your arse kicked,' I shrug,

disinterestedly. 'Oh, and it's doubles only. Holly joins us, so you better look around for a mate to play with.'

Sean dashes off and comes back with some random bloke who had been minding his own business, reading a newspaper with a pint and a pie.

'This is Joe,' says Sean breathlessly. 'We've known each other years.'

'It's John,' says "Joe".

'Anyway,' breezes Sean, 'let's play.' With an enthusiastic nod to us all, we stand up and join him at the pool table.

So, I have been living with Sean for two years and nine months. Much to my Mum's initial horror and half the family asking if I'm pregnant. Sean plays with the band every Thursday, Friday and Saturday. Sundays are boys' nights out, so it's a fairly part-time relationship. Sean doesn't like me to go out without him, so half an hour after he leaves on a Friday night, I get out of my pyjamas and into my party frock, heading out in Dundee City centre with Holly. I, of course, do nothing untoward behind his back, but it's best he doesn't know. I occasionally hear rumours doing the rounds about Sean's antics. He sweeps them off dismissively and informs me that the other band guys play around, but why would he go for a burger when he has steak at home? I don't believe the gossip anyway. It's no secret that Sean is fancied the length and breadth of Dundee. There was even a ridiculous story from one gay friend of mine that Sean had slept with his ex-boyfriend. One of the many reasons why I didn't believe anything I heard.

I worked Saturday and Sunday nightshift in Safeway. Not the best job, but a good crowd to work with. I remember being exhausted for two years juggling work and College. I hated College. I had assumed it would be very grown-up and cool, calling the teachers by their first names and all going out for lunch together. The reality couldn't have been further from my expectations. It was exactly like school had been, but now the lecturers -good choice of name for them I thought – would inform us that we were supposed to be College, not High School students. Tardiness and bunking off was not acceptable in College. Funny that, my High School teachers used to say the same about not being in Primary School any more. What next? Due to my bad behaviour, my employer asking if I still thought I was in College? I really expected people to have stopped bossing me around by the ripe old age of 18, and was most indignant. We had four tortuous weeks of College before our placements began. Did we need to know so much before being let loose on the children of the world? Or perhaps they were so awful that we needed to be educated on how to deal with them before we even met.

The day finally arrived when Miss Smith, the Senior Lecturer, handed out the slips of paper with the name of our nurseries on. Jan leaned forward in her seat and delivered a sharp punch to my shoulder blade. I tutted and turned to glare at her.
'Oi, frizz-head! What nursery you got?'
'Do you really need to punch me to get my attention?' I scowled.
Jan ignored me and studied the name of my nursery.
'Hey, Cragtonhill! You got lucky, one of the nicer nurseries, jammy bugger.'
'Oh, great!' I beamed my relief at her. 'I was so worried I'd get a rough one where you have to check the kids for knives on the way in. Well, thank God for that.' I turned back and smiled at my piece of paper. This would be a doddle.

Monday arrived. Placement day one. I waited anxiously at the bus station. It'll be fine, I reasoned. Jan said it was a nice nursery. All of them are, our lecturer had said.

Dundee is a decent city, friendly people. Apart from the dodgy mob of three at college, everyone else had been nice to me. No reason not to believe her. There are one or two places with more 'challenging' children, Miss Smith had added cautiously (she did love to do those air inverted commas), but she had given those to the girls with previous childcare experience. I should be safe then; apart from babysitting my cousin Craig, I didn't have any prior experience. Craig was fairly feisty but nothing three tubes of Smarties and *Button Moon* on repeat couldn't control.

My bus arrived. I explained to the driver it was my first day and could he please shout me when we got to Cragtonhill School. He glanced behind me:

'You on your own, are you?'

I nodded blankly. The driver gave a throaty chortle,

'No problem, I'll shout you when we get there.' He gave another hearty laugh as if he found himself hilarious and shook his head. I walked to the back of the bus. This being my first mistake.

'Missus. Oi! Missus. Yeh you, wifie, wi' the nice hair.' A snort from the other boy caused me to turn around. 'You got a smoke we can have?'

I stare in shock at the two seven-year-old boys on the back seat.

'No! Indeed I do not, and if I did, I certainly wouldn't give it to two young boys like you.' Ten minutes pass by and the bus lumbers halfway up a steep hill.

'Cragtonhill School,' bellowed the driver, followed by yet another chortle. I get off the bus and walk up the remainder of the hill. Nervous, and now cigarette-less too. Seven- year-olds can be so cruel. Took my two pounds lunch money too, for another pack. It was my fault really; I should have had more than three smokes on me. I walk past a group of teenagers watching a rubbish bin blaze as they discussed possible accelerants for the next one, and into the school. The corridor was long and eerily quiet. The smell of disinfectant and carbolic soap hung heavily in the air. I walk the half a mile to the office and give a tentative knock.

'Come in,' says a friendly woman with a smile in her voice.

I open the door, which creaks on its hinges, and nervously sit down opposite Miss Jamieson.

'You must be Lucy,' she beams proudly at me. 'Our latest protégé.'

'Nice to meet you Miss Jamieson,' I squeak politely.

'Now let me tell you all about our little nursery and adorable children.' I smile and nod, trying not to notice her black eye and chipped tooth.

An hour of induction later and I am sitting in front of twenty little upturned faces. With a shaky voice I begin to introduce myself.

'Can't hear you,' taunts a small grubby boy with gelled, spiky hair and a smudge of mud on his cheek. I take a deep breath and begin again, louder and with what, I hoped, carried more authority. Grubby boy stands up and introduces himself.

'I'm Billy and this here is my sister.'

'Lovely,' I smile, looking from one to the other in confusion. Billy, blond and sickly pale with freckles, his sister, dark-skinned with a mass of curls.

'I'm not finished,' stated Billy, indignantly. 'This is also my sister, and this is my brother. He pointed to two other equally grubby-looking kids.

'Good grief! Did your mother have quads?'

'Er, no,' Billy says patronisingly, and rolls his eyes at me. 'We all got different Mums.' 'OK.' I exhale loudly and smile around at the children, now gigging at my stupidity. Shall we sing some songs?'

A chorus of 'yessssss!' Am I mistaken or did they sound sarcastic? I rack my brain to think of a song. We haven't done this module yet. I must know one.

'Old MacDonald,' I burst out in relief. 'Let's sing *Old MacDonald*.'

'OK,' says a small, pretty, blond girl, 'but we always get to choose the animals.' She nods seriously at me. I hear a chuckle from Miss Jamieson's desk.

'That's fine, sweetheart. Of course you can.'

We begin to sing and as we reach . . . '*and on that farm he had a...*' I point to the little girl.

'Hedgehog,' she states defiantly. Half a minute passes until I eventually carry on my '*ee-ii-ee-ii-oooo, with a snuffle, snuffle here, and a snuffle, snuffle there.*' Ha! Got you, you little bastards. They look at me in disappointment. Each time I manage to think of some absurd thing that silent (or perhaps I just don't know the sound they make) animals could possibly do .Giraffe, easy; munch, munch. Worm; wiggle, wiggle. Tortoise; plod, plod. And so it went on until Miss Jamieson clapped her hands in delight.

'Oh, the little beggars, that's their favourite trick. Well done you, Lucy.'

Having exhausted my repertoire of one children's song, I cunningly suggest they take turns to come up and sing. Billy urgently puts his hand in the air.

'Come on then Billy, up you come.' He leans against my knees and informs me:

'I'm gonna sing *Twinkle, twinkle* but diff'rent, OK?'

'Fine.' I scratch my head nervously as he begins.

'*Stinky, stinky, little fart, how I'm glad you're not a shart...*'

Twenty cackling little voices fill my head.

'OK, let's stop there, Billy. I don't even know what a shart is?' I wonder aloud.

'It's when you think you need a fart, but it's really a shi...'

'Right! How about a story?'

'Aww, my Daddy teached me that last year when I see'd him.'

'Me too,' squeaked another three little voices.

'Yes, very nice. Thank you, Billy.'

Miss Jamieson stands and says she is off to make a few calls as I seem to be coping. This is so unfair. I'm a student. Both room teachers are off on stress leave and Miss Jamieson is supposed to take the class. She arrives back twenty minutes later with a frantic Jemima, who had run screaming to the office telling Miss Jamieson that I couldn't cope.

'You left her alone. With *us!*' Jemima shook her head in disgust at Miss Jamieson on their breathless arrival back to the classroom. One page into *The Very Hungry Caterpillar* all hell had let loose. I had since been frantically trying to regain control as they tipped out boxes of Lego and painted the curtains, while one of the better-behaved children sat thoughtfully chewing a page from a book.

'*Enough!*' screamed Miss Jamieson. Where did that voice come from? 'Now sit down until I fetch Mrs Gowan from next door to mind you. Lucy, office!'

I sat shamefaced on the squeaky *faux*-leather chair. Imagine – being sent to the headmistress's office on day one. 'OK, let's cut the crap,' she announced as she walked into the room, slid behind her desk and took off her glasses. 'You know now that these kids can be a bit of a handful.' She pinched the bridge of her nose. Understatement of the decade. 'But they're basically good kids, just not had the same opportunities in life that some kids get. Take our twisted little Brady Bunch through there. All four mothers find out within months of each other that their partner is having an affair. He pays nothing for any of them, it all goes on his – ahem – habits, and he rarely sees any one of those kids. That's just one example. Now, the College assured us that you had childcare experience and could cope. I don't usually advocate shouting at children, except in extreme cases, but you need to find a way to keep control of the class. I trust you won't let me down, Lucy.'

I walk back to the classroom, stopping only at a two-sided easel with chalk in the tray. I rub my hand with pink chalk and carry on back to class. I'm playing hard-ball now.

Break time, but not for me it would seem. I'm on playground duty. Fifteen children surround me and stare in wonder at my hand.

'Ten of the belt,' Billy shakes his head in awe and admiration, 'and we all thought you was a wimp, di'nt we?'

Fifteen nods. We reach an agreement that day. I'd bring in sweets tomorrow and we'd start over. Miss Jamieson did not mess around. They didn't want to be next for the belt, it was the first time she'd ever done that. I didn't feel the need to inform them that the belt had been banned before I'd even left school.

After stressful weekdays of College and Nursery, I'm shattered when I head into work at the supermarket every weekend. It's a good laugh, as I said, but I really could do without it. Tim, the nineteen-year-old nightshift supervisor, knew where we could smoke and not set off the alarms and he got the grocery boys during the week to write-off and then hide various alcoholic beverages. We'd look at the Write-Off book occasionally and laugh. 'Aisle three: one litre of vodka dropped by customer. Item discarded due to Health and Safety reasons.'

We would then get stuck into said vodka with a bottle of written-off coke.

'Past sell-by.'

The button of the tannoy in Customer Services was held down by a carefully placed can of Kestrel Super Strength, blaring the sounds of The KLF and The Urban Cookie Collective all around the store. This continued successfully until 13th of February of that year. The Head Grocery Boy was caught with two hundred stolen Woodbine in his locker and struck a deal with the Manager that if he tipped him off about the night staff's antics, the police wouldn't be involved. So, at three o'clock on a Sunday morning, in the middle of a 'price gunfight' with Tim and some frozen chickens, the tape switched off. An announcement, in the form of our Manager's voice, came over the loudspeaker for all staff to meet by the Customer Service desk. Despite a gin, tonic, cider and Martini Rosso stupor, we knew we were in the shit. Ashamed, we made our way to Customer Services, only to be unanimously fired on the spot. We were stripped of our tabards and informed not to ask for a reference. We made our way *en masse* outside. Tim was really ticked off when he spotted that the ribbon had been pulled from his tape and discarded on the floor; he was seemingly unconcerned at the loss of £60 per week in wages.

I arrived home at 3.20am with a cheery, 'I'm back.' I am met by silence. I take off my boots and creep into the living room. Looking for signs of a Valentine's surprise. No card, no flowers. He wasn't expecting me home yet, I reason, dismissing the fact that he wouldn't be up until lunchtime tomorrow and then out with the boys. I tiptoe into the bedroom and immediately step into a discarded, half-eaten doner kebab. I pull off my sock, now covered in a combination of chilli and garlic sauce. My eyes grow accustomed to the darkness and I can make out the snoring figure of Sean. I smile and walk towards my side of the bed. My foot catches something. A stiletto-heeled shoe. Confused, I strain my eyes in the darkness and make out another figure. Blonde, heaving bosom like a Sumo wrestler deflated. Charmaine! On my side of the bed – naked! I observe the scene for a second. The power I wield. Then I notice Dillon, our cat, curled between them. This is the worst moment of all for me. The traitor! I gather up my few belongings from around the comatose trio. Luckily, I never moved all my stuff in. Just a few outfits, tapes

and the like; something must have held me back subconsciously and made me keep the majority of my belongings at my Mum's. I pause in gathering mode only to pick up the card I bought Sean for Valentine's Day. I pick up a pen and write:
'Roses are red,
Violets are blue.
You treat me like shit.
So I'm leaving you.'
I place the card in its envelope, calmly lick and seal it, and slip out into the mild winter's night.

Chapter Four

I move back to Mum's for a month with the intention of looking for a new job. Almost immediately, I am driving everyone crazy and really not coping with being at home again. It makes me feel a complete failure, as if I've backtracked to childhood and couldn't make it on my own. Mum and I are far too similar in nature. Two adult Taureans under one roof does not bode well. One bull to a field, I reckon. I can't deal with rules any more. When I lived in my own place, if I wanted to leave my dinner plate on the table until the next morning, I could. Well, it was Sean's place, granted, but I paid enough towards his bloody mortgage to gain the right to claim part ownership. At least in my mind, if not on paper. I also hate sharing a bedroom again with my excessively tidy sister. Mary, used to her own space, seems to hate it even more than I do. I'm certainly not the neatest person to live with. I suddenly go back to finding items of my clothing missing, which, of course, she has never seen. Amazingly, they turn up in my washing basket the day after I enquire of their whereabouts. It's time to move on.

I decide to head to Edinburgh on the coach and I move in with some old school friends who are studying at the University. This way, I figure, I can be a rich working woman while still being signed into all the student unions. My wage will go much further like this. I apply for a position in a Care Home for the elderly. I'm more used to looking after the opposite end of the age scale, but I figure that wiping arses is wiping arses, regardless of size. Fortunately, I am very good at interviews, embellishing as I go. I do, however, have a genuine love for elderly people and I think that shines through. The day of the interview dawns and I arrive at the Home. After my college placements nothing can faze me, so

I'm not particularly nervous.

Interviewer: 'So, tell me, er... (looks at my CV)... Lucy. What makes you want to work with people redundant from society?'

Anti-discriminatory trick question, handle with care.

Me: 'Well, Mr... er.... (I glance at my job specification)... Roberts, I find it very unfortunate that elderly people would be considered no longer a valuable member of society. Are you familiar with the phrase, "you can't teach your Granny to suck eggs?"

Point taken. Mr. Roberts laughs and relaxes into the interview. I am aware my comment could have backfired badly on me, but I was willing to take the gamble. Discrimination is not something I tolerate, having worked with some of the poorest, but nicest families with a variety of problems. I don't judge a book by its cover.

'So, Lucy,' he smiles. 'I see that you normally work with children, apart from a position of a nightshift worker at Safeway. Why do you think you are suited to Care Home work?'

'I have spent two years training in childcare, but a lifetime of assisting with my Grandparents,' I reply. 'They have relied on my help over the years and I feel that I have contributed to the best of my ability, in relation to their needs.

They don't *need* care, of course. Gran has a slight paralysis from a stroke and therefore isn't quite as good a shot as she used to be when chucking ornaments at Granddad's head. Be it whether he's had too many down the Crown or when he's spent the housekeeping at the bookies and bingo. Due to my Granddad's failing eyesight, my 'assisting' involves catching said ornaments mid-air. Bet they're sorry now they never let me on the netball team (instead of the embarrassing position of reserve for the B team). I seem to have painted a picture to Mr. Roberts that my grandparents are somewhat frail and in need of a lot of support. He nods approvingly at me.

'What kind of role do you see yourself taking in our centre?'

'Purely an *ad-hoc* need basis,' I reply, 'someone who will respect the independence of the clients and promote their individual rights and abilities.'

Think covering for Granddad down the pub. No, he told me he's going to the allotment for the potatoes for tea, Gran. Honest!

'Also, I am someone who will respect the fact that these people can still be very active in mind and body, and maintain the right to express so.'

Think telling Gran that, no, I don't think she's stupid and that is where Granddad said he was going. Hoping that this doesn't lead to any cranial blows of the bone china kind.

'I will happily contribute to the daily activities, taking into account the interests of the service user but also encourage new skills and interests on a continual basis,' I finish, with a hopeful smile. Think telling both Gran and Granddad: 'Why don't you go to the bingo/tea dance/bowling, and forget what he/she has done?'

I am offered the job on the spot.

If I ever make it to a ripe old age, I am very much looking forward to being as cantankerous as possible. Blue-rinsed and shouting randomly at inanimate objects, terrorising shopkeepers and bursting the ball of any small child that bounces into my garden. I'll have 20 cats and the children will chant: 'Witch! Witch!' when they see me. Old age may inhibit the body, but it liberates the mind. You no longer give a toss about what anyone thinks of you. You don't need to worry about your weight, being skinny will just make you look more wrinkled. You don't bother making new friends – at your age they'll only go and die on you anyway. The ante is upped on the mortal lottery. You don't have to worry about finding a new man, what for? Will you really want sex in your eighties? I doubt it very much. A nice cup of tea, a packet of chocolate digestives and *Countdown* – that's what you'll want.

Actually, I'm already into my Granddad's old habit of playing dirty word *Countdown*, though nowhere near in his league. He used to chortle over his afternoon tea, perusing the jumble of letters to make into words, while Gran looked on with distaste.

'F, great. Can do a lot with an F. C, smashing. T, tricky one, keep 'em comin' Carol. Keep 'em comin' girl. K, excellent.' He'd sit up in his chair with renewed enthusiasm. P, edge of his seat now. 'Right, enough of your bloody consonants.' A – a tut of displeasure, 'Vowel, yes, vowel,' followed by a delighted cheer and triumphant air punch at the arrival of U.

'Fuck!' he shouted with glee, followed by mutterings of how nobody ever announces these words on the show. The highlight of his life was not the birth of any of his children, his marriage or even the end of the war. It was the day of 10th November 1988 when the letters he had been waiting for – for years – eventually arrived. He joyously phoned around the family. We were convinced he'd won the lottery. That the unlikely scenario of choosing numbers one to six (they have as much chance as any, apparently) had come good. In fact, he had finally been able to make 'bastard'. He died a week later; perhaps it was the shock? Bless him, he died a happy man. Finally at peace. Naturally, we were all devastated, but so happy for him that his much-awaited letters had come up before he went. Even Gran had to agree with that. I caught her several months later muttering swear words under her breath as she watched *Countdown* from Granddad's old chair, complete with his bum-print, over her afternoon cup of tea and half a packet of Hobnobs. Yes, she missed him but, never one to be outdone, she had to find a similarly long rude word. She never did. The Master could never be beaten.

The time comes around for me to begin my new job. Day one and I'm placed in my wing. The Home is devised to make the clients feel that they are in a Five Star hotel. I spent all last week on training courses and am now qualified in many wonderful things, such as changing colostomy bags, giving medication and realising the difference between the onset of dementia and a urinary tract infection. They are strangely and intricately linked it would appear. My first job is to help a stroke victim with his breakfast. His name is Harry, and he is Eighty-seven years young. His speech is slightly slurred, but I can understand the majority of what he says.

'Not a bad arse,' I hear, as I bend to pick up his washing from the floor.

'Excuse me?' I laugh.

'Am I getting my breakfast or not? I probably won't be alive by the time those clothes come back from the laundry anyway, but I am hungry.'

'Now don't you be saying things like that,' I scold. 'You better keep in with me if you want a wee dram of a winter's night. I know where the keys to the booze cabinet are.' With that, we are firm friends. Harry looks for me each day that I am working, and sulks if I'm on a day off.

'Those weekend staff don't know if they need a shite or a haircut,' he complains.

Two weeks into my job and I'm allocated Harry as my key client. It hasn't gone unnoticed that we get on so well and, where possible, the seniors try to match up the clients and key workers if they see a rapport. I read up on Harry's fascinating history. He had been in the Royal Navy and had fought in World War II. He'd never married nor had children. It seemed such a waste. He cared for his elderly parents and inherited their house when they died, which he had now sold to pay for his care.

'Bloody ridiculous state of affairs,' he had said when I had discussed this part of his care plan with him. 'You spend your life working your arse off, paying your taxes and serving your country. Then how do they repay you? I'll tell you how. They say: "I'm very sorry Mr. Mackay but you're no longer any use to us. Tell you what, you sell your house and give us back every penny that you and your family have ever earned." That's what!' I nod in agreement. It is ridiculous. Considering some of the other residents had never owned their own homes and yet still receive the same care as Harry, but for free. Not their fault either. Life can deal you some crap, but still it seems unfair that your achievements can be snatched away so cruelly, just because you need help to support yourself. I ask Harry discreetly if he had ever been close to marriage.

He laughs. 'Do you think I have never been with a woman?'

Mortified, I splutter: 'No! That wasn't what I meant at all. I just wondered why someone as handsome as you never got married?'

I glanced over at a faded black and white picture of Harry and his brother in their Navy uniforms, their goofy pose captured in time. Jimmy had never come back from the War. Just weeks after the picture was taken, they had been sent off to different vessels and Jimmy had died in a torpedo attack on his ship; Harry had been on the aircraft carrier flagship and he had seen the flames and explosions from a distance.

'The one and only time I prayed,' he solemnly informed me. 'I prayed that he was alive and that if he wasn't, that it was quick.' I looked at Harry in silence, not knowing how to reply to that. His alarm clocked ticked away to fill the void. Harry glanced at a bird pecking at some stale bread thrown out the window of the kitchens and then, in an attempt to lighten the mood, said:

'Besides, being the hunk that I was, I never got around to choosing just one woman. There was just too much damn choice.' His eyes sparkled at the memory. 'And another thing; don't think all the girls were virtuous in those days. So long as you didn't get in the club you were fine.' I stifle a shocked laugh at the biggest player of his day.

Despite Harry's chattiness to me, he never repeated his intriguing tales in our regular reminiscence groups.

'Can't get a word in for all those bloody wimmin,' was his excuse.

It was around this time that I met Paul. He had come to give us a talk on Dementia. He was around for three days, to make sure he covered those on days off and all the senior staff. Paul wandered around the centre, whistling tunelessly. Everywhere he went I witnessed the old dears taking out their hearing aids, shaking and fiddling with them in a confused manner. Paul was very shy with me, despite being able to stand up and talk to a room full of people, and blushed even if I asked him if he fancied a cup of tea. Every time he popped into the day room, Maisie, an eighty six-year-old 'Dementia sufferer' would nudge me knowingly.

'Don't be daft,' I'd say. 'He doesn't fancy me!'

'You're lucky I have no memory, hen,' Maisie stated. 'Otherwise, I'd be most offended that you called me daft.' It was our little joke.

'Well, I guess I am lucky, Maisie'.

'Lucky in what way, dear?' Maisie would reply. We would both laugh.

It was her little play on "forgetfulness." If the Social Work department knew she had more marbles than she cared to admit, she would be out on her ear from the place she'd loved on a respite visit and put into sheltered housing.

One afternoon Paul wandered into the kitchen with his empty cup. He started a little at seeing me and blushed beet red.

'Erm, so… What you up to tonight then, er, Lucy?'

Fifteen wrinkled and expectant faces look our way.

'I'm on early tomorrow,' I say apologetically. 'Planning a bath and an early night,' I lie.

'No! She's on the back shift,' informs Bessie. 'Don't you play hard to get, Missy.'

'Carry on, son,' encouraged Sadie.

Paul looked at his feet and shuffled uncomfortably, giving me the perfect opportunity to shoot a warning look at Bessie. She smirked and winked in return.

'Well, if you like, there's a new restaurant opened on Rose Street. I thought, maybe ...' he trailed off.

'She'd love to,' shouted Maisie from the kitchen. OK, I think we can rule out deafness along with marble loss.

'Well, yeah, all right,' I agreed reluctantly, feeling under duress and knowing full well I'd never hear the end of it otherwise. I can't be bothered with a boyfriend at the moment. I like my life the way it is. But, at that moment, I had no say in the matter – and we left the room to a lavender-scented round of applause.

Our evening out goes really well. The restaurant was the perfect setting for a first date and I do manage to actually eat instead of awkwardly pushing food around my plate. Paul pays for everything. We head on to a few pubs along Rose Street, laughing and joking and feeling very comfortable in each other's company. Paul confesses that he doesn't have a huge amount of luck in his relationships and tends to get too involved too quickly, which seems to scare off potential girlfriends. OK, so he's not the best looking guy I've dated, but he seems a true gent, attentive too. At the end of the evening Paul walks me home, coyly taking my hand and smiling. At my door he quickly leans over and gives me a peck on the cheek. How sweet. He promises to call again soon to arrange another date – if I'd like to, he anxiously adds. Of course I would, I tell him, putting my key in the lock. Perfect. He didn't even try it on.

I arrive at work on Monday morning and immediately the ladies in the day room give me the third degree. Having to start again several times as new clients join us, on top of repeating everything twice for Meg, who has lost her hearing aid yet again and is leaning forward, attempting to listen intently from the corner chair. I wander down the hallway and rap my knuckles on Harry's door.

'Come in,' is the grumpy reply, quickly followed by a wide smile when he sees it's me. I give him a hug and after a quick chat, I open his medication cabinet, unscrewing bottles and tipping pills, second nature into the little pill cup as we talk. He's not too interested in my date. Harry is strangely hesitant about Paul.

'Here we go, Harry.' I hand him the med cup and go to pour him a glass of water from a jug on the side table, with the very un-Harry crocheted doily on it. It was a gift from one of the well-meaning lady residents. An attempt to bring a woman's touch to Harry's barren room, which is sparsely furnished with a three quarter-sized bed, side table, an old tea trolley, with a black and white portable TV on it, and two armchairs. One for Harry and, sadly, a barely used guest one.

A lone picture hangs on the wall. His niece in London, Kirsty, has a daughter, Emma. She painted a picture of Harry's old black and white collie, Laddie, from a photograph and sent it to him. Harry was thrilled to bits with the sixteen-year-old's gesture. Good on the girl! Considering she had never met Harry, it was sweet of her. This was the main reason it seemed to touch Harry. Laddie had meant so much to him. He felt Emma must be a kindred soul. Harry talked proudly of her two letters to him; OK, so not much, but more than her mother did. She had passed nine GSCEs and wanted to study law. She spoke fondly to the elderly man she had never met, discussing her plans to visit her 'heritage' and travel around Scotland. She would definitely come and see him. The last time he had seen Kirsty had been at a family party twenty years ago.

I hold the glass of water out toward Harry. He gently grasps my wrist with one hand as he removes the glass with the other and places it on the table. He opens my hand and looks intently at my palm. I hold still. Looking at the top of his grey tufty head, I think how much he looks like a baby bird from this angle; the hair, the small eyes and the slightly beaky nose. Finally, he glances up, eyebrows raised.

'Sit, Lucy.' I sit down in the armchair opposite, leaning forward. Harry gazes intently into my palm, twisting the ring on my middle finger absent-mindedly.

'Mum is very important,' he says almost to himself. 'Dad is an enigma. This is why you have such an innocent... what's the word I'm looking for? Almost, awe of men. That is your downfall, Lucy. Paul isn't the one. You don't need me to tell you that. The man you end up with will be the man you see as only him. Not some figment of your imagination of the perfect man – because *he* doesn't exist. Don't have idealistic views of us Lucy. We are just the same as women, only worse.' Harry gives a small laugh. 'You have a strong family bond, in life and in spirit. It's where you find your strength. You are a good person. You do what you want, when you want, so long as it doesn't hurt anyone. That is a good way to live.'

A knock on the door interrupts us. As if snapped out of a trance, Harry drops my hand.

'Tea trolley.' I hear the irate voice of my colleague. I was supposed to be doing the drinks after my drugs round.

'Sorry Harry, I have to go help out.' He nods graciously, with a small bow as I make my way to the door.

I have now been dating Paul for three months. The opportunity to discuss the impromptu palm reading with Harry has never arisen again. What he said did have a lot of relevance, however. I kept it on board. Besides, as a distraction, there's much dusting off of hats in the Care Home and mutterings of:

'Perhaps she won't be a maiden after all…'

A little premature. Well, quite a lot premature. I'm having the time of my life hanging out with old school friends and exploring the clubs of Edinburgh, even though Paul is everything I want in a man. Funny and charming, generous the week before pay day when I'm broke, and gracious the week after when I'm, albeit temporarily, solvent.

We see each other almost every night and his cute pretend sulks when I make plans that don't involve him, and elation when I reluctantly cancel them, don't bother me at all. One Saturday night we head off to a club in the Grassmarket. My flatmates have hooked up with some of our old school friends and there's a big weekend planned in the city. As we walk over the George IV Bridge through driving rain, Paul is quieter than usual.

'Everything all right?' I shout from under my umbrella.

'Yep,' his reply is barely audible. He has refused my offer of sharing the umbrella. We walk in silence. I'm trying to work out what I could have said or done to annoy him. I'm so looking forward to tonight. So many people I haven't seen since school. I'm a little miffed at the wet blanket literally trailing behind me.

The music pulsates through our bodies as we walk into the club. I spot some of the girls on the dance floor. Jess, one of my flatmates, runs over and grabs us both, chatting twenty to the dozen.

'Seb's here – and Jase. Louisa and Donna are dying to see you! This is gonna be great,' enthuses Jess. I can feel the cloud over Paul darken. I decide to ignore his mood and throw myself enthusiastically into the throng. So many hugs.

'How have you been?'

'I must give you my number!'

'Where are you living?'

I glance at Paul. He doesn't have many friends. Certainly, I haven't met any, only heard about them. Quite a few seem to be off travelling and a lot live out of town. I guess he feels left out. Despite his reluctance, I pull him by the hand and introduce him to everyone.

'Kat, sat next to her in Geography.'

'Stacey, bunked off many a gym class together. Same medical condition, out of control menstrual problems, strangely coincided with each other's every time.'

'Tom, High School boyfriend for a year, although we did no more than hold hands.' Paul's face clouds over with rage. He announces that he is going to the bar. I continue chatting, whilst out of the corner of my eye watching the bartender pour three tequila shots in front of him. Paul is talking animatedly and gesturing a lot at the barman, who throws me a cautious glance. Tom saunters over smiling.

'Luce, it is so good to see you, what are you doing now? Last I heard you were training to be a babysitter.' I give him a jokey slap.

'Oh, how dare you!' I exclaim. It's a bit more in depth than supervising a sleeping child I'll have you know. I'm working in a Care Home now. I love it, old people can be so funny.'

'Same old you,' Tom laughs, 'never one to do things by halves. From the youngest to the oldest in the space of two jobs.' He leans in and plants a peck on my cheek. 'It really is so great to see you, Lucy,' he says. I cast a nervous glance in the direction of the bar. Paul silently fumes. The bartender is keeping a close eye on him over the top of the pint he is pouring. I try to ignore him and continue my conversation with Tom. I hear about the law practice he has opened with two other guys from our year, and about Jane, his live-in girlfriend who is definitely 'the one'. No offence to me, he laughs. None taken. I give him an offended sniff, and laugh along. Jane hadn't been able to make it this evening as she is a nurse and on night shift. Tom glances around to make sure no-one is listening, and then he leans into me to whisper in my ear.

'We just found out Jane is six weeks pregnant. I can't wait to be a father. Keep it to yourself though, you know, first three months and all that.' I squeal and squeeze Tom's arm, oblivious to the fact that Paul is heading our way. Until I hear Jess mumble:

'Uh-oh, trouble ahead,' and turn in the direction of the bar.

With the sickening thud of knuckles on bone, Paul's fist smashes into Tom.

'You slag!' screams Paul in my face. 'Who the fuck do you think you are? Showing me up with your ex-boyfriend, *ignoring* me!' I stand there in stunned silence. Tom holds his hand over his nose, blood pouring through his fingers.

'Listen, *mate*,' begins Tom, through gritted teeth. I can tell he is struggling to control his temper, but doesn't want to retaliate. 'I can assure you…'

Bang!

Tom wavers for a moment before crashing to the floor. The bouncer has Paul in a double arm lock and is thrusting him towards the door. All around us chaos breaks out. Tom lies unconscious on the floor, surrounded by broken glass from the pint he had been holding. I stare at him in horror. Silently willing him to wake up. Please don't let Paul have just killed the father of an unborn baby.

'Call an ambulance,' someone screams.

After four hours in Casualty at Edinburgh Royal Infirmary – and a hundred apologies later from me – Tom is released. Two black eyes and a severely bruised jaw for his troubles. He graciously declines the offer of a stay at my house and the experience of my very amateur nursing skills, and heads back to Seb's in a cab.

Somewhere around 5am I crawl into bed, after cleaning up as much broken glass as I can. A brick has been thoughtfully thrown through my bedroom window. I fall into a restless sleep.

I dream that Harry walks into my bedroom.

'Oh, you perv,' I laugh. 'I am not one of your wanton women!'
He chuckles heartily. 'Oh, I know you're not,' he says. 'If only
you had been fifty years younger...'

'Try sixty,' I smile wryly.

'Anyway, Luce, I only wanted to say that you deserve so
much more.'

'Yes, Harry. I know. He is so dumped first thing in the
morning. I'd do it now if I had the energy.'

'Lucy, you're a good girl. Remember what I told you now,
never settle for second best.' Harry places a kiss gently on my
forehead.

'I'll see you again, honey.'

'I'll see you tomorrow, Harry. I'm on a late. Now let me sleep,
you old git.'

I drift off as Harry leaves my room, with a backwards glance
and a smile.

I phone into work the next afternoon to say I'd be ten minutes
late. Dashing into the kitchen, I almost run into Maisie.

'You're late,' she observes astutely.

'I know, I *know*.'

'There was an ambulance here last night. 2am. What do you
know? Nobody tells us anything. Bloody night staff!'

'Maisie, I'm sorry. I know nothing. I have to go to the
handover meeting. Make me a coffee please – and I know you
can, before you start.'

I walk quickly to the office, saying hello to clients as I go. The
group quietens as I enter.

'I'm sorry,' I begin. 'I know it's the second time this week I've
been late, but...'

My senior, Ellie, stands up.

'Lucy...' She pauses, breathes deeply and closes her eyes:
'Harry's gone.'

I stare at Ellie, confused for a moment. A sea of concerned faces all around me. This isn't real. Not my Harry. This can't be happening. I run from the room and down the corridor, tripping over a discarded hoist and bump my forehead on the skirting board.

'Lucy?' shouts Maisie, from somewhere behind me. I pick myself up and keep running until I'm outside. I take in huge gulps of freezing, drizzle-soaked air.

He came to say goodbye.

Chapter Five

It has been two weeks since Harry's funeral. His only living relatives, the niece in London and her family, want his remaining money, but no personal items. This angers me so much. After hearing this, I walk out of the handover meeting at the beginning of my shift and storm along to Harry's old room. I glower at the picture his great niece has done. Where are you now? Where are any of you? You will never know what you've missed. I hope you enjoy your money. I angrily punch Harry's bed before sitting down and picking up his photograph; Jimmy and Harry, now together with people who really care. Ellie appears at the door, silhouetted against the bright light behind her, making it impossible to read her expression. I sigh wearily and ask her if I may have the photo? I hear a smile in her voice as she tells me it's mine, I look down at it again and when I look up, she has gone. I rummage around in Harry's bedside drawer and find a sticky bag of boiled sweets covered in fluff from being in his dressing gown pocket. I won't eat them, of course, but it was just so Harry. He used to suck them in bed, even though the night staff confiscated many bags as it was a choking risk. Today we are having a clear-out of Harry's things. There's a lady moving in tomorrow. This is the last day I can sit here and feel like I'm totally with Harry. Come tomorrow, the new lady will be busying herself with turning the room into hers, and trying to get rid of the old man smell that so reminds me of Harry.

His niece didn't attend the funeral. Only Care Home staff and a smattering of Harry's old Navy friends, including one elderly lady nicknamed 'Vera Lynn'. Fond of the Navy boys in her younger days, she had entertained the troops in a whole different way to the real 'Forces Sweetheart.' The organ played the opening bars of *Abide with me* and the choir joined in. I stared sadly at the stained glass windows, my chest tight with the grief I wouldn't let go, and thought how ridiculous it was that the closest I have got to my George Bailey was an eighty seven-year-old man. Albeit sometimes dirty-minded, but one who was charming, funny and kind. Harry wasn't religious but the ceremony was, as he hadn't stated what he wanted.

'I'm not going to be at the party, so why would I care?' he had said.

At the end of the service, I walked over to the coffin and popped the boiled sweets and a half bottle of whiskey at Harry's side. He looked peaceful – a cliché, I know – but he really did. A small smile seemed to have been playing on his lips when he went.

'I'll miss you, old bugger,' I smiled sadly, 'don't go terrorising those poor angels too much.' I kissed his cold cheek, feeling the roughness of bristle from an overdue shave that never arrived.

Things settle back down at the Care Home and I don't hear from Paul again. I heard that he was spotted out with another poor unsuspecting soul, both looking miserable as they drank their pints. I swear off men for a good long while. Instead, I seem to have a different view of life. Maybe, after Harry, I realised how quickly it can be snatched away, but I'm not sure. I start by quitting smoking. I give away my last fourteen cigarettes in a pack to Bessie, along with my ashtray and lighters. I also stop drinking for a few weeks as my resolve to stop smoking weakens terribly when I add alcohol. I walk the forty minutes to work and back, more for something to take my mind off cigarettes than anything else, and find I am quickly shedding the pounds too. I have no appetite. There are good days, when my intention is to live my life as fully as I can, and others when I'm angry and flop into bed pulling the covers over my head, not wanting to talk to anybody. Everything reminds me of Harry.

After a few weeks of feeling really low and grumpy due to nicotine withdrawal (OK, I admit it, borderline psychotic) things start to look up again. I spend my time seeing movies and going to the gym with friends. I'm beginning to feel more positive than I've been in a long time. Like a tiny stream of light has appeared from behind a dark cloud after days of storms.

After a couple of months hiding out like a recluse, seeing only non-smoking friends and allowing myself a maximum of two wines total on a weekend night, I decide it's time for the re-launch. I've gone from a size fourteen to a ten, so Jess and I hit the town for some power shopping. For the first time since I was a teenager, I enjoy buying clothes. Instead of being bright red in the face, struggling to button up a fourteen whilst grunting like a stuck pig, I slide easily into a size ten jeans and they sit snugly on my hips. I want to cartwheel through the changing rooms. The last time I had gone shopping I had, to my shame, got stuck in a slinky satin top. Mortified, I struggled for ten minutes with my arms over my head, stuck from the chest up, before I gave in and shouted on the pre-pubescent stick insect assistant to help me. Chewing her gum loudly in my ear as she attempted to release me, she eventually ripped the seam and pulled the top free. Just in time for me to notice three of her colleagues disappear, giggling, around the corner. Of course I had to pay for it even though, technically, she had ripped it.

Why do they allow these foetuses to work in clothes shops? It doesn't make me want to go in there. Flaunting around in their size six clothes with ridiculously trendy names as they shout across a crowded store.

'Jaz, can you check if we have this in a size fourteen – or maybe a sixteen, actually – for this customer?' While looking disdainfully at me through a too-long fringe.

I want to be served by women whose arses are bigger than mine and who have shared the experience and humiliation of being stuck in a garment. I want them to say in hushed tones that they have the same trouble as me finding trousers to fit. I mean, the average UK size is a sixteen. I'm not alone here in being a real woman.

I do not want to hear the size six brigade tittering behind their hands and saying in mock awe: 'It *really* suits you.'

Wait 'til you hit real womanhood, sweetie, with your boobs swinging round your knees. So now I want to walk back in the manner of Julia Roberts in that scene from *Pretty Woman*:

'Big mistake. Huge!' I want to smirk as I flaunt my new look at them. I figure they won't know the relevance of my statement. Probably haven't ever watched a movie that wasn't Disney. So I stick to getting my own back by dangling my arm out of the changing room curtain, shouting: 'Service please, would you happen to have this in an eight?' It's fairly lost on them, sadly. In their minds anything over an eight is obese.

Laden with shopping bags, I head for the final part of my re-launch preparation – a new haircut. I exit an hour later with glossed, long choppy layers. It's just what I needed. Twirling around in the street, Jess and I squeal at my reflection in a shop window. Much to the annoyance of people attempting to pass by. Serving staff in the shop look at us curiously.

'Now, lunch,' states Jess and we head to our local to chill out and discuss which of our new purchases we will wear tonight. As Jess hurries back from the bar, with two glasses of Pinot Grigio, she pushes my head down to near table level.

'Stay there,' she hisses. She rummages in my River Island bag and chucks a pair of boot-cut jeans and a slinky top at me. She takes off her skyscraper heels and throws the lot in a carrier along with my makeup bag.

'Toilet, now!' she orders. 'And don't come out 'til you'd make

Kate Moss look like a complete dog.'

'Eww, gross! I'm not putting on "still warm" shoes. Reminds me of that time we went bowling, I swear I got a verruca...'

'I don't have any verrucae – now seriously, go!' Jess hisses, giving me an almighty shove. I have no idea why I am doing this, but I also know there will be a good reason. Even if temporary insanity is the cause.

I exit the bathroom ten minutes later, having preened myself thoroughly, and walk down the stairs to find Jess sitting at the table shoeless. She grins widely and points to the bar, where Sean and a sulky-looking Charmaine are waiting to be served. I teeter past as quickly as I can on four inch heels and sit down.

'What the hell are they doing in Edinburgh?' I ask.

'I overheard Sean saying they are through for the day to fix up some gigs for The Magic Mushrooms,' whispers Jess. 'You have *got* to go over.'

'No!' I look at Jess in horror. 'And let them have one up on me as they flaunt their relationship? I think not.'

'Lucy, you look amazing. She looks like the side of a house and, by the sound of things, all is not rosy.'

I listen closely to their muffled words. Indeed, it does sound like Charmaine is having a go at Sean over something. I take a deep breath, pull in my tummy and head over. Jess claps her hands with glee.

'*You* said that we would have one drink and go. You've had no luck in finding a gig and I'm tired. We've done five bars now and I'm not having you throwing up in my car again on the way home. You either come now, or I'm leaving on my own,' threatens Charmaine.

Sean looks tired. I try not to smile. I note the solitaire engagement ring on Charmaine's finger. Knowing Sean, it's not a diamond. It'd be from a Lucky Bag if he thought he'd get away with it. He storms off to play the bandit.

I order another two glasses of Pinot Grigio and smile sweetly at the gorgeous barman, Callum, who has been flirting outrageously with Jess and I since we came in. Charmaine turns in recognition of my voice.

'You!' she stares at me in disgust.

I look at her in confusion. 'Sorry, do we know each other?' I ask politely.

'Charmaine!' she exclaims, looking me up and down. 'You used to go out with Sean. Don't make out you don't know me,' she says indignantly.

'Sorry,' I smile. 'I think you're mistaking me for someone else.' I saunter back to my seat as Charmaine heads over to Sean, shaking her head and pointing in our direction. He walks toward us, smiling:

'Lucy, oh my God, you look great!' he announces, giving me an approving once over.

'Oh. Sorry, I realise who you are now,' I whisper to Charmaine.

Jess dashes to the bar where she is waving her arms and chatting enthusiastically to Callum. I smile at Sean and ask how he's been.

'Just been signed up for three gigs in Edinburgh,' he says smugly. Charmaine shoots him a 'what the hell are you talking about?' look.

'Only went to five bars. Had to turn two down and take the best three. You know how it is.'

Suddenly, I am swept backwards. Callum plants a kiss on my lips and says:

'I'll only be half an hour longer, gorgeous. Then I'm all yours. I've booked the restaurant for 7pm. You were right, when I gave my name, suddenly there was a table after all, Sir.' Callum turns to Sean: 'I don't *usually* like to name drop, but a rich music biz Daddy does work wonders.' He smiles knowingly and walks away.

Sean's face is a picture. 'Who... who is that?' he stutters.

'Like the man said, he doesn't like to name drop,' I shrug. 'Sorry, I can't help.'

With that, Jess and I wave sweetly to Callum and gather up our bags. We'll have lunch somewhere else.

'Sean, it really was a pleasure. Best of luck with the gigs and Chantelle, good luck, sweetie.' I glance pointedly at Sean when I say this. She's going to need it.

'It's Charmaine!' she screeches after us in disbelief.

Laughing loudly, we walk out into the sunshine, leaving an open-mouthed Sean and a silently fuming Charmaine staring after us.

I head in to work on Monday morning, after a hectic Saturday night and a very relaxed Sunday. I never got out of bed, other than to answer the door once and for a couple of calls of nature. Just read, watched TV and ordered a pizza. I arrive at work to discover we have lost another client in the Home – Bessie. For a lot of people the mortality rate in this job is not easy to accept – three of our people in as many months – but I admit, I have a philosophical approach to it all. There have been a couple of issues since Harry went, but nothing serious. Muddled up shifts and a couple of sick days. Nothing that the other staff don't do. I walk into a supervision meeting with Ellie, precariously balancing two coffee cups with a plate of biscuits on top of one. Ellie looks troubled. Getting straight to the point, she kindly informs me that, with the best of intentions, she is referring me to go on a bereavement management course. I roll my eyes and tell her I'm fine. I'm coping! She looks at me intently and says that the course will do me no harm anyway, and it may help me. I agree to do it – I have to. The company is very into preventative measures. Of what, I'm not sure. Nipping things in the bud is how it's referred to. They don't want people off on stress leave, I guess. Understandable really and great in theory, but not when you're coping as well as I am. I'm just wasting their money and my time. But I sit and listen, making the right noises until I can head back to the clients. I decide to go out at lunchtime and call around a few agencies for nanny work. Hopefully, the prognosis will be better when the people you care for are younger... I speak to Elaine at Edinburgh Nannies. We had a flyer handed out to us from her agency when we all graduated. She came in to do a talk and seemed friendly enough.

'We're really slow at the moment, Lucy,' she says. 'But why don't you pop in and register in case something comes up?' I head down after work and fill in an application form that makes *War and Peace* look like a pamphlet. Exhausted, and with a cramp in my wrist, we discuss the options.

'Just in: family with five children, new-born to nine years in Corstorphine. Laundry, cooking and some light housekeeping.'

'No way.'

'OK. Shared care with mum, twin boy and girl, two-months-old in Haymarket. 7am to 7pm.'

'Good God, no!'

'Buckstone. Weekend nanny...'

'No!'

Elaine looks defeated.

'OK,' she says. 'Sole charge, four-year-old boy, in nursery mornings, hours 9am 'til 5pm...'

'I'll take it,' I say firmly. 'Whereabouts?'

'Islington,' says Elaine hopefully.

'Don't know it,' I shrug. I thought I knew Edinburgh inside out.

'Islington... London,' ventures Elaine.

'Oh no you don't,' I eye her suspiciously. 'I know your game, trying to palm me off with London jobs because you get more money for them. Bet you have loads for Edinburgh really. My life is here, my home, all my friends, I'm not too far from my family.'

'Lucy, let me show you something.' Elaine swivels the screen round for me to look at, and types in 'Daily Positions in Edinburgh'. Like she says, only three come up.

'There are five live-in posts, but you don't want that.' She then types in 'Daily Jobs in London'. Immediately the screen fills up. They appear to be endless! The computer informs us it's on page one of forty-seven.

'Woah! Back up a bit. How much is a "daily" on in London?'

She highlights one. It's double my current weekly wage.

'That's after tax and National Insurance,' explains Elaine. 'The parents are responsible for your contributions.'

I exhale with a whistle. It's very tempting.

'Look, Lucy, London's great fun. You're young, single, you should at least try it. Maybe even just go for a few interviews. Get a feel for the place. I can speak to the parents, they're clamouring for qualified girls down there. If I set you up for three or four interviews, tell them they have to share your fare, I bet they'd do it. It's a drop in the ocean to the likes of them. We are talking serious money here. You're losing nothing but a little of your time.'

I sigh: 'I guess so. OK – I'll go for the interviews at least. Only if they pay my fare, though.'

A week later I arrive at King's Cross for my three lined up interviews. My backpack and I follow the swarms to the underground sign. I'm jostled to and fro all the way to the turnstiles, swearing under my breath at all these people in an apparent hurry to go places. I walk up to the barrier and look blankly at the closed gate. What am I supposed to do here?

'Ticket!' barks a fat, sweaty suit from behind me.

'Excuse me?' I reply.

'You need to put your ticket in here,' he says slowly and patronisingly, aggressively jabbing a finger at the slot.

'I don't have a ticket,' I say.

'She doesn't even have a ticket!' he bellows.

Several people laugh. It seems the 'no talk' rule on the tube that I've heard about doesn't apply when there's a dippy tourist in their midst.

Blushing, I make my way back to the machines I saw on the way down. Perhaps I can get a ticket there?

I stand in the queue, only to be shouted at for holding it up as I try to figure out what I need. A kindly, but slightly whiffy man pulls me to one side.

'You're new.' He states the obvious.

'Yes, I need to get to Islington,' I say, gratefully.

'For a small fee, I will be your personal guide,' he says, holding out a filthy hand for me to shake. I know – I shouldn't. But I'm not about to head down any dark alleyways or accept a lift from him. Plenty of people around, I figure.

He fleeces me for £2 to take me outside the station and informs me I can take the bus from opposite McDonald's. I thank him, despite knowing full well that I have been ripped off, and take in a panoramic view.

Two McDonalds.

You know those people who wander around London aimlessly, swearing and muttering to themselves? People give them a wide berth. They are not mad; they are *lost!* I'm doing the very same thing that they do at that moment. I spend fifteen minutes at the wrong McDonald's stop before asking the guy next to me why there are no Islington buses going by. I spend twenty minutes at the correct McDonald's, unable to figure out which one I should be on. None say Islington on the front. Finally, I meet a sweet, old lady.

'Where are you going, dear?' she asks.

After my recent fleecing, I inform her I have no more money and she looks offended.

I do, however, want to kiss her when she sees me safely off at my stop. It turns out she lives nearby and gives me clear and concise directions on how to get to my Bed and Breakfast.

A passing 'businessman-in-a-hurry' hits my backpack and sends me into a tailspin.

'Watch it, asshole!' shouts the old lady.

I think I've just made my first friend in London.

I fall asleep on the bed's stained top sheet (it looks suspiciously blood-like) in the B&B for two hours after my arrival. I wake at 9pm to the honking of horns and a hell of a racket outside. Food, that's what I need. I head outside and look along the street. Lots of lights on in the shops – a good sign. I walk up past the Angel tube and onto Upper Street, taking in the new sights and sounds. Kebab shops, hotdog stands and many drunken people swigging from cans, some asking me to spare some change. A large rat scurries by me from some bins. My squeal startles a homeless man in a doorway.

'Shurrup, stupid cow,' he slurs at me. 'I have a seven o'clock meeting in the morning.' He chortles at his own joke before the laugh turns into an emphysema fit.

I wait in a takeaway on the main street through Islington, trying to decide what to have to eat, from the garish, yellow menu board. I hear a voice addressing me from behind. I turn to see a friendly-looking Australian girl smiling at me.

'I saw you looking a bit lost wandering up the street there, just checking you're OK.'

'Oh thank you, I don't know this area well but it's kind of you to look out for me,' I smile politely and turn back to the menu. Why are you off home so early?' she asks.

'Oh, I'm new in town. Just here for interviews. I don't know a single soul in London.'

'Well, you do now,' she says triumphantly. 'Let's go grab a beer.' She pulls me outside despite my protests of interviews tomorrow. I give in and follow her across the road. It turns out Emily's friends have been stuck on the tube for over an hour. She has been waiting in 'Walkie' for them and was told by some 'random' that the Northern Line was down due to a 'jumper'. Once she has explained that this is a member of the public who has perhaps committed suicide, or possibly been pushed, I am shocked beyond belief.

'Doesn't that bother you?' I ask.

'Shit, yeah! Was late into work twice last week 'cause of them.' We have a great night in Walkie. Emily's friends turn up after two hours, seemingly none the worse off for having trawled through blood and guts on a track. I'd probably never get used to living in London, I decide. Oblivious to the fact that only six months later I too will be moaning about the inconvenience of 'jumpers' (do it off peak if you must at all!). I also go on to complain about 'tourists' who take longer than thirty seconds at the ticket machine.

I have three interviews the next day and I'm offered two of the positions. It seems Elaine was right; they are desperate for qualified nannies, with Scottish nannies being particularly desired for some bizarre reason. The latest trend in London, Elaine explained when I called her. It'll be Spanish ones next year, or Australians. Cash in while you can. I take the lowest maintenance job. The four-year-old boy with, in nanny terms at least, short hours. It is also on the same celebratory night out with Emily and friends that I meet James. I start my new job and have moved in with Emily, Amy and Jill in a shared house. Emily works in marketing. She and Jill, who is also from Adelaide, have been living in London for just over a year after leaving Australia on an extended working visa. These two are in constant competition with each other over, amongst other things, who weighs less, who can pull the most men and who has the most expensive wardrobe, Both girls, much to the annoyance of Amy and I, have year-round tans thanks to a sunshine-filled upbringing and long, lean bodies thanks to years of outdoor sports. Jill has long honey blond hair. She is definitely the prettiest of us all and never fails to pull, though I would never say this to Emily. Em hates her mid-length dark curls. They have a tendency to grow out the way, rather than down. Looks-wise, she is stunning, but isn't a patch on Jill. Both Amy and I are blonde too, but unfortunately look a bit on the plump side compared to Jill and Em. I mean, we both fit comfortably in a size twelve (I've crept back up) and are far from being fat. But being fairly short and standing next to two stunning size tens at nearly six foot tall each, who wouldn't feel like a podgy little frump? Jill's downfall, in Emily's opinion, is her job. As a waitress, she is on half Em's salary and therefore Em wins in the wardrobe department. Their constant bickering drives Amy and me to distraction. It can be entertaining at times, but mostly it's irritating. Amy, like me, is a nanny. Which probably explains why we're slightly heavier than the other two. In the homes where we work there are too many tempting kid's treats and lovely food. I spend most of my mornings in Starbucks with her and Phoebe, her two-year-old charge, who is generally purple-faced with temper. We then head along to our respective nurseries for Amy to pick up Harold and me to pick up Jake. The family I work for are great. They appreciate that I do have a life and therefore don't want to babysit at weekends. Occasionally we all go out for dinner and I know that, compared to a lot of nannies, I am very lucky.

Anyway, James is a Londoner, shows me all the sights I should see – and quite a few I probably shouldn't. I am, after all, a good Scots girl who has had a relatively sheltered life. He is fun, sociable, just your average Joe really. Or so I thought...

James, my friends and I all hung out every week at Walkie,

went out for dinner or had movie nights in. He spends a few nights a week at mine and I spend a few at his. One night a week I go out on my own with the girls; Usually a Friday or Saturday. We date for a few uneventful months and as I reflect on some of the horrors I've encountered in the past, I do feel quite relieved.

On one of our Friday nights out after work, Emily, Amy, Jill and I are in our local. We are mid-conversation, listening to Amy tell us about Phoebe's latest tantrum, when she pauses and stares at the window.
'What is it?' Emily asks. We all follow Amy's gaze, then look towards her blankly.
'I thought I just saw James looking in,' says Amy.
'Can't be,' I shake my head, 'he's off to Brighton with the boys tonight.'
'Oh, OK,' shrugs Amy, looking slightly confused. 'Lucy, I'm not sure about him,' she whispers. 'I caught him one day reading some of your mail from off the dining room table. When I questioned him on it, he said you had asked him to bring up the letter from the bank. Did you?'
'Not that I recall' I reply. 'I'm sure I did though, if he was rummaging.' Amy purses her lips in silent disapproval. I know she can't stand him. James thinks she fancies him. Typical man. You ignore them, so you must fancy them; if you rebuff their advances, you must be a lesbian. I have heard every one of their pathetic little excuses to justify the fact that, actually, they're just not your type. Amy brightens up a bit and informs us that she hasn't given us the latest low-down on her now married ex-boyfriend from years ago. He tracked her down a few weeks ago and has been harassing her by email ever since. It started out friendly enough, joking about how she dumped him three months into their relationship as the spark just wasn't there. He asked how she was, told her all about his life and then suggested they meet up for a drink one

evening in the week. Amy replied that that would be great – she'd love to meet his wife. Not what he was meaning, it appeared. Of course, Amy knew this. She's not stupid. He became more and more insistent, pestering her almost daily until, eventually, she emailed him to say: 'Look, I didn't fancy you when you were seventeen and loosely resembled Brad Pitt. I most definitely don't fancy you now your pushing forty, fat, bald and with a wife and four kids. Now *piss off!*'

Our laughter attracts a few stares from other tables. This is just so not an Amy thing to do. I am seriously impressed.

'What did he say?' Jill shakes her head in disbelief.

'Nothing, he pissed off like I told him to,' smiles Amy, enjoying a rare moment of being the centre of attention.

The evening continues raucously. We chat to a group of lads from Ireland on a stag night and share their tray of shots. After an hour Emily disappears with the best man, Matt, smirking at us over her shoulder. Jill fumes silently at being outdone so early on in the evening. We carry on until the early hours. The groom, Tony, informs me that, before proposing he had visited a fortune-teller; he had been constantly teased by his friends that his marriage to the 'psycho bitch from hell' – as was the name given to his fiancée by all the boys – was doomed. Apparently, they'd divorce in seven years and two kids later, but Tony was willing to take the gamble as it was, 'a load of old shite anyway.' The fortune-teller had told Matt that the name Emily was significant in his future. We all troop out to the kebab shop across the road. Amy stops and sways slightly.

'Luce, are you *sure* James is away?'

'Yes, Amy,' I say, pulling her along, 'He'd have said if it was cancelled. Now come on, it's just tequila-induced hallucinations.'

We leave the kebab shop with our steaming packages and say goodnight and good luck to the boys.

'Oh! Wait, Lucy,' says Tony. 'Can I give you Matt's number in case he doesn't give it to Emily? It's too much of a coincidence to let go. Besides,' he laughs, 'I don't want to be the only one with a ball and chain.'

Tony scribbles Matt's number on my arm with the kebab shop man's biro and we say our goodbyes and head home. Emily never contacts Matt again, despite me giving her his number. It was a one-night stand, and he was a rubbish kisser apparently. There must be a different Emily out there for him. I hope so. As a fatalist, I like to believe in these things. Amy looks nervously behind her all the way home waiting, I'm assuming, for another James-type hallucination. I choose to ignore it.

The next night, James comes around. He talks about what they all got up to in Brighton and how he could have pulled at least two girls. I listen with a smile and well placed nod. Tired of hearing his tales of delusion, I tell him I'm going to put in a pizza for tea. As I pad into the kitchen, Amy is making pasta for her and the girls. She gives me an uneasily sidelong glance.

'Want some?' she asks.

'No, I'm good thanks, we're having pizza.'

'How was James's weekend in Brighton?' she enquires.

'Sounds like it was fun – he could've pulled twice over.' Amy nods non-committedly and stirs her pasta. I walk back to the bedroom to see James hastily putting my phone down on the bed.

'What are you doing?' I question.

'Oh, it rang, I was going to answer but...' I check my phone. No missed calls.

'So... You meet anyone at the weekend?' James asks conversationally, shuffling into an interested, sitting position.

'Like, who?' I ask, distracted by scrolling through my call register.

'Oh, any random club-type men who gave you their number,' he says.

'No. Though Em met a guy who seemed really keen. Hasn't called him, though.'

Nothing more is said. I fetch the pizza and we eat in silence through the movie. I feign tiredness. 'I'm really knackered,' I say. 'I think I'll turn in.'

'Fine,' says James, using the side of my bed to push off his trainers, leaving a muddy smudge on my white duvet cover and his big toe poking out from a hole in a greying sock. He assumes that he is staying; annoyance suddenly flares up in me. I have a sudden urge to push him and his holey sock off my bed. Amy has unsettled me, she doesn't usually dislike a person for no good reason. Having thought about it, he didn't appear in my room at any point with a bank statement. What's with the snooping?

'Sorry, but I'd like a full double bed just for me tonight.' I attempt to hide my mixture of anger and disgust at the mess on my lovely clean duvet cover that I only changed today. James raises his eyebrows and stands up.

'Fine, I have a few calls to make,' he says ominously, 'so I'll be off.' He shoves on his trainers without undoing the laces and pulls on his battered denim jacket. The front door slams loudly. Relief washes over me. I get up and walk into the living room. The girls are watching the third series of *Friends* for the zillionth time and laughing uproariously.

'Strange night,' I say, breaking the mood.

'How so?' says Emily, her eyes still on the screen.

'Well, just James really. Being weird.'

'Hmm,' replies Emily, then goes back to laughing at Rachel and Ross's latest argument. Only Amy glances over at me, giving me a warm smile that tells me that she cares. I shrug and smile back. Another boyfriend on the way out, probably. We're beyond surprising these days.

Next morning, I have a call at 8am from my mum. Poopsy threw up on the bed an hour ago, forcing Mum to get up and attend to it. She's awake early and assumes everyone else is too. My mum would normally sleep until 11am. I think having me so young made her miss too much of her teenage years, and she is now making up for it. She sleeps late, parties with her family and friends and has a much more familiar chart knowledge these days than I do.

'Hi babe, still up for next weekend?' she asks.

'Of course, I can't wait,' I gush. It's my Uncle Robert's 40th birthday. These family events are usually quite fun, messy affairs.

'Grand. We've done a poster, it's the most horrific yet,' she states proudly. The 'poster' basically involves any horrendous photos from the past of the person in question, accompanied by text as horrid as possible.

My last, on my 30th was a faded black and white photograph of me, the fattest baby ever born and carried the thoughtful caption, 'I ate my twin.'

The poster is never pretty. It's never complimentary, but always hugely funny at the expense of the recipient.

The week passes quickly and, before I know it, I am boarding the train at King's Cross. James smugly informs me that he won't notice I'm gone, he has such a 'mental' weekend lined up. Great, I think with relief. I can let my hair down and be myself.

I arrive at Arbroath station and take a cab up to the 'Cliffy' – our local hotel and party venue. It's seen many an occasion from us; parties, weddings and, sadly, funerals. I can't wait to see everyone. It feels so long since I saw them all. I walk to the door of the function room and observe for a moment what my family does when I can't see them. I gaze through a gap in the frosted glass doors, picking out the familiar shapes of my loved ones. They laugh and they hug. Life goes on without me. I ponder for a moment on how much of their lives remain unseen to me. Yet it happens. Like my life does too, and they don't see. Some things we will never experience about each other. I have a pang of wishing I could do this every day. Not to miss a moment. Funny statements made by my auntie, my mum's smile, my niece's silly dancing surrounded by clapping relatives. It all occurs, funny at the time, but not funny enough for them to remember and tell me later. A million moments we miss in each other's lives. I walk in and break the spell.

'Auntie Lucy,' Josh gasps, as he sees me first. He runs over and I pick him up, wrapping myself in his baby hug. Suddenly, I am surrounded by warmth. Hugs, kisses so fast on my cheek that I can't see the person who delivered it. My hand being squeezed by another unseen loved one. Then my mum's smiling face.

'Hiya, my girl, I have *so* missed you,' she says, enveloping me in Chanel and baby powder. I feel safe and warm, surrounded by my family, all chatting ten to the dozen, telling me of new boyfriends, exam passes and, in the case of Jessie, the littlest girl of the family, a brand new tutu for ballet class. I try my hardest to answer everyone and keep up. Mary pulls away from hugging me and gives me an excited smile.

'Oh my God,' she says, 'we have a total surprise for you.'

My family step aside to reveal… James.

'I just couldn't miss this,' he smirks. 'Hope you don't mind, Luce.'

Chapter Six

'Oh my God! This *is* a surprise,' I exclaim. 'I didn't even know you had any way of getting in touch with my family.'

'Password, Lucy. Every phone needs one,' James whispers patronisingly, then laughs loudly. Everyone around us thinks we are sharing a private joke and laugh along.

'I see,' my tone makes several of the female family members straighten up like meerkats, sensing danger.

'Bar?' suggests my cousin, Jo.

'Back in a moment.' I aim a sickly sweet smile at James.

Mary, Jo, Claire and I head towards the bar. We buy four vodka and Diet Cokes and I'm quickly pulled into the ladies. Mary opens a window, sparks up two cigarettes and passes one to me.

'I don't smoke anymore.' I stub it out quickly and hand it back to her, before I'm tempted to take a puff.

'So, what's the story?' Jo asks.

'I don't know,' I explain. 'I'm just not comfortable with this. He's obviously been looking through my phone and one of my friends seems to think he's following me. There's been a bit of an issue with my mail too and after him turning up here tonight, well, I feel like I'm being stalked.'

'I'm sorry, Luce. He sent me a text saying he wanted to surprise you. I'm totally responsible,' Mary sighs apologetically.

'No, it's not your fault. He's very sly,' I insist, 'we just need to keep an eye on him. I'm not comfortable with him getting so close to the family.'

A knowing nod passes around all three.

'He does seem a bit like he's trying too hard. OK, we have to make out we suspect *nothing*,' conspires Claire. 'Keep your friends close and your enemies closer. Pretend to befriend. It's the only way.' A dramatic hush ensues.

'Let's go,' orders Mary.

We walk over to the crowd around James, who is clearly loving an audience.

'So, by then she's looking through my video collection and she shouts through, "what's Head Cleaner about?"'

Everyone laughs along at the latest 'blonde moment' of mine that James is describing.

'You've done well this time, Luce,' says my Uncle Jim, with a nod to James.

I watch as a worried glance pass around the girls in the know.

The evening continues and, much to my disappointment, I'm not enjoying it. James follows me around incessantly. When I spot someone I haven't seen for ages on the other side of the room, he's there. 'Just want to meet all the family.' And when I go to the bar: 'I'll just help you carry the tray of drinks.'

'He's very attentive,' says Mum. 'Seems really keen.'

'Too keen,' I mutter bitterly.

The final straw is when I find him waiting for me outside the bathroom. The girls and I have met for an update. They too can see how irritating he can be, and have given up the befriending mission and now favour a very public dumping instead.

'For goodness sake, can I not even have a pee without you hovering around?' I snap.

He looks hurt.

'Sorry, Lucy. It's just that you keep going to the one place I can't come with you. I miss you,' he whines.

James begins sinking his pints faster, now that we've had words. He takes my aunties up to all the Scottish reels, looking over at me for approval at how much part of the family he is. He pulls my small niece, Jessica, onto his lap. She squirms to get away, a look of disgust on her face. Sensible girl, I think – another one immune to his charms. James sits and looks sullenly into the bottom of his pint glass. Several family members ask if he's all right. He smiles wanly at them and nods. The music starts for *Strip the Willow*, my favourite Scottish reel and very important to get right. Many a person attempting it for the first time has been shouted down. Scots take their reels very seriously indeed. My cousin, Craig, and I look over at each other and immediately make our way to the dance floor. We stand in line ready to go. James appears behind Craig.

'Would you mind if I dance with my girlfriend, please?' he simpers, holding his hand out toward me. Craig shrugs and looks at me.

'Sorry James,' I say dismissively. 'Craig and I always do this one.'

Mary is swiftly by James's side.

'This one's mine, I think,' she announces, giving me a wink. As the first couple start to spin each other around, James looks at me as if he's a puppy I've just kicked, and continues to do so for the rest of the dance. Afterwards, he comes over to speak to me.

'Bugger off!' I say angrily, and storm back to my only sanctuary – the ladies loo – with an unlit cigarette and lighter in my hand that I had grabbed from the table on my way past. Mary bursts in.

'Come quickly!' She grabs my arm, disposing of my cigarette down the toilet. 'And don't you dare smoke because of him.'

'Ladies and gentleman, we have a young man here who wants to make an announcement,' yells the bandleader over the mic in the manner of a game show host.

'Oh sweet Jesus, no,' I hear Claire mutter.

'Hi everyone. I'm James. Some of you know me already.' He clears his throat awkwardly, and looks around the hushed room with an adoring smile.

'I would just like to say how happy I am to be here and how welcome you've all made me.' He chokes emotionally over the last few words.

'What an arse!' booms a male voice behind me.

'I'd also like to say that, although Lucy and I have only been together a few months, she is undoubtedly the most wonderful thing that has happened in my life.'

'No way, man,' snorts Craig behind me.

'So, it's on this note,' continues James, 'that it gives me great pleasure to ask Lucy to be my wife.' James gets down on one knee to a now horrified throng. 'Lucy, will you marry me?' James gives me a watery smile.

'No!' I shake my head violently. 'James, come down please, so we can talk about this.' Several people laugh uproariously.

'Lucy, please,' implores James, with an anxious glance around the crowd.

'It's been two months James – I can't marry you! Don't do this.'

'And, you're a knob,' mutters Jo, just loud enough for me to hear. I walk over to the stage.

'Come down, James,' I urge. 'We can carry on having a nice evening. But I'm sorry, I'm not going to say yes just because it's in front of all these people.'

I gesture to the crowd behind me. Some open-mouthed with shocked amusement, others looking away in embarrassment. The compere gently prises the mic from James's clenched fist.

'Take your partners for the *Eightsome reel*,' he bellows jovially.

James runs from the stage and doesn't stop until he's outside.

'Craig, go and see if he's all right,' orders Auntie Betty, giving my cousin a shove and making him spill some of his pint down his shirt.

'You're shitting me, right?' exclaims Craig in disbelief. 'He's bats! He'll murder me.'

'Do it!' demands Betty and cuffs his ear. Craig wipes his shirt with his mother's cardigan sleeve, which is hanging on the back of his chair, and saunters reluctantly outside. Uncle Robert throws his arm around my shoulder.

'This has made my birthday!' he laughs. 'I think that's the funniest thing I've ever seen.' He wipes a hand across his eyes. A small crowd has gathered at each window overlooking the gardens. Three valiant couples are attempting an Eightsome Reel with a meagre six. James is hunched over on a bench whilst Craig awkwardly pats his back, glancing around uncomfortably. He spots us looking out, smirks and flicks the V-sign at us. They speak for a few minutes and then I see Craig talking on his phone. Five minutes later we hear the screech of tyres and James is gone. Craig walks back in and announces that James is going to get the sleeper back to London. The room exhales as one.

Back at mum's for an after-party party. We dissect the evening with great mirth.
'What's the deal with all these failed relationships, Lucy?' Mum asks through a mouthful of crisps.
'Obviously an invisible tattoo on my head that says "all nutters stop here,"' I suggest. Mary laughs, and sings along to the Foo Fighters song that's playing, about moving on to the next man.
'Hey, lyrics you've actually got right for once,' says Robert. He picks up the pickled onion Mary has thrown at his head from the floor, examines it for fluff – and eats it.
'Yep, get back on the horse,' says Jo. 'Preferably a rather large muscley one to scare off James. You've not seen the last of him I'm guessing.'
 And I hadn't.

 I arrive back to London to find six answerphone messages and a massive bunch of roses in the front room. All flatmates are instructed to, under no circumstances, let James in or pass on any information about me. One week on, I buy a new sim card. Poor Jill, with no way of contacting me, he starts on her. Well, until Mark, her boyfriend of the week, phones and tells him to piss off or he'll phone the police. The next evening our landline rings. We look at each other nervously. With a loud tut, I announce that this is getting ridiculous. We shouldn't be worried to answer our own phone. But I click on the loudspeaker, just in case I need witnesses to this call.

'Hello?' I say tentatively.

'May I speak with the man of the house, please?'

Open-mouthed with shock, we all stifle a giggle. We love these calls; never stop until the telesales person either hangs up or cries.

'Ooh, hello. Are you calling from the 1950s?' I ask.

'Er... No, I...'

'Well, I do apologise,' I interrupt. The only people here are me, my lesbian lover and our two adopted daughters.' The room erupts. 'So, to whom would you like to talk to now?' Click.

It's been a while since we had a 'man of the house' call. It's our favourite!

'Oh he sounded quite cute, actually,' Amy sounds crestfallen. 'I'm fed up being single, my nanny friend told me about a site I should try called 'Millionaires Looking for Love.'

'That is so mercenary,' I announce.

'They all seem to turn out to be arseholes,' she explains defensively. 'May as well have a rich arsehole than a poor one.' She spends all evening tapping away on the computer, putting in comments and uploading photographs. She adds the message:

'No photo, no chat. You are obviously either married or ugly. Either way, I don't want to know you!' She clicks 'add profile' and waits.

'It's going to take at least 24 hours for the site to check you're not a bunny boiler,' says Emily. 'Why not do a search now and find all the gorgeous ones?' We group around her and wait expectantly. A romance novel hero appears on the screen.

Swept back, black hair and an enigmatic smile.

Miles: Owner/ Managing Director of I.T. chain. Thirty seven-years-old, likes classical music, fine wine and dining out. Twice divorced, four children from two marriages, wltm…
'Christ, no!' I exclaim. 'Miles has more baggage than Heathrow.'
We search again. Anthony: sole inheritor of father's satellite installation company. Hoping to meet kind, attractive woman for no-strings fun.
We observe his photo.
'Eeuww! Fugly,' exclaims Jill. We look at her confused. 'Short for fucking ugly,' she rolls her eyes at our ignorance. 'I mean, look at the beak on him! Funny how he mentions no-strings – he looks just like Pinocchio,' she giggles.
'Here's one,' says Amy. We all read his profile.
Justin, a DJ in a London club, tours twice a year to Ayia Napa and Faliraki. Didn't want to follow his brothers into the family business. Used his trust fund to buy decks and take a Sound Engineering degree. Gorgeous to boot!
'Email him,' I demand. Amy sends him a short, sassy message.
'Hi Justin, like your profile. Living in London and would love to meet up. Email back if you like the sound of me. Not a gold digger, I have my own fortune. Sick of blokes only wanting me for *my* money, so thought I'd try a financially independent catch.'

We search for another hour and Amy sends out two more messages. For the most part, it's fairly obvious why a lot of them are single. We switch off and send for a takeout. Watching a movie an hour later, Amy's eyes keep wandering back to the computer.
'Leave it 'til tomorrow,' says Jill. 'You don't want to seem too keen.' At 9pm – and bored – we decide to make a round of hot

chocolates and head up to our respective beds for an early night. I stifle a laugh at the creaking floorboards an hour later, as Amy makes her way back down the hall to check for messages. I plan to creep down and give her a fright five minutes later but with no man occupying half my bed, I doze off like a contented starfish.

Chapter Seven

My alarm goes off at 6.40am. I hit the snooze button unnecessarily hard and roll over. My nap is short-lived, however. I hear a 'Woo-hoo!' from the living room. I pull on my dressing gown and make my way along the hall.

'What's so good about a Monday morning that could possibly warrant such celebration?' I blink as the sunlight streams in through the blinds.

'Two replies,' says Amy dismissively, focusing on the screen. I hover behind her, reading over her shoulder.

'Justin wants to meet, says he likes my pics, my profile is up now. Says I sound "cool."'

She flicks to a new message from Alex.

'Hi Amy,' she speed reads aloud, 'Thanks for your email, you do sound great. I am actually currently seeing a girl from the site and feel it would be unfair to meet up with you. However, my friend Alfie (and I am aware this sounds juvenile) does like the look of your friend in the pic entitled 'Me and Luce' and wonders if she's single and would like to meet up? He's a widower, his wife died three years ago in a yachting accident. Please don't quote me on this though as he is very private about it. He has come to terms with it, but I'd prefer it if Luce didn't mention this part of his life should she decide to meet up, but I do think it's important to mention up front as he's quite nervous about getting back "out there". I'm sure it will all come out in due course from Alfie anyway.
Kind regards,
Alex.'

'Shit!' I exhale, 'Poor guy, how could I say no? OK, email back and say I'll go along and meet Alfie. Even if I don't fancy him, I'm not going to refuse to go. That's awful...' I shake my head at the unfairness of the world at times.

It's a fairly uneventful week of crash dieting, face packs in the bath and early nights. All in preparation for the weekend. Before I know it, Friday comes along and, thanks to a combination of Amy and Alex, I now have a date for this evening at 7pm with Alfie.

The girls and I trawl through my wardrobe for a suitable outfit.

No black. Too funereal.

No red. Reminiscent of blood.

We settle on a modest pastel blue top and jeans.

I have a quick glass of wine to settle my nerves as Amy and Em tease my hair straight and touch up my make-up. By ten minutes to seven, I am waiting in the bar of our local on Upper Street. I'm on my second glass of wine and my nerves are beginning to fuzz at the edges. I take out my phone and send a few random text messages to pass the time.

To Em: 'Shitting a brick.'

To Amy: 'If he's ugly, you are so a dead woman!'

To Mary: 'New date! Urgh! I hate this.'

Mary texts back immediately: 'Is this one an alien, perchance? Nothing you brought home would surprise me anymore. Good luck! PS don't shag him!'

'Lucy...?' a kindly, well-spoken voice enquires.

'Yes, that's me,' I answer. Woah! Cute. Alfie smiles and asks if he can buy me a drink. I nod politely and say a white wine would be lovely. He heads off to the bar, giving me a great rear view. I may have struck lucky this time I think.

We have several drinks and the conversation flows easily. He tells me how he has worked for his father's textiles company since he left school.

'Nepotism – a game the whole family can play,' I state.

He bursts out laughing.

'That's quality,' says Alfie. 'Not quite true, though. The company was in serious trouble and I was cheap – no, make that free – labour for Dad. Well, for the first year anyway, but we managed to turn it around and it's doing great now.'

What a nice guy, I think, feeling bad about my nepotism wisecrack.

'So, are you lurking on that Millionaires website too then?' I ask.

Argh! That makes me sound shallow and money-grabbing. I cringe.

'No,' Alfie smiles. 'Not quite in that league. Maybe one day.'

This man can do no wrong.

'It's a bit shallow I mean, why not go on a regular website to meet men? Why millionaires?' I try to cover my *faux pas*.

'Why not?' shrugs Alfie. 'Financial security is important to a lot of people. I don't see it as shallow, necessarily.'

'So, do you date much?' I ask.

Foot in mouth disease or what? There's something wrong with me tonight. I have lost the ability to speak without dropping clangers in every sentence. Alfie looks sadly down at his lap.

'I've been out of the loop for a bit, actually. Just didn't feel like dating for quite a while. Back on track now though,' he smiles reassuringly.

I text Mary after Alfie drops me home. We're meeting again for Sunday lunch.

'Date was excellent. Seeing him again. He is, dare I say it, normal! P.S: I'm going to bed. Alone.'

Things go from strength to strength with Alfie. On our fourth date he tells me about Polly, his wife. I cringe in anticipation. He has no idea that I know about it already. I have to look unfazed at this point, which is so difficult when I know what is coming.

Alfie and Polly had been at a party on a friend's yacht. There were quite high winds that day and they had been warned the sea might be choppy. They headed out anyway, as it was for his friend's wife's birthday and nobody wanted to be a killjoy. They had all had quite a lot of champagne and canapés. The friend had hired a Captain for the day so he could enjoy a few drinks. A band played on board and everyone was in good spirits. The sky had darkened over with black clouds at around 7pm. The Captain decided they had best head back before dark, with what looked like an imminent storm heading their way. Stupidly, Polly and Alfie had been sitting chatting on the edge of the boat. Polly had asked for another glass of champagne and he had left her there for a few minutes. Alfie had been talking to his friend's wife about their plans to extend their house, when they heard a scream. Running back along the deck, a panic had broken out. The yacht was quickly moving away from a now unconscious Polly, who was just visible in the water. Alfie knew it was bad, there was a pool of blood around her head. He dived in and swam towards her. For a while he managed to keep her head above water, but exhausted, it was becoming increasingly difficult for him to keep them both afloat in the waves. His friend, Chris, had pulled him from the water and insisted he stay on board.

A couple of the men jumped in and managed to pull Polly onto the deck. It took twenty minutes to get to dry land and another fifteen for the ambulance to arrive and take Polly to the nearest hospital. She had lost too much blood and was pronounced dead on arrival. I sat in horrified silence. Feeling sick.

'How do you even begin to get over something like that?' I asked quietly.

'You have to,' said Alfie sadly. 'I never thought I'd ever find someone who even came close to Polly. Aren't I lucky I met you?'

Wow! I hadn't expected that.

It was also this night that I saw Alfie's apartment for the first time. It was a huge, three-bedroom place in Chelsea.

Tastefully decorated, a woman's touch definitely. It obviously hadn't been touched since Polly's death. One solitary photograph sat on the mantle. A wedding picture. I picked it up and had a good look. Polly was very pretty. Dark, curly hair swept off her face with a white rose stuck loosely in the back. It was a paparazzi-style shot, like they hadn't expected it to be taken. Laughing, with their heads close, holding a glass of champagne each.

'Oh, I'm so sorry, Lucy,' Alfie says as he walks back into the room with a bottle of Rioja and two glasses. 'How insensitive of me. It's just been so long since I had anyone back here...' he trailed off, sadly.

'Don't be so silly!' I exclaim. 'Of course you should have a picture up of Polly. She's gorgeous. It looks like it was a great day for you.'

'The best,' Alfie smiles wistfully, lost in thought for a moment. 'Anyway,' he says, coming back to Earth, 'wine?'

I spend most of my time in Alfie's opulent surroundings. To the extent that whenever I call any of my flatmates they say, 'Lucy, who?' and laugh. They are very pleased for me, particularly given my track record. Alfie is quite obviously loaded, his flat alone must have been worth a million, easily. We spend almost every night together, apart from when Alfie is away on business. Often, annoyingly, at the weekend and sometimes for up to a week and a half at a time. He insists on leaving the freezer full and inviting my friends to come around whilst he's away. He also calls every single night. All these trips are a small price for him to pay, I guess, for the lifestyle he has.

The months with Alfie seem to fly by. Never before have I had such an attentive boyfriend. He brings me flowers, takes me out for dinner at least twice a week and constantly tries to take me on shopping trips. I often tell him not to spend money on me. I am in a full-time job too and should pay my way. I never wanted to be one of those girls who expect men to pay for everything. They irritate me beyond belief. It's so difficult when he comes home with his 'little gifts' as he calls them. Designer dresses and diamond jewellery are not little gifts. The one time I attempted to refuse, Alfie looked so crestfallen, I felt awful. I'm nowhere near in the same league financially, but I do buy him the odd CD that he's mentioned sounds good, or cook him one of his favourite meals. That's about the limit I can stretch to. But I guess it's the thought that counts. I'm not a material girl in the slightest, and joke to him that the wrong type of girl really could take advantage of him.

On one rare weekend that Alfie is around, Mary, Jo and Claire all come down to London for a girly weekend of shopping and shows. Of course, Alfie insists they stay at his instead of booking into a hotel. They are astounded, not only by Alfie's amazing apartment, but also his charming manner. The perfect host, he paid careful attention to the tiniest of details. By day two he knew what every girl took in their coffee and came home with a huge bunch of roses for Mary. His reasoning: she had complained the day before that never in her life had she received a bunch of flowers from a man. On the Saturday night, we were applying the finishing touches to our hair and make-up before heading off to see a West End show, when the buzzer to the apartment went.
'Ladies, cab's here,' shouted Alfie from the hallway.
A chorus from the bedroom of 'shit!' and 'bollocks, it's early' and 'where's my new pissing top' amongst other expletives led Alfie to joke:
'OK! Perhaps I was wrong about the ladies bit.' Much to our hilarity.

We headed downstairs to the cab, buttoning up coats, applying lip gloss and generally cackling like old hens. The concierge opens the front door and we thank him profusely and clatter down the marble steps. There, in front of us, is a gleaming black stretch limo. The girls squeal in unison.

'Have fun,' shouts Alfie from the balcony.

'Thank you,' we yell back, blowing kisses and waving with glee.

We all pile in and arrange ourselves in the back of the limo.

'Fucking hell,' yells Mary, 'this bugger's bigger than my living room.'

'Sssh!' hisses Jo, trying to conceal a laugh. 'Have some bloody class, woman.'

'Good evening ladies,' a voice comes from hidden speakers, causing us all to glance around nervously. 'How are you all this evening?'

'Erm, hello Sir. We've come to see the wizard,' Claire says in her best Dorothy voice. 'Me and my dog Toto.' She indicates Mary, who looks at her aghast, giggles, then slaps her arm. The driver gives a deep laugh.

'Finally, some normal people in here. You couldn't imagine some of the stuck-up arseholes I meet.' In just thirty seconds he has gone from a BBC English accent to a broad Cockney one.

The driver, Mick, advises us to sit back and enjoy the view.

'We shall head through Chelsea to Kensington,' he continues, 'and also will be taking in views of the Palace, Hyde Park, Marble Arch and Embankment this evening. You will alight at Claridge's, where you will have dinner. Afterwards, we will carry onto the Dominion theatre in time for your show.'

'But the show starts at five,' exclaims Jo.

'The show starts at seven thirty, ma'am,' states the driver. 'But, as Alfie said: "I'll never get the bloody prima donnas out if I don't tell them it's three hours earlier." Now sit back and crack open the champagne. Please feel free to choose any music you wish from our selection. You will find snacks in the back there too. Mr. Hughes chose them specially.'

Mary locates the champagne while Claire rummages for the snacks. We crack open the bottle, singing loudly and tunelessly to the Foo Fighters while we sink our champagne.

'If you ever break up, he is so mine,' declares Mary.

'You'll have to fight me first,' argues Jo.

As light-hearted bickering ensues, I sit back and smile, feeling very, very fortunate indeed.

The weekend ends, all too soon. Mary, Claire and Jo take Alfie and I out for lunch to say thank you for all that Alfie has done. We choose a cosy Greek restaurant in Sloane Square. The wine flowed, as did the jesting from the girls. Jo enquired if Alfie had a brother or cousin, even some single cute friends like him. Alfie promised to try and fix her up with some of his mates next time she comes down. She booked her train the second she got home. We headed up to King's Cross to see them off. I waved sadly from the platform as three heads popped out of the window, waving enthusiastically.

'I love your family,' smiled Alfie.

'Me too,' I sighed, turning and walking back along the platform.

Christmas time comes around again. Alfie declines my invite for a visit to Arbroath as he needs to go into work on Christmas Eve and Boxing Day. I'm desperate to show him off to the family but reluctantly agree that sometime in the New Year would be better. After a rare, but thoroughly enjoyable, girl's night out, Emily declares that they need to see more of me. We have all missed each other and this one night has served to highlight the fact. Em suggests the next time Alfie is away on business we should have a girly weekend in Brighton. I agree, non-committedly. I have now turned into one of those pathetic coupled-up people who don't want to do anything when their boyfriend is away. I'd be quite happy watching movies and waiting for his call. Maybe a cinema trip or lunch with a girlfriend, but definitely not a club. Those are for people on the pull. I, most definitely, am not.

So, it's with great trepidation that I agree to go on a girl's weekend two weeks later.

'You'll have a great time,' says Alfie. 'And I will have a much nicer business trip knowing you are happy. Please do it. For me?' he smiles.

'OK, I'll go,' I say reluctantly. 'Maybe some time I should accompany you on one of these trips? You can't be in meetings all of the time.'

'No. I'm not,' laughs Alfie. 'All right. How about you accompany me to Venice next month? I'll be busy during the day, but in the evenings I'll be all yours.'

'That sounds like a plan.' I smile broadly.

I arrive home to the flat on Saturday morning, to be told that we are no longer going to Brighton, but Southampton. Better nightlife, apparently, and also Amy is to meet a website 'Millionaire'. We head off around lunchtime, Emily driving, the rest of us sharing a bottle of wine and Jill smoking out of the window. We play a 90s CD and sing along loudly.

We pile out at our B&B and make our way to the room. I am actually beginning to enjoy myself. It's been so long since I saw the girls like this. We head out to the pubs at around 5pm, laughing and joking along the street. We visit two dodgy-looking pubs on the main street, full of bikers who stare at us when we walk in. I wait for someone to inform us:

'You ain't from around these parts, are you?' We hastily drink up and wander off along the main street, stopping off for an Italian meal. An hour later and we are sitting in the Ship, a bar on the sea front. Jill announces that she is out of fags and goes off in search of a shop. We all find this ridiculous as there is a cigarette machine in the pub.

'I refuse to pay £6 for three fags,' she announces huffily, and storms out to find a corner shop.

Half an hour later, Jill hasn't arrived back. Amy calls her on her mobile. No answer. Another ten minutes passes by and I try Jill's number again.

'I'm outside Lucy. Come out a minute,' she says seriously.

'Oh, for Christ's sake, Jill,' I slur. 'Just get yer arse in here now. We're working our way through a tray of shots and we won't save you any if you don't hurry.'

'Luce, I am serious. Come out here now! Please.'

'For fuck's sake, OK!' I manoeuvre around the others and head towards the door.

'What is it, Jill?' I demand, hanging up my phone.

'It's Alfie.' She points in the direction of the pub opposite.

'What do you mean, it's Alfie?' I am starting to lose patience.

'He's in *there*,' she says exasperatedly.

'Jill, he's in Barcelona. Come on, let's go back to the Ship.'

'Just take a look, Lucy. It definitely is him.'

We round up the girls and head off to the Anchor, which is across the street. The others take Jill seriously, while I fully expect to see an Alfie-alike.

We walk in and find a booth from which to observe. Amy heads to the bar and buys a bottle of wine. I glance around. Coming through the door from the rest rooms is, indeed, Alfie. The girls gasp as one. Em places a restraining arm across me, keeping her eyes firmly on Alfie, like a cat watching a bird.

'Easy,' she warns. 'Watch and learn, sweetie.'

Alfie re-joins a table full of men. They are raising their glasses in one friend's direction and toasting something – I can't hear what. Alfie's phone rings. He takes it out of his pocket and smiles when he reads the caller's name on the screen. He chats away, laughing and smiling affectionately.

'He's talking to a woman,' whispers Em. 'That is an "I fancy you" smile. Not a blokey "I'm talking to my mate" smile.'

I agree, but say nothing. He hangs up the phone, after

mouthing what looks like, 'love you'.

I take out my phone and press Alfie's number. We all watch as he takes his phone out of his pocket a second time. He shakes his head and laughs, saying 'sorry' to the boys. A flash of concern clouds his face as he checks his caller I.D. He whispers something to the man next to him and heads outside.

'Luce, honey, how are you?' I watch his nervous body language as he paces back and forth in the doorway, taking long drags on a cigarette.

'I'm good,' I reply. 'The girls and I are pubbing it. Having a ball. How's Barcelona?'

'Dull, dull,' he says quickly. 'Wish I was with you.'

'Well, you could be,' I reply.

'I have to work, Luce. I want to keep you in the manner to which you have become accustomed.' He laughs nervously and scratches his nose.

'So, what are you doing right now? I mean, where exactly are you?'

'Well, I just had dinner on my own and was contemplating a pint. I am standing outside a bar, near my hotel. I am wearing the top you bought me for my birthday and jeans and trainers, anything else?' Alfie laughs, but there's no smile behind it.

I begin to walk towards the door and push it open.

'That's not the top I bought for your birthday,' I say. 'I bought you the red one.'

He turns and does a double take. The girls have their faces pressed against the window.

'Lucy,' he yells, before giving me a huge hug. 'I thought you were in Brighton!'

'And I thought you were in Barcelona,' I deadpan.

'Trip cancelled, last minute, I didn't want to say as it's a mate's stag party weekend. I never mentioned it so you couldn't persuade me not to go,' Alfie babbled quickly.

It did make sense. I would have persuaded him to stay in

London with me. God, what kind of girlfriend had I become that he had to lie to get time out?

'I'm sorry, Alfie,' I say, hanging my head. 'I feel terrible that you think of me that way.'

He wraps his arms around me and kisses the top of my head.

'I don't think of you that way and, believe me, I would rather be with you. I do, however, want to hold on to my friends, so this is a necessary evil,' and he gestures toward the bar. 'Well, since both of our plans have changed and we find ourselves randomly thrown together, why don't you get the girls over to our table? I can hardly see that bunch of Neanderthals complaining,' he indicates to his group of friends.

'Great idea!' I smile and head inside to gather my brood.

'What the fuck?' exclaims Amy, 'you actually believe that shit?'

'It's not shit,' I snap irritably. 'Come on. Let's join them.'

The girls reluctantly trail behind me. Jill immediately starts to grill Alfie. He good-naturedly answers all her questions.

'Of course it's not suspicious that I said I was in Barcelona,' he laughs. 'I mean, Lucy said she was in Brighton, didn't she? I don't find that *suspicious*.' He leans in to Jill and says the last word conspiratorially.

My friends aren't convinced, but go along with the evening as planned. We all head to a club at midnight, the earlier drama quickly becoming a distant memory as we drink and dance. The girls flirtatiously eye up Alfie's selection of gorgeous mates. Later, I go to stay in Alfie's suite. Much bigger and posher than our tiddly B&B, and I can't be bothered with the interrogation I'm bound to get.

I awaken contentedly the next morning and roll over to give Alfie a hug. He starts a little at seeing me and I laugh affectionately.

'Sorry to wake you but the girls will be checking out soon and

I promised I'd go back with them.'

'Yeah, of course. Sorry, I'm all disorientated this morning. Drank way too much last night.' He replies.

I text Emily and tell her I will wait outside the hotel in half an hour. The atmosphere on the way home is tense. In the cold light of day, the unlikely scenario of Alfie's trip being cancelled, and him just happening to be in the same pub in Southampton as us, has reared its head again. I can tell it has been discussed in much detail. I decide it's up to me to bring up the events of last night. Taking a deep breath, I launch into the subject.

'Look, I want to discuss with you this whole Alfie-in-Southampton thing.' Em's foot presses hard on the accelerator. Flicking her brown eyes at me in the rear view mirror, her pretty face set in determination. She is the one who is most protective of me; maybe because I met her first, she saw me at my most vulnerable. She is a no-mess Aussie girl. Jill, Amy and I cling on to the nearest fixed object. Amy looks at me, with pity.

'I'm worried, Luce. Sorry, you know I don't like to interfere but, I just feel there is more to this.'

'I know. And I know you're all only looking out for me because you care. My instincts say he's not hiding anything, but Hell mend me if I'm wrong. We all know I have previous on that! So, I guess what I'm saying is that I give you free rein to delve into what you can find and, well, I guess I will hear you out if there is anything dubious.'

My friends brighten at this. They do love to play detective. I just so hope they are wrong, but even I am now beginning to have my reservations.

Somehow we make it back in one piece. Em's erratic driving leaving us all in silent terror throughout the whole journey. There seems no going back from this weekend. I have to face it. Can I trust Alfie? My friends don't seem to think so. Is it so weird that he was in Southampton? I didn't tell him our location had changed and I was doing nothing wrong. What's to say he was? I mentally replay the reaction on his face on seeing me. Shock? Surprise? Maybe a bit of both? He was almost unreadable. The sign of a liar? Or the sign of someone who really thought nothing of the situation he found himself in? My head pounds. Every time I replay the scene, Alfie's reaction changes, until I no longer know which the real one was anymore.

We get home and immediately go our separate ways. Emily heads straight to her room, slamming the door. I hear her talking angrily to someone on her mobile. Jill runs a bath. She has a shift in the restaurant later tonight. Amy heads to the computer and turns the screen away from me, before looking up apologetically and telling me she is just going to give her no-show 'Millionaire' what for, for standing her up. I shrug and head into the kitchen and switch the kettle on. I know what she's doing. Looking for evidence. I know this for a fact because, an hour later, I check the history and find the name Alfred James Hughes has been searched. Fair enough, I gave them the go ahead. Emily comes to find me in my room later and finds me half-heartedly reading a week-old magazine on my bed, a cold coffee next to me.

'Come on, I'm taking you out,' she orders. It's Em's way of saying she cares, without actually saying she cares. An hour later and we're all sitting in Jill's place of work for dinner. It's quiet, so Jill sits with us and sneaks drinks from our glasses when no-one is looking.

'Jill and I have been thinking,' announces Em, 'We're going to back off from this whole Alfie thing, it's your decision and I guess it's not so weird. I mean, we said we'd be in Brighton and we weren't. I guess it's not so suspicious. And if there is anything dodgy about him, well I guess you'll find out eventually.' I feel as if a weight has been lifted off me.

'I'll drink to that.' I raise my glass and Jill and Em follow, clinking hard and spilling some of the liquid onto the tablecloth. Jill ducks down as her boss walks by, staring lasciviously at the merry group. A hesitant Amy eventually raises her glass and clinks solemnly. She's yet to be convinced, but convince her I will. Right after I convince myself.

Chapter Eight

Two fairly uneventful weeks on, and I'm fidgeting nervously in the airport as Alfie and I wait for our flight to Venice. I absolutely hate flying. I do know that, statistically, it's safer than being in a car. That only serves to make me more scared about getting in cars, not less worried about flying. I anxiously down my glass of wine like an alcoholic fresh out of a failed rehab attempt. Boarding announced. Alfie steers me down towards the tunnel of death, as I've named it. The walk between the safety of *terra firma* and the plane is probably one of the most nerve-wracking things for me. My knees buckle. He laughs and pulls me forward. 'I'm going, I'm going,' I insist irately 'Stop dragging me.'

Part of my anxiety isn't just about the flight. It's that I know in my heart that I am right. There is something he isn't telling me. I feel a bit insecure leaving my friends to be alone with someone I can't trust one hundred per cent any more. I know he's been through a lot but still, in the back of my mind, it's there. Tormenting me. I do listen to my instincts – and often – despite wishing desperately that they are wrong. I find that they never are.

I fiddle nervously with my magazine as we taxi to the runway. The jets kick in and I am pushed back in my seat. I begin mumbling the Lord's Prayer to myself. Didn't even realise I remembered it.

'Thy Kingdom won't be done on here, love,' laughs Alfie, 'and you'll be lucky to get your daily bread with this airline. Maybe a packet of peanuts. As for forgiving your trespasses, you're in England now. Trespassing laws do exist.'

I dig him in the ribs and attempt some deep breathing I saw on a childbirth video at college years ago. If it helps with pushing something the size of a melon out of something the size of a pea, then it may just help with flight nerves. As the seatbelt sign is switched off, people begin to leave their seats and mill about the plane. They head to the toilet or loiter in the aisles, chatting to friends from whom they have been separated. I watch as one man in his early thirties makes his way back to his seat from the toilet. He stops two seats ahead of us and exclaims:

'Alfie! How's it going mate?' Alfie looks at him, then at me. He seems uncomfortable. Probably an ex-employee he had to fire or something. That's all we need.

'Jamie, mate! Good! Good. You? You off on holiday?'

'Yeh, mini break, Sarah insisted,' he rolls his eyes. 'The kids are with the outlaws. So, you on – er – business? This a work colleague?' Jamie looks pointedly at me. Alfie doesn't reply straight away. An uncomfortable pause hangs between all three of us. Why isn't he telling Jamie that I'm his girlfriend? Instead, he says:

'Yeh, business trip, isn't it, Lucy. Probably boring as arse but, well, needs must. You know how it is.'

'Yes, buddy,' laughs Jamie. 'I know *exactly* how it is. Have a good trip.' Jamie heads back to his seat. Alfie looks out of the window. I glance over my shoulder in time to see Jamie pointing in our direction and whispering. His wife, Sarah, gives me the up and down look that only females are capable of. No straight man will ever understand the up and down look. They are incapable of seeing it. Gay men can see it and do it to each other and women. Women only do it to other women.

'She probably was just admiring your outfit,' has been said to me by many a boyfriend. It's a completely different kind of look to the 'admiring an outfit' look.

'What's her problem?' I say to Alfie, giving Sarah an up and down back.

'Snooty cow,' dismisses Alfie. 'She knew Polly. Probably doesn't approve of me seeing someone else after two years. Probably not socially acceptable yet in her eyes.'

'Three years,' I remind him, gently.

'Hmm?' he says distractedly, glancing at London decreasing beneath us. 'What's three years?'

'Since Polly died.'

'You're right, Lucy. It is nearly three years. Feels like yesterday.' Alfie gazes sadly out the window.

Poor guy. He's still so traumatised he forgets how long it's been.

Of course, I make out flying was no big deal as we arrive in Venice. I will repeat the procedure two days later on the way home, but for now, it was nothing. We arrive at the hotel and I look around in amazement. Alfie pulls out a bottle of Champagne from the mini bar. I checked out the prices on arrival. He has just uncorked half my weekly wage! I flop backwards onto the firm, springy mattress.

'Oh, I could so get used to being your wife,' I think aloud. A momentary flash of terror crosses Alfie's eyes. He turned away quickly, but I caught it.

'Oh my God, I'm so sorry.' Fuck! How insensitive.

'I'm glad you brought that up, Lucy,' he smiles and sits beside me, playing with the fringe on the cashmere bed throw. 'It's something I do want with you, one day. I'm not quite ready to go there again yet. I do imagine it though.' His smile is wistful. It's enough for me, this 'one day' thing. I'll work on it.

'Do you like the name Zuzu for a girl?' I enquire, coyly.

'Why not,' he laughs and shrugs.

We have an amazing weekend of sight-seeing and meals out. I have had the best time and am sorry to be heading back to London – and normality. I actually don't feel too nervous on the flight home. It's been a great bonding session and I know now that I have to trust him. If Em and Jill can put their suspicions aside, then so can I. We both have a week off now, and it will be nice to continue our holiday back home.

We arrive back at the Chelsea pad, order a takeaway, switch on a romantic comedy and crack open a bottle of wine. We are just thinking about heading to bed when Alfie's mobile goes. He looks at the screen.

'Shit, work,' he mumbles, turning away from me.

'Don't answer! You're on your holidays, for Christ's sake.'

'I have to Lucy. It's "Boss Home."' He turns the phone to show me the screen. 'It has to be important.'

He leaves the room and I feel my heart sink. This is the downside of a luxury lifestyle. The money to fund it has to be earned somehow. Alfie walks back into the room and gathers up his laptop.

'I have to go to Geneva, I'm so sorry Lucy.' He kisses me, briefly, on the cheek.

'No! What about our week off? This isn't fair, Alfie.'

'I know, I know,' he soothes, 'It's not like I want to go. There's a crisis over there, the CEO just walked out and I'm the only one who can do it.'

With that, he is gone. Deflated, I switch off the television and put the wine bottle back in the fridge. I switch off the lights and stand for a moment picking out shapes in the darkened front room. A streetlight hums and flickers out on the street. It's a familiar sound that doesn't bring its usual comfort. I pull the front door closed and, with a deep sigh, head for home. I don't want to be here on my own anymore.

I arrive back home to find Em, Amy and Jill getting ready for a big night out. They seem to never stop partying. Where does all that energy come from? I certainly don't have it. I'm in a foul mood and try to sneak to my room unnoticed.

'Come on Lucy, you know you want to come. We're going to Walkie,' Em tries to tempt me by grabbing my arms and dancing suggestively with me.

'Nope, I'm going to put on my jammies and veg out in front of the TV,' I announce.

They attempt to badger me for another half an hour as I run a bath, take off my make-up and put a face pack on.

'Fine, have it your way,' Em shouts through the door. 'You know where we are if you change your mind.'

I lie in the bath and call Alfie. His phone rings. I had expected voicemail. Maybe he's arrived already. It has been two and a half hours since he left.

'Hey you,' I say, when he answers.

'Hi,' he says quietly, 'What's up?'

'Nothing,' I reply, a bit miffed at his brusque manner, 'just wanted to say hello to my boyfriend.'

'Look, Luce I forgot my charger and the battery is really low. We may get cut off here.'

'Where are you?'

'Geneva, Lucy,' he mumbles impatiently.

'Alfie?' I hear a voice at the other end of the phone. Female.

'Who's that?' I demand.

'Work colleague. Miranda. We are going over the minutes of the last meeting,' he sighs dismissively. 'Look, I'll call you when I get back, probably the day after tomorrow. I think my phones about to cut…'

'off.' I finish for him – and throw my mobile to the floor.

I ponder on the call as I top up the water. There was something funny about that call. No, not Miranda being there. I've met her, totally loved-up with her husband and twin boys. She would be safer to leave Alfie with than, say, a nun? Besides, it's such a big company that he's rarely away on his own. He often comes back with stories of how they start out with good intentions of working and end up hammered. I can't put my finger on what it is that's not quite right. Obviously, it's not that important or it would come to me straight away. It's just the disappointment of thinking we were in for a nice few days off together. On a sudden urge to be with my friends, I pull the plug out from the bath and quickly get dried. Chucking on some clothes, I give Em a ring to say I'll be along soon.

'Yay!' I hear her cheer above the noise of the club. Ten minutes later and I'm on my way.

Pushing through the double doors of Walkie, I search around. Some lairy shrieks and high-pitched laughter directs me towards them. On taking in the girls' drunken behaviour, I decide not to drink tonight. Is that how I usually look? I'm in far too strange a mood to add alcohol.

I order a soft drink and attempt to join in the conversation my friends are having. I can't help but feel a bit left out. It's been so long since I socialised with them regularly, that I now no longer know half the people they talk about.

'Did Dan and Mickey say they'd be out tonight?' asks Jill, with a coy smile.

'I can't remember.' Amy tilts her head to one side: 'When is it they go to Greece?'

'Not sure.' Jill looks deflated at the thought of not seeing them.

'Call them,' says Emily.

'No!' yells Jill, 'they might think I fancy them.'

'Well, you do,' states Amy. 'I may just call Dan and tell him,' she laughs, shaking her mobile at Jill.

'Oh you bitch! You dare!' Jill makes a grab for it and knocks two pints off the next table.

'Uh-oh, bouncer moving in at three o'clock,' says Em, quickly looking down in denial of association.

'So sorry, can I buy you another?' stammers Jill, to the obviously pissed-off couple wearing a pint of lager each. The bouncer pulls himself up to his full height and glares at Jill.

'I'm sorry, I really am, don't throw me out,' she begs, whilst simultaneously fluttering her eyelashes. 'I have offered to buy them another drink. You won't hear another peep out of me.' He nods briefly to the other bouncer closing in, and they both back off.

'For fuck's sake, Jill! Are you trying to get us barred from our local?' hisses Amy, taking her phone back out, pressing a few buttons and holding it to her ear. Jill gives a little squeal of protest and glances at the bouncer, who is watching her carefully.

'Oooh, aren't you a lucky girl?' Amy says sarcastically. 'Long ring tone, they are in Greece. But luckily, my credit won't stretch to more than three seconds.'

She snaps shut her phone and pops it back in her denim jacket pocket. We all giggle at Jill's obvious relief.

Hang on a minute. Long ring tone. That's what was missing when I called Alfie. How can he be abroad with a UK ring tone? My mind searches for a reasonable excuse. He answered, it's not even like he left his phone at home. I saw him pop it in his briefcase before he left. I can't think of a single reason to justify this one. Where the hell is he?

I argue with myself for an hour before deciding to tell the girls about the call to Alfie. They look on seriously as I explain. The reason I struggled with myself over whether to mention it or not is because it would only alienate them further from him, which would make it stressful for me any time I wanted an objective view from them. Or to bring him around to ours. But, on the other hand, when do I do that? And I do need the support of my friends.

'Oh Lucy,' Emily gives me a squeeze. 'We did some research. Alfie has a house in Southampton. Amy found a planning permission application for him on the Internet. We weren't going to tell you tonight, but since you've brought it up...' she trails off.

Personally, I wouldn't know where to begin finding someone on the Net, but Amy, having friends in high places combined with being a bit of a computer whizz-kid, could find out pretty much anything she wanted about anyone.

'So, what's wrong with that?' I ask.

'Nothing in itself I guess. But I think we should pay him a

visit when he's next "away",' Amy concludes.

'Fine,' I shrug, 'he's away now. Let's go.'

'All right, but I need to call in a sickie tomorrow,' says Amy.

'I was joking!' I snap. 'God, leave it be won't you!' I don't know why I'm feeling so defensive. What did I expect them to say? They wouldn't leave it be. Three pulled sickies and a total waste of a day's holiday for me and we are back on the drive to Southampton at 10am the next day. Waste of bloody time, if you ask me. But I know, deep down, that it's just that I'm not sure I want to know the truth.

Armed with Alfie's Southampton address, we follow Jill's directions and only get lost four times. A record – by her standards. We pull up outside a gorgeous Victorian house in a leafy suburb. Amy puts a head scarf and dark glasses on and walks up to the door with the latest home-wares catalogue, which had been delivered to our house yesterday. The excuse being that she, the agent, had muddled some of her orders and was having to retrace her customers to check if they had placed an order and, if so, what they wanted. We watch as she walks up to the door and rings the bell. Nothing.

'See,' I say. 'Big wows if he has a Southampton home. Probably wants to make sure I'm not a gold digger before he mentions it. Besides, he's on a business trip, so why would he be here anyway?' Amy returns to the car and a discussion ensues, without my involvement in any of it. The decision is made that they will all take another sickie tomorrow and check back into our B&B from last time. Jill places the call to book us in and we park up for the night in the pub car park and continue our stakeout from the bar closest to Alfie's house.

Taking it in half hourly turns, Jill, Amy and Emily walk the 200 metres to his house.

5pm: no lights, no answer.

5.30pm: nothing.

6pm: dog barking when Em rang the bell, still no answer.

6.47pm: all a bit drunk now, so missed the half hour slot, still nothing.

7.42pm: drunker still. Jill rushes back in from outside, exclaiming there are now lights on in an upstairs window and also one on in what appears to be the front room.

'Did you knock?' asks Emily.

'No! exclaims Jill. 'I didn't think they'd listen to a pissed Home-ware woman. One of you will have to do it.'

'But we're all pissed,' I say, 'And besides, I think he might find it a bit funny if one minute I'm a nanny in London and the next I appear to be a catalogue delivery person down his street in Southampton. So that's me out.'

'I'll do it.' Amy raises her head in a dignified manner and walks out the door. Closely followed by a gaggle of hysterical females. We hide behind the hedge, like something out of *Scooby Doo*, and watch as Amy knocks. After a minute or so, a young girl in pyjamas, aged around eight, comes to the door.

'My Mummy and Daddy aren't here, but my Auntie Jane is. Jaaa-aaaane!' she shouts. 'Home-ware lady.'

Turning her attention back to Amy, the little girl makes conversation:

'I'm going bowling tomorrow with Mummy and Daddy.'

'Oh, how nice,' slurs Amy. 'Whereabouts?' Amy's silhouette takes on the appearance of *The Chitty, Chitty, Bang, Bang* child catcher.

'Just at multiplex, down there.' The little girl points to the left.

'What's your name, honey?' asks Amy.

Auntie Jane appears behind the child.

'Sorry, we don't want anything, thanks.' She ushers the girl inside and closes the door. Bugger!

The next morning Amy insists we are up at 11am for the bowling alley's opening time. We begin stakeout number two. She could have at least got the time out of the child I think, unreasonably. We order coffee and bagels and chat amongst ourselves until 1pm.

'There's no getting around it, Lucy,' Em shakes her head solemnly, 'why hasn't he told you about the Southampton place? Did you know he had kids?'

'He doesn't.' I roll my eyes. 'At which point did you hear the child say: 'My Daddy's name is Alfie,' I mock.

'True,' Amy picks up the possible explanation. 'I mean, he could have a Southampton home and rents it out. In which case it probably just didn't occur to him to mention it to Lucy.'

'Thank you, Amy.' I hold my hands out towards her, to show that she is the only one with a bit of solidarity. Amy flicks a long blonde lock off her shoulder and smiles in a superior way at the others.

'Good explanation,' Jill nods her agreement. No-one can think of a way around that one.

'See, wasted trip,' I smile with relief. 'But we shall sit it out here, like idiots, 'til the kid turns up with her Mum and Dad just to prove the point. Then we can head for home, so I can actually have some kind of holiday.'

An hour later. Emily is the first to prick up her ears as she hears a familiar voice. Alfie! He walks in, with Auntie Jane behind him, and three children.

'Once again he lies. He's supposed to be in Geneva,' states Emily.

I announce that I'm bored with this and go outside for a walk. I wander along the street and look in the shop windows. I can't focus on anything I see, but I don't want to be at the multiplex either. I look like a stalker.

I meander back after half an hour and bump into Jill.

'Where the hell have you been?' she exclaims. Then adopting a more sympathetic tone, suggests we wait in the car.

'No, I don't want to, I want to know what's going on.' I make my way back towards the bowling alley. Jill pulls me back.

'Luce, there is something you should know first. His wife,

she's in there…'

I am now imagining some bizarre kind of wake. The anniversary of her death perhaps, when Alfie exhumes her and does something fun, with his sister and the kids. How weird.

'So, Jill, you're trying to tell me he's in there with his sister and three kids and has brought his dead wife along for a laugh?' My head buzzes with confusion. Anyway, how would Jill even know what Polly looks like? None of it makes sense. I have to see this for myself. Storming away from Jill, I walk purposefully back to the building, just in time to see Alfie and family exit *en masse*. I take in Alfie, Auntie Jane, the little girl from the doorway and two boys.

'Chloe, don't forget your fleece,' I turn toward the exit where a pretty, dark, curly-haired woman is shouting. I recognise her immediately from the photograph. I feel like I'm going to throw up. I stop dead in my tracks and Jill looks at me anxiously.

'It can't be. It just can't,' I stammer, shaking my head violently.

'Lucy, come on, we can go now. You know the truth, leave it be and deal with it next time he calls. Look at them all. Do you want to break their hearts? *They* have done nothing wrong.' I feel fury rise up inside me and I walk purposefully towards them.

I'm going to do them all a favour and tell them everything.

Chapter Nine

'You absolute *bastard*!' I scream at Alfie. My head feels like it's spinning, I am puce with rage. 'Were you actually going to ever tell me you were still married?' My voice rises hysterically.

'Lucy...?' Alfie stares at me in shock and confusion, like he doesn't recognise me out of context. 'What...what the hell are you doing here?' he stammers.

'Alf?' queries a confused Polly, looking from Alfie to me and back again.

'Polly, take the kids to the car, please. I'll explain in a minute, once I've calmed this woman down.'

No, Alfie,' says Polly. 'I think I'll stay and hear this.'

'Pol, I have no idea who she is. She could be dangerous. Take the kids to the car!' he shouts.

'You are Alfred James Hughes, your wife died three years ago in a yachting accident – *allegedly!* You live in King's Road, Chelsea, your telephone number is 07745...'

'OK, Lucy! I think you've made your point here. Now piss off!' snarls Alfie. I laugh in disbelief.

'Excuse me? I have been with you for just over a year and I have no right to an explanation?'

'You know what, Lucy, you do,' Polly intervenes. 'But you also deserve the truth. So, therefore, Alfred, *you* take the children back to the car. If you didn't know who she was, you wouldn't have known her name. Don't insult my intelligence.'

Alfie looks helplessly at Polly.

'Do it!' she yells. Alfie scuttles off with a now sobbing Chloe and the two boys. Polly runs after them, and kisses her daughter on the top of her head,

'Mummy will see you soon, baby. Be a good girl and go home now.'

'You absolute wanker!' She shakes her head at Alfie, and

walks back to Jill and I.

Jill looks uncomfortable.

'Lucy, if you're OK I think I'll head back and let you talk. I can come along if you want, though,' she trails off, sadly.

'Oh, I don't know. I suppose I'll see you back at the B&B.'

'Don't scratch her eyes out,' Jill warns Polly. 'She really had no idea. None of us did.'

Jill walks off, her head down. I can tell she feels awful about being the messenger. It just makes me love her all the more.

'Coffee?' says Polly, business-like and with a slight chill.

'Wine?' I suggest.

'Why not?' Polly sighs.

We stop off at a wine bar Polly knows and order our drinks.

'So,' she sighs, 'why don't we start this at the beginning?'

I explain how Alfie had contacted me through a friend on the Millionaires website.

'He seemed so genuine, saying how you had died in a yachting accident.' Polly chokes on her wine, coughing loudly. 'I remember that trip well. Sadly, it was our friend Malcolm's wife that died.'

Unbelievable! He stole some poor man's real tragedy for his own gain.

'Melanie was a great friend of mine. My two eldest children are only months of difference in age of her and Malcolm's. He has never found a new person to share his life. He was devastated. Still is.'

'I'm so sorry,' I tell her quietly, not able to look at her face. 'I would never knowingly go with a married man. Or even with any man with a girlfriend. I have morals – and besides, if they do it with you, they'll do it to you.'

'Well, there's a prophecy that's come back to bite me on the backside,' murmurs Polly absent-mindedly.

'You and Alfie? Was he married before then?'

'No', replies Polly, 'but he did have a girlfriend. I was

flattered, I guess. He said I was the one.'

'Hmm, he talks the talk, right enough.' I reply.

'I did notice he seemed to spend a lot of time away from home, though,' says Polly. 'I just thought Dad was working him really hard. He always answered the phone when I rang, nothing made me feel there was anything suspicious going on.'

Conference calls, I think. All those times with me, when he darted out of the room – that was his excuse. How could I have been so stupid?

'I suspected after Chloe was born that he was having an affair,' continues Polly. 'He started to spend a lot of time at the office. Said he had responsibilities now and I guess, well, I just believed him. Suppose I wanted to.'

'I made a lot of compensations for the fact he was a widower,' I reply. 'Uncomfortable silences during any movie with a death or funeral scene. I put it down to sorrow, but really, it was guilt. Actually, I don't know how anyone with a conscience at all could have kept up that for a year. I guess he had too much to lose.'

'Probably,' Polly mused. 'I mean, Dad won't want him in the family business now. He won't have use of the apartment in Chelsea, no family home, nothing. In fact, I'd be amazed if he even got another job in Management. From what Dad says, it's loyalty and not skill that keeps him there at all.' She gives an ironic snort.

It's my turn to choke.

'You mean it's not Alfie's family that own the business and properties?' I splutter.

Polly laughs. 'So, he said it was all his? Why, after all this, am I surprised?'

'He'll have half anyway, if you decide to split,' I shrug.

'No, Dad made him sign a prenuptial agreement,' says Polly, swirling her wine absent-mindedly around her glass, a catch in her voice. 'I was loved up and stupid. Maybe Alf would have left me by now if he knew he was guaranteed half, but he gets nothing. Well, access to the kids, but no monetary entitlement. He doesn't even seem to care too much about the kids. I mean, he missed Chloe's birthday last week due to a business trip. That's why he took her bowling today. He promised her when he called last Tuesday.'

So, he really had no intention of staying with me this week. It was all pre-arranged. He also cared so little for his eldest child that he'd miss her birthday to go away with his mistress. God, I hate that word. That's *me*! Albeit by default, but I still was his mistress for more than a year. But what warms the chill in me most is that, for what Alfie has done, he ends up homeless and jobless. It's difficult for me to feel devastated; rather, I feel I've had a lucky escape. Like I've narrowly avoided being hit by a car. Shock, relief and counting my blessings – it could have been a whole lot worse. The Alfie I know now is not the Alfie I loved. He doesn't exist; he was an illusion. I feel strangely elated. Sick but elated. It's as if he has been erased completely.

'Will you try and make things work?' I ask Polly.

'No. To let you understand, Lucy, I see him two nights a week if I'm lucky. I'm practically a single parent. I'd be better off just me and the kids, without the financial leech. I've always worn the trousers in our relationship. He'll do as he's told. He even has my numbers in his phone as 'Boss Mobile' and 'Boss Home.' Besides, there is a very cute single Dad at school making eyes at me every pick-up. I may just make eyes back.'

Polly smiles weakly and stands up. I stand too.

'I really am so sorry,' I say.

'No, I'm sorry that my shit of a husband put you through this. Good luck, Lucy. I do wish you happiness, but right now I have a soon-to-be-ex-husband to kick out.' Polly gives me a quick peck on the cheek and disappears into the early evening haze.

I down the rest of my wine and head back to the Bed and Breakfast. The girls stand up immediately on seeing me. Hugs all round. Jill pulls off my coat and Amy guides me to a chair. 'I'm fine,' I laugh off their concern, sounding slightly hysterical. 'Get this. The best bit of all is that the money is all Polly's. He has nothing. She has a pre-nup and he's out on his ear. He even had her in his phone as 'Boss' so that I would think it was his real Boss. I'm sorry,' I laugh loudly, 'I just can't believe he has nothing now.'

'What goes around comes around, Luce,' smiles Jill.

The next morning I receive a text from Alfie informing me that I owe him somewhere in the region of one year's rent.

'Get lost, if I owe anyone, it's Polly and I'm sure she won't ask for it. Contact me again and I'll send some big burly mates round to sort you out!'

'Don't think Em and Amy could take me,' he replies.

I laugh, but it's immediately replaced with anger that I can still find him funny. He doesn't deserve that. There is nothing funny about what he has done. I throw my phone across the room with an angry shout – and instantly regret it. I can't afford a new phone. I walk to the furthest away wall and reach down behind the dressing table to find it and inspect the damage. There's none apparent. I need to know just one thing. It will bug me forever if I don't ask him. I type out a simple question.

'Why?'

Less than thirty seconds later, the phone beeps his reply.

'Because I could!'

I kind of wish I hadn't asked. He doesn't contact me again, but is occasionally spotted by friends. These days his suits are more Man at C&A than Armani. It does appear that what comes around goes around. Amy found out that the second her divorce came through, Polly married again. I can only assume cute Dad from the playground had won her over.

Chapter Ten

So there we have it, just a few of my biggest disasters relationship-wise. There have been others, but I won't bore you with them – barely worth mentioning really. But let's get back to where we started. This Christmas-time, and my family's disillusionment with, and amusement at, my love life. We are in the middle of a noisy Christmas dinner. I'm currently being harangued by the females in the family about the fact that I am a complete failure in the romance stakes.

'What you need,' insists Mum, putting down her knife and fork, 'is to have a chat with Gran. She'd sort you right out.' Betty and Sarah nod in agreement.

'I don't want to risk upsetting you,' I say, chewing thoughtfully on a brussel sprout, before realising what it was and pulling a disgusted face at Mum. She patiently holds out a holly-decorated napkin for me to deposit it in. Some things you never grow out of. It must have been hidden under the mash. I shudder.

'We had the misfortune of losing Gran twelve years ago,' I continue.

'No, stupid,' says Betty. 'The big psychic telephone. Go see a medium.'

I look at them cynically. I'm not as convinced as they are that this stuff works, though they swear by it. Regaling me with their tales of how the mediums they've seen could not have possibly known these things about them. But to me they sound vague, layered with a generous amount of guesswork. It doesn't take a genius to see an engagement or wedding ring, even a mark where it should be if they've tried to disguise the fact. For example, I could spot a mother of young children a mile off, even without the kids in tow. The utterly exhausted, yet elated to be momentarily free, expression on their face. At some point, if you observed them long enough, a flash of panic would cloud the euphoria and they would frantically look around before relief set in. It's a hazard of spending most of your time with children. Sometimes you forget that you shouldn't have them with you, and terror sets in. I do it all the time – and I'm a nanny, not a mother. Right now, I am hearing these stories for, possibly, the third time from my family members, yet feel obliged to attempt to show an interest as if it's the first.

'Last time I went Mum pushed me to go for a promotion at work which would mean I could afford a new car,' Betty points to the driveway and holds her hands out as if to say, 'ta-daa.'

'She told me we would be happier in the countryside, renovating the old farmhouse. However, she didn't mention the roof would fall down and it'd take fifteen months instead of the estimated six,' says Sarah, wrinkling her nose.

'Your Gran told me I had two daughters to be proud of; one would have two children and the other was unlucky in love,' mentions Mum, patting my hand.

'OK, I'll go,' I give in. 'Not here, though. It has to be someone I've never met who does the reading. Too many people know me round here.'

Satisfied with this, they all back off and re-join the conversation of the party. Current topic, Claire's own personal dating disaster. My protégé, I often think. We join in halfway through the conversation.

'So, we went to the Ball together, me in my gorgeous floor-length midnight blue gown – I tell you, those designer discount stores are great. Nowt wrong with the stuff, just end of line or last season's styles.' She shakes her head in wonder.

The others nod frantically. Get to the point, we don't care what you were wearing they seem to say. Claire looks around, takes the hint and continues.

'Yeh, anyway, so he said he would call me, and then…poof!'

'No! He was gay?' asks an incredulous Sarah.

'No! Oh my God, I did not turn him *gay!*' Claire looks at Sarah in horror. 'He disappeared,' she says slowly, as if explaining it to a three-year-old. 'I never saw him again. Wouldn't answer his phone, reply to my emails…'

'Cos you shagged him,' announces Craig, shovelling his second heap of trifle in his mouth. 'Why buy the cow when you get the milk for free?' He nods sagely.

'I so did *not*,' flushes Claire, glancing nervously at her Dad, who is now taking a sudden interest in the conversation.

'I didn't Dad, honest, you know I'm saving it for marriage.'

Several of us explode with laughter at this. Hmm… how many twenty-five-year-old virgins do you know? Still, it wouldn't be Christmas Day without an argument.

I'm back in London a few days later. Becky returned last night and is itching for a night out and a girly catch-up. She greets me at the front door with a squeal.

'Oh my God, I've so missed you. Mum says hi, she's coming over for the sales and wants us to take her clubbing again.'

Becky's Mum, like mine, never quite grew up. Both still enjoy the thrill of being chatted up by young things, dancing, drinking and hanging out with the girls. They are great fun, but a bad combination together. The one and only time their visits coincided it was just like Becky and me, but one hundred times worse. They got on well. Too well! For the safety of the residents of London, we have made sure they're never over at the same time again. It was the one and only time I've ever had to put my mother to bed.

As usual, we head out to the Frog and Bucket. We are greeted like heroes returning from war. These poor people have had no time off and are desperate for stories of what it's like 'out there'. We have a quick catch-up between the times the staff spend serving the crowds, and then retire to our usual corner. Thoughtfully, a 'Reserved' sign has been put on the table by one of our smart-thinking, bartending friends. I tell Becky about how I have promised to go and see a medium. She is enthralled.

'I've never been to see a medium. I could certainly do with some spiritual guidance in my life right now. It's about time I got back out there,' she shrugs. 'Put myself back on the market, so to speak.'

I have a flashback to before Christmas and my promise to be a better friend.

'How are things now? I ask. 'Do you still miss Bob?'

'Not too badly,' she replies. 'I had a look through some old photographs of us when I was back home. It was more nostalgia, I think. I don't miss him so much as miss a relationship. That's why I want to get back out there.'

We book into our local Spiritual Church for a reading later in the week. I sit nervously as we wait for the medium to call us in. The church is peaceful, very much like a traditional church. Blue stars light up the ceiling and an altar is draped with purple velvet. It doesn't look as if it's been used to sacrifice a goat – or any other animal for that matter.

'Lucy?'

I jump.

'Sorry, yes,' I say breathlessly.

'First visit to us, is it?' the woman asks gently. I read her name tag: 'Brenda,' it says. Should be OK, I reason. Brenda is not the name of a psycho serial killer, is it? She has a warm, homely, brown face and the 'lived-in' look about her of people comfortable in their own skin. She wears a purple tie-dye floaty skirt and smells of jasmine. She has a soft Caribbean accent that I find soothing and hypnotic. I feel safe. I follow Brenda to a pew at the back of the church and she indicates for me to sit. She closes her eyes and breathes deeply.

After around thirty seconds she begins to talk.

'I have a lady present. When she passed she had a very sore left leg. It's fine now. She passed over more than ten years ago in her mid-... no, early seventies. It's Gran,' she smiles, still with her eyes closed.

Spot on! I have said nothing so far, and don't intend to.

'I also have a handsome, young gentleman. Gran tells me that he is your Father. He sends his love. You look very like him but barely knew him. He will always walk with you through life, protecting you in a way he never could in his lifetime. He was taken before he was ready, he says.' My throat constricts. I take a deep breath.

'Gran tells me you work with children and you're not happy there. You should be doing something creative. You get the love of that from her.'

My mind drifts back to being seven-years-old in Gran's kitchen; Mary and me up to our elbows in dough. The comforting warmth of the room and the smell of a Sunday roast wafts from the oven. We were in charge of the baking.

'Gran says you have had bad luck in the past with men.' I stifle a giggle at the understatement. 'Very bad luck,' frowns Brenda. I can imagine Gran filling in the details as Brenda raises her eyebrows and looks at me. 'What you need to do, Lucy, is ask the Universe.' She explains further, on noticing my puzzled expression.

'Basically, what Gran is saying is that all that we want from life is there for the taking. You simply have to ask. Visualise the kind of man you want to meet, write it down even. The same with the kind of job you want. But only use positives. Don't say: "I don't want another man who will be unfaithful." Instead, say: "I want to attract a man who will be faithful to me." Do you understand?' Brenda smiles kindly.

'Yes,' I say. 'Kind of like divine ordering?'

'Exactly,' Brenda laughs softly, closing her eyes again. She definitely isn't trying to read my expressions. Only glancing at me occasionally to put across a point. She is impressing me, in spite of my belief that it's all a crock.

'You worry about your family too much,' Brenda continues. 'Mum's health in particular, but she is fine. Stress is her biggest enemy.' I nod in silent agreement. Mum lives on her nerves. Her Health and Safety job only shows her how the most obscure things can happen – making her worry unnecessarily more about us – on top of all the more likely hazards.

'Your sister's relationship will break up soon, but it will be a Godsend to her. He annoys her more than anything and does nothing around the house. Wait, he is fond of the vacuum cleaner, so it's obviously not all housework he has an aversion to.'

I burst out laughing at Gran's joke, startling Brenda out of her trance.

'I'm sorry,' I giggle. 'That has more relevance than you'll ever know.'

'Gran wants to take you overseas,' continues Brenda. 'I see a coastline with palms and good friends surrounding you. But it's more than a holiday, and more in reach of your grasp than you think. It's a long held dream for you.'

Gran continues to tell me, via Brenda, that I'm too skinny (despite going back up to the wrong side of a size 12!). It's the belly that keeps the back up! Brenda laughs at this, and quite possibly it's the one thing that convinces me most. It is word for word exactly what Gran used to say to us. I should have a proper breakfast, like porridge. I think back to this morning's first meal of the day. Leftover pizza and a can of Irn Bru. OK, point taken. I should eat more fruit. I should drink less wine, but she's glad I've stopped smoking. I am very happy with my reading and thank Brenda profusely. As I walk to the door of the church, Brenda calls out to me.

'Lucy, there's an elderly man walking next to you. He is blowing you a kiss and saying thank you. It's all he wants to say.'

'Thanks Brenda,' I smile, 'that'll be Harry.'

I head outside to wait for Becky. The frosty blue daylight is sharp after the dark warmth of the church. Becky skips out smiling.

'Wine?' she asks.

'Yes!' I reply, pausing momentarily to look up at the sky. 'Sorry, Gran,' I smile cheekily. 'Come on Harry, let's hit the pub.' Becky throws me a strange look.

Becky was happy with her reading too. She will meet a man soon who will be very significant in her future. One of her friends will introduce them.

'I already know everyone that you know,' she says dismissively. 'So, it must be another friend.' Her Grandfather was more general in what he said, just things about everyday life and family. She would be beginning a new job in the next few months, though she was fine where she was and didn't see that happening.

'Did you give my name when you booked the reading?' I ask Becky.

'No, just mine, why?'

'She knew it was Lucy, that's all,' I reply.

The next night is Hogmanay. Being a Scot, I refuse to call it New Year's Eve just because I live in England. Becky and I plan to head down the Frog with some friends. We are having a few warm-up drinks at home and watching *Breakfast at Tiffany's* with a huge bag of tortilla chips, when my phone rings.

'Hi Lucy, It's Mike. From the train?'

'Hello, Mike from the train. How was your Christmas?' I ask.

'Home was great. I now have another pile of useless things I will never use but, hey, I believe it's the thought that counts.'

'Guess I got the share of good presents this year,' I laugh. 'So what are you up to for Hogmanay?'

'Well, there's the thing, bugger all. What are you doing?'

'Heading to the Frog and Bucket just off City Road. Bit of a pain to get to from Chiswick, but you're welcome to come along and crash at ours if you like.'

'Cool, see you there. I'm leaving now.'

'Oooh, who's Mi-iiike?' Becky asks snidely.

'Nobody that you or I are interested in,' I say. 'He has a girlfriend and she's going to fix my Denis Healey's.'

Becky gives me a 'whatever' look and goes back to Audrey Hepburn, sobbing and searching for Cat. I head off to change and stop as I notice a notepad sticking out from under my bed. Why not? It can't hurt.

List of qualities I want in a man:

1) Kind and generous, but not a pushover!

2) Minimal baggage. Def no kids. I ain't spending my weekdays AND weekends in a park.

3) No drug or alcohol dependency problems, or tortured poets.

4) Fun-loving, faithful and someone with direction and purpose in life.

5) Reasonable intelligence!

I add the last part as I remember, with frustration, yet another ex-boyfriend. One particularly hot summer we were out for a pub lunch. I asked if he wanted to eat *al fresco*? He informed me he didn't like pasta. Same guy asked me to arrange a dinner party for his boss and his wife. I called him at work and asked if he'd pick up some canapés. I didn't think I'd bought enough. He arrived home and plonked three tins on the counter.

'What's this?' I asked in confusion.

'A can of peas, like you asked for. Only you didn't say if you wanted garden, processed or mushy. So I bought one of each.' Enough said.

I finish my list and sign it with a flourish. Oh, bollocks! I was supposed to write it all in positives. Well, I've no time left – I'll do it tomorrow. Maybe casting on the first day of the year will bring good fortune? Or should I cast my wish properly on the last day of the year? Out with the old and in with the new? My hand hovers over the pen.

'This is *your* doing, Granddad!' I say to the ceiling. He has made me unnecessarily superstitious. As the bells chimed in New Year, he would open the back door to let the old year out and the open the front door to let the new one in. He would then stand guard out front to make sure the First Foot (first visitor after midnight) was a tall, dark male and carried a gift. Traditionally, that's a lump of coal. But a packet of custard creams would do.

I'll never forget the year that Mary, bursting for a wee, had sprinted from the Steeple, our gathering point in Arbroath. A place where you snog so many people that you're guaranteed a Happy New Year cold sore from at least one. Granddad had refused her entry, on the grounds of being a girl, ginger and coal/biscuit-less. He left her diddling about on the spot for twenty minutes until Uncle Jim turned up and was granted entry. Mary was furious.

'You happy now?' she aimed a dirty look at Granddad, 'You made me piss my pants for the first time since I was five.'

Gran intervened with a plate of pickled onions and cheese and pineapple on sticks. Mary took one grudgingly. Gran took it back and removed the cocktail stick, before plonking the lot back in Mary's hand.

'No way to start the New Year, with your Granddad's eyeball on the end of that.'

Hogmanay always makes me nostalgic about my family. I've now been sat on the bed pondering for twenty minutes and haven't even started to get ready.

'Lucy, we're going,' yelled Becky from the top of the stairs, wrenching me from my reverie.

Decision on 'the list' has been made for me. I'll have to leave it for now. I change clothes quickly, slick on a layer of lip-gloss and tousle up my hair.

'Just finishing up,' I shout. I hear a big sigh in response. Patience isn't one of Becky's strong points. I put on my gloves and hat and shrug on my coat. We arrive at the Frog fifteen minutes and forty frozen fingers and toes later.

We head into the warmth and noise of the pub. It's bursting at the seams with happy revellers. Many drunk already. I look around for Mike and Sam, then realise I wouldn't know Sam if she fell in my soup. I spot Mike lurking uncomfortably at the bar and tap him on the shoulder. He envelops me in a bear hug and says how good it is to see me again.

'This is Becky,' I announce. Mike smiles broadly, as does Becky.

'Come to Mama!' she mutters. I dig her in the ribs.

I look at Mike for a moment, viewing him through Becky's eyes. He is good looking. Guess I was too stressed out from work to notice before. He has overgrown dark brown hair that has a tendency to stick up in tufts. He looks very masculine, strong jaw line, wide shoulders and dark brown eyes you could melt into.

'So, where's Sam?' I enquire pointedly for Becky's benefit, and look around.

'Bitch dumped me and moved out before I even got back,' he shakes his head in wonder. 'Think her family indoctrinated her while she was home. She's gone back to Hampshire – to her ex.' Another forty watts is added to Becky's smile.

'Sorry about your eyebrows,' mumbles Mike. I shrug and shake my head sympathetically.

An hour into the evening, Becky and Mike are smitten kittens. Staring too long at each other and laughing a little too hard at anything the other says. Becky glances over at me and I mimic sticking my fingers down my throat and gagging. I smile and leave them to it. The others have arrived now and I'm too busy catching up with Em, Amy, Jill and their men of the moment. We're dancing around near the bar when some idiot whacks into me, spilling my drink.

'Oi! You pillock!' I shout.

'Sorry,' he smarms over me, attempting to wipe wine from my front.

'Touch me again and you're a dead man walking,' I inform him, turning away.

'Apologies for my mate,' smiles a friendly-looking guy.

'Is he always such a twat?' I ask him.

'Nah. Well… yes, actually,' he laughs.

'Lucy Ramsey,' I say, holding out my hand.

'Nick Bailey,' he replies, imitating my formality.

'You're shitting me, yeah?' I laugh.

'No,' Nick shakes his head in confusion.

'Bailey. Your surname is Bailey?'

'Yes,' he says slowly, 'and yours is Ramsey I believe.'

I can't believe it. Bailey, as in George *'It's a Wonderful Life'* Bailey.

'OK,' I say in awe. 'Fast movers up there aren't you?'

I look up at the roof of the pub.

Nick follows my gaze and looks at me in puzzlement.

'I'm not being funny,' he says, 'but are you a bit unhinged? It's just I've had enough nutters to last a lifetime, so I may just get my coat now.'

'Stay!' I put my hand on his arm and laugh, trying not to sound manic. 'Believe me, I am not one of those.'

Chapter Eleven

So, Is Nick is the one? I am almost convinced. It's all so coincidental. My visit to the Spiritual Church, the surname of *Bailey!* OK, so it's not George Bailey. But the fact that I met him the night I cast my wish to the Universe, albeit not the way I was meant to. And the Universe understood that I was being harassed by a deranged flatmate and had to meet another friend in the pub that very moment. Things are most definitely working out for Becky and Mike. They have turned into one of those barf-inducing loved-up couples that make you want to scream, 'Get a room!' at the top of your voice. They seem to be perpetually snogging whenever I enter the room. We no longer have girly lunches alone, as even the suggestion of one invariably results in a hair ruffling for Mike, and Becky baby-voicing:

'But what about poor schnookums?'

We mainly have foursome lunches out, which is nice. I am happy with Nick, but we don't have the kind of suffocating relationship as the other two. I quite appreciate a bit of space, and so does Nick. I'm no longer one of those girls who have to be joined at the hip with her boyfriend. I'm moving much more slowly from now on. Proceeding with caution. Nick seems relieved when I'm fine about him going out with the boys.

'Of course I don't mind,' I say. 'Why are you even asking me?'

'Just out of respect,' he replies. 'I love being with you. I just also like a catch up with the guys too.'

It's a healthy relationship. I have learned a lot since 'Alfiegate', as it's now referred to in my circle of friends. It's all going so well. Two months into his and Becky's relationship, Mike moves into ours. It's easier to get to work is the excuse. Becky is over the moon. Nick can't help using the fact that we met on the same night as a guide for our relationship. He starts to ponder that maybe we should be moving on at the same rate.

'Really, Nick, we're fine as we are,' I say. 'They have moved at an abnormally fast rate.' To be honest, I really want to go at an easy pace so that we don't crash and burn after a few months. I'm done with wanting things to move quickly and prefer to keep an air of mystery around us. I would like Nick to move in – one day – but, by making him think I'm not that bothered about him, maybe I will have more success this time.

I have a stressful Friday at work. Georgie is being potty trained and has had seven so-called accidents that day. I head home full of intent to look for a new job that very weekend. It's the same plan I have every Friday, but by Saturday morning I've always forgotten how bad my job really is. Until Monday again. I walk over to the fridge to see what I can scrape the mould off for tonight's tea. Hmm, Lasagne? Either it's now hairy mouldy all the way through or I made it with Verdi pasta. Not sure, best not risk it. I quickly dispose of it in the bin before turning to an oblivious Mike and Becky snuggled on the sofa.

'Takeaway, anyone?'

'Sure. Nick round tonight, Luce?' asks Mike.

'Yeh, in about an hour,' I answer from inside the fridge. I have decided to venture further into its depths and have a clear-out. 'Gads! Is that last month's Chinese I was going to take to work?' I ask. No reply. Looks like it is. My mobile rings. I wipe my hands on my jeans, which are covered in wee anyway, thanks to Georgie. I don't recognise the number. Normally, I wouldn't answer an unknown number but something about this one looks vaguely familiar. Hope it's not a mad ex, I think. Too late, I've hit answer.

'Lucy Ramsey,' I say, warily. Pause. Scottish accent.

'Lucy? Hi, it's Ellie.' Oh my God, my old senior from the Care Home. If she asks me to go back, I'm going.

'Ellie. Hi! How are you? So good to hear from you.'

'I'm good, Lucy. How's the job?'

'Oh Christ, crap. I hate it. Are you calling to beg me back, because I can be on the next train,' I laugh.

'No, Lucy, though of course you're welcome anytime,' laughs Ellie. 'Anyway, do you remember Maisie?'

'Yes, how is she? Have Social Services found out she doesn't have Dementia yet?

'Yes, they did, Lucy. She moved into sheltered housing six months ago. Hated it. But it's turned out be to your benefit.'

'How so?' I enquire.

'Well, otherwise, as a Dementia sufferer, any changes to her will would be null and void if they were made within five years of diagnosis. And because she was of sound mind, well… they are not.'

'I'm not with you, Ellie.'

'Lucy… Maisie has made you sole benefactor in her will. She died five weeks ago. We attended the hearing, as she has no family. She has left you just over £63,000.' I sit down heavily on the floor.

'How did she die?' I ask, stupefied.

'In her sleep, lovey. You'll need to come to Edinburgh and see her solicitor in the next week if you can.'

'OK, yes, I can do that. Why though, Ellie? Why me?'

'I think you perhaps underestimated how we all touch their lives, Luce. She always did have a soft spot for you. You never treated them like they were a waste of space, like I've seen a lot of people do with the elderly. They already feel that way a lot of them, they don't need a reminder.' Ellie sighs: 'But I obviously don't know for sure. Maybe she knew she was on the way out and that you would get bugger all unless she 'fessed up to being of sound mind. Anyway, give me a call back to let me know when you'll be up. You probably need time for it all to sink in.'

My Maisie. Gone. I stare at my phone as if I have just dreamt the last five minutes. I feel sick. Too many people I have cared about, gone. I do, of course, appreciate the money she has left me. But to me, money is a means to an end.

'Can't take it with you,' Gran's voice pops into my head.

I'd give it all back to have just five minutes with all those that I've loved, who aren't here anymore. What a blast we'd have in those five minutes.

'What is it?' Becky asks cautiously. I explain. Nick arrives, and I start over.

'Bloody hell,' he states, incredulously. 'What are you going to do with all that money?'

'Tell Sylvia to shove her job up her arse, for a start,' I say.

'Well, here's where my plan comes in,' Mike says cautiously. 'I was going to ask you anyway, it's not about money.'

'Yes, we were going to ask you tonight. Both of you,' Becky agrees emphatically.

'I have around fifteen grand saved,' Mike explains 'Remember on the train at Christmas, Lucy. What we discussed? The plan?'

'Tenerife?'

'Yes, well, Becky and I,' Mike takes her hand, 'were going to ask if you and Nick want to make a go of things with us? Have our bar stroke restaurant thing?'

'Yes,' I nod slowly, mulling the idea over. 'But with Maisie's money too, we have an even better chance. Mike, you're a genius.' I fling myself onto his knee and give him a squeeze. Nick and Becky look at each other in surprise, shrug and then share an awkward hug.

'Wait, get off,' shouts Mike, from somewhere underneath me. I remove myself from him. 'Luce, don't invest all that money, just match me – and only if you want to,' he adds quickly.

'Don't be silly! It'll be a great success with us four. I'll be investing in our future. I look around at my three smiling new colleagues and feel elated. I can finally get out of the job I hate and live the dream I thought would never become a reality.

Morning arrives. I feel my head pound from last night's celebratory bottles of wine – of which, I reckon, I sunk a fair amount, due to shock. Nick is sitting on the edge of my bed, looking thoughtfully out of the window.

'What's up?' I ask sleepily. The effort of attempting to sit up is just too much. I slump back onto the pillow feeling like my skull will shatter at any second.

'I don't know,' he sighs. 'This plan of yours and Mike's. Long hours, no time to actually enjoy where we are.'

'That's the whole point, though,' I attempt to sound enthusiastic. 'We work all summer and then take the whole winter off. Go wherever we want and not work for a few months. My old school mate Janey's out there working in a bar; the pubs in Tenerife are making a killing.' 'What would my role be?' asks Nick.

Mike's voice shouts from outside the bedroom: 'With me, on the bar! And the girls in the kitchen, where they should be...'

Mike dodges what sounds like a blow from Becky, and laughs.

'Lucy, obviously, will need to do a food hygiene course, judging by last month's Chinese takeaway on the worktop. But her actual cooking is up to scratch.'

'What the hell are you doing eavesdropping outside my bedroom? Pervert!' I shout, then groan, immediately regretting it as my brain pounds.

'Nothing, was just passing and overheard. Come have a coffee so we can talk properly.'

An enthusiastic discussion is taking place downstairs. I'm feeling a bit better, two coffees and three slices of toast later. We discuss menu planning, cocktail evenings, themed party nights and quizzes. Becky types furiously on the laptop and then prints the results.

'Now,' says Becky, officiously, 'Location.'

'Well, obviously, we will have to visit Tenerife to look around

for a place to rent. Are we agreed on Tenerife then?' Mike asks, looking around hopefully at us all. 'Big business on tourists from the UK. Immediately after landing, they head straight for the nearest pub selling fry-ups and other Brit food. Different crowd in Greece, they seem to actually want to try Greek food and, sorry Luce, your Moussaka is shit.'
'Oh, I can't wait to tell Sylvia to ram her job!'
'A month's notice, Lucy,' says Nick. He had to burst my bubble.
'Shit, I need to get up to Edinburgh next week too, to claim my inheritance.' 'Bless you, Maisie,' I smile at the ceiling.
I'll come with you,' says Nick. 'I've never been to Edinburgh.'
'Great! I'll need to call in sick for a couple of days.'

Monday morning arrives, all too soon as it always does. I don't have my usual feeling of hoping to be hit by a bus rather than go in to work. Not hurt badly, you understand. I'm not suicidal! Just enough to perhaps break a leg or something. No head injuries though, and something that will heal without a limp. But, oh how I've dreamt of six weeks off that job, even if it was in plaster.
I arrive early to work. How I hate that. Ten minutes of my life spent hanging around outside their house that I will never get back. I hover and read my *Metro* until thirty seconds to start time. It takes me twenty-six seconds to open the gate, walk up the path, put my key in the lock and hang up my coat. That leaves four seconds for Sylvia to look at the clock and realise that no, actually, I am not late. I have synchronised my watch with their kitchen clock to the millisecond. Like something out of *Mission Impossible* – or was it *The Matrix*?
'Morning, Lucy,' Sylvia gives me a look of contempt, 'how are you?'
Of course, she doesn't care. She also never listens. I suspected this all along until one Monday morning when she enquired how my weekend had been; I joked that I'd spent all day

Saturday and Sunday on a bad comedown from some dodgy crack.

'Lovely,' she replied, while Henry slapped the table and laughed like a donkey for ten minutes.

'Oh, just a quick word, Lucy. When you do my laundry, can you make sure it is separate from the children's, please? Katie's ballet leotard has colour run into my favourite Donna Karan blouse. I know it's last season, but it was a particular favourite of mine. Oh, and also, you forgot to put the bin out last Friday when you left. Do be a dear and ensure it doesn't happen again.'

My brain and mouth fight each other. Mouth wants to scream: 'Go fuck yourself, you arrogant cow!'

Brain reasons:

'You have two weeks of holiday pay to claim, don't blow it.' Brain wins.

'Sure.' I smile.

I make up two packed lunches. Henry leaves with Sylvia to be driven the 200 metres to school – in the jeep, naturally. I dress Georgie and we leave to drop Katie off at her school. On the way out of the door, I grab some notepaper from the bureau. What better insult than to hand in my resignation on one of her favourite scented, poncey notelets I know they cost the equivalent of what I'd spend on a spree in Topshop. I head with Georgie to the Soft Play centre and settle down to write. He throws himself into the ball pit, ready to growl at and terrorise anything smaller than him. Occasionally, a mother or a posh nanny from a 'proper' nanny school will say:

'Who *is* that child with? He is being just beastly to Florence and Gertrude.' I shrug and shake my head in understanding, pointing to the nearest cute little toddler – today's choice, a sweet little girl with bunches, sucking her thumb and clutching a teddy.

'No idea, that's mine there,' I smile sympathetically.

Backfired on me once though. Turned out 'chosen child to be mine' on that day actually belonged to the complaining mother. She clutched her to her bosom and gave me a look as if to accuse me of child snatching.

'Don't worry, believe me the last thing I want is my own kid, let alone yours,' I informed her with a reassuring smile.

'Time's up for George Wilkington-Jones,' says the bored, pimply youth in charge of soft play. I pretend not to hear.

'Scuse me, Missus, your kid's had his forty-five minutes,' he says, louder this time. I take £5 out of the kitty purse.

'Forty-five more and this is yours,' I wave it towards him.

'I don't accept bribes!' he splutters, looking around nervously. Sure you don't. A pustule on his neck throbs ominously. Maybe it's a self-defence thing, like those lizards that can drop off their tails. Get too close and splat!

'Fine,' I say. 'I'll just head down to reception and pay my fiver to them, then we'll stay here *all* day.' I smile sweetly.

'You wouldn't!' he stares.

'Wanna watch me?' I raise my eyebrows defiantly.

'OK, fine.' He snatches the fiver with bad grace. I go back to my letter of resignation. I have done two. One horrible and truthful, just to entertain myself; the other – the one I'll give them – is a polite version, and without a hint of truth.

I read through the joke one.

Dear Sylvia and Simon,

It is with pant-pissing pleasure (Get me! Alliteration! Unlike you thought, I'm not on an intellectual level with a badly trained chimp after all. Woohoo!) that I give you my one-month notice to quit. I have decided that I have had enough of being treated like a hired help and have decided to bugger off with my current shag and two best mates to run a bar in Tenerife. Where I intend to get completely legless every night and flirt with horny Spanish waiters. Safe in the knowledge that I will never see you or your brats again since Spain is beneath you – and just isn't Barbados, Jamaica or Antigua, dahhhling. Lucky for me, a wonderful friend from a Care Home, (real people – they do exist!) has left me a hefty sum in her will. It would almost be on a par with what you paid for your garden shed. Yes! That much.

I am now in the most fortunate position of being able to tell you to stick your job up your arse and to let you what I really think of you. Simon (crashing bore), Sylvia (so far up your own backside that you'd need to open your mouth to wipe it), Henry (perv, needs restraining order and shares in Kleenex), Katie (see Sylvia), Georgie (an ASBO waiting to happen).

So, from one month and ooh, let's see, seven and a half hours, you can find some other skivvy to run about after you all like a blue-arsed fly.

Yours (no more),

Lucy Ramsey

PS: It is not acceptable for a nanny to have to unload your clean weekend crockery from the dishwasher, before refilling it with your dirty breakfast ones, take out the overflowing bin bag – again, from the weekend – and spend six hours a week doing you and your husband's laundry and ironing. Note: nanny, not maid!

PPS: With knickers like Simon's, I am quite frankly amazed you would want me to handle them. He can make it to position of Managing Director, but he sure as shit (pun intended) has never learnt to wipe his own arse.

I cackle like an old witch as I read it back. Pustule-boy gives me a wary look. I stare him down and begin the real letter.

Dear Sylvia and Simon,

It is with great reluctance that I am giving you my one-month notice to terminate my employment. I have, thanks to a very kind elderly friend, received an inheritance and have decided to pursue my dream of being a chef. I will from next month be moving to Spain with my partner and friends to run our own restaurant business. I have thoroughly enjoyed my time spent with your family and feel blessed that you have allowed me to help in the raising of your children. I will genuinely miss them all. I would love to see you all should you

ever consider a trip to Spain and, of course, I hope the children will keep in touch.
Many thanks again. The next nanny is a very fortunate girl. I hope she has as many happy hours as an employee of yourselves as I have.
Kindest regards,
Lucy Ramsey.

I find Georgie lying in the bottom of the ball pit and put on his coat and shoes.
'Me troll,' he says, menacingly.
'You sure are,' I say. 'Was that why the little girl was crying?'
'Yes, me bad monster,' he laughs. I ruffle his mop top head. 'Come on, Chucky, let's go home.'

We walk back towards their house, stopping off to collect some brochures from the travel agent. I need to see blue skies and sea. Not slate grey, with a *soupcon* of drizzle, and the filthy canal, with attractively placed shopping trolley, that I see now. I put Georgie in the cot for his nap and start unloading the washing machine. Nooo! Red sock, new white Dior top. Sylvia's. Shit! Bleach. One hour. Now yellow Dior top. Not nice yellow, patchy, piss-stained and still streaked with bits of red from sock. Bin. Sock and top. Imagining how much top cost. Probably equivalent to a fortnight's Caribbean holiday for a family of four. Feel sick. Fuck it! Leaving. Never saw it anyway. I take the bin bag out and place it in next door's bin. Hiding the evidence. They really aren't smart enough to think of that. Actually, that's not quite true, but they wouldn't think that I was smart enough to think of it.

The rest of the day passes remarkably quickly. Henry has football practice and Katie disappears to her room to play Cyber Pets with the girl from next door. Thirteen and a bit old if you ask me. But, apparently, she's a good influence on

Katie, according to Sylvia. I think she is actually 'grooming' her to be a future babysitter. Free child labour and definitely wouldn't let the little ones eat five Easter Eggs, like Henry did when Sylvia popped out for the weekly shop. Before I know it, I hear a key in the lock and Sylvia walks smiling down the hallway. Katie takes the wine out of the fridge and Georgie opens the cupboard to fetch a glass.

'Oh, my babies,' she smiles, 'so good of you to look after Mummy. Not the crystal though Georgie-pops.'

'Lucy, you pop off home early. The traffic is terrible out there.'

'Oh, thanks,' I say, surprised. This is how brainwashing affects nannies. Like a kicked dog, we immediately forgive one hundred acts of bitchiness for one act of kindness. I have a momentary pang of guilt thinking of the letter in my bag. I hover in the vestibule while I place the letter in the envelope.

'Georgie! Psssht. Over here, honey,' I whisper.

He continues to wheel his truck along the bottom stair and blatantly ignores me.

'Georgie,' I cajole. 'Want a sweetie? Don't tell Katie.'

Immediately he lumbers towards me on chunky legs. I hold out a chocolate orange square, complementary from our Indian restaurant and definitely less than a month old, though it's hard to tell with my handbag. I'm sure there are lost ancient tribes lurking in the bottom there. He goes to grab the chocolate.

'Ah, ah, ahhh,' I say. 'Take this to Mummy and come back for the sweetie.' He practically takes my hand off for the letter and runs in the direction of the kitchen.

'Mummy letter,' I hear his muffled babble.

'Thank you, Georgie.'

She has it. I hand him the sweet, say thank you, and slip out into the Baltic chill of the evening.

Chapter Twelve

I arrive home to find Nick and Mike smiling like Cheshire Cats. They've only gone and booked us flights to Tenerife for this weekend. This weekend! Mike pops a bottle of champagne and a beaming Becky walks into the living room with four glasses.

'Here's to the business buddies,' announces Mike.

'Cheers!' we chorus, clinking glasses together.

We sit around the table and call out for a Chinese. No time to cook, too much to discuss. We look at my brochures and argue good humouredly about how we need to be in a commercial-ish area, but not one full of spewing Club 18-30-types. I don't know anyone aged thirty who goes on these holidays. It should be call Club Eighteen to Twenty-two and a Half. By then you are fed up of being urinated on in the pool and treading through rivers of vomit to get to your room. Or at least, I was. We finally decide to travel around the island at the weekend, looking for possible sites and take it from there.

'Oh, Lucy, so how did the resignation go?' asks Becky.

'Well, I kind of gave it to Georgie to give to his mum on the way out the door,' I say with a grimace, feeling slightly ashamed.

'So, you got a two and a half-year-old to hand in your notice for you,' laughs Nick.

Well, of course it sounds really bad when you put it like that.

'Oh, wait till you see what I was going to write,' I giggle, trying to change the subject from my spinelessness. I delve into my bag and – with a flourish – hand over my hilarious resignation. All three huddle around and read. Becky smiles as she mouths the words, the boys focus hard, faces serious. Becky finishes first,

'Very nice,' she smiles.

'Not funny, though,' frowns Nick.

'What? Have you all had a sense of humour bypass? Simon's shitty pants? Sylvia's head up her arse? Henry's shares in Kleenex?' I finish lamely. 'Well, I thought it was funny.' They all look at me confused.

'Look,' I say, snatching back the letter. 'Maybe it's funnier read aloud.' I skim through.

Dear Sylvia and Simon,
It is with great reluctance that I am giving you my one month's notice...
NOOOOOOOOOOOOOOOOOOOOOOOOOOOOOOOOOOOOOO!
I stare at their three worried faces in horror. Becky bites her bottom lip and stares back at me. Mike's eyes are wide and shining. Nick shakes his head and gives me a lopsided smile.
'You gave them the wrong letter. Didn't you?'
I pace the room anxiously as the other three practically wet themselves laughing and demand to know what was in the other letter. I can't even bring myself to remember, I am so mortified.
'Oh, come *on*, Lucy!' Nick holds his stomach. 'You are so fired anyway. Embrace the moment.'
I tentatively think back, cringing, and sink my Champagne quickly. I recite as much as I can remember. Pretty much all of it word for word, unfortunately. I have never seen anyone laugh as much as those three that moment. My mobile rings.
Oh fuck fuck fuck!
Becky snatches it up.
'Sylvia, home,' she exhales.
'Put it down,' I order. *'Put it down!'* Silence. We all wait, shoulders hunched and grimacing, for the voicemail beep.
Beep-Beeeeep. It sounds pissed off.
Becky presses the replay and speaker phone buttons like they may burn her.
'You have One. New. Message. Message. One.'
'Lucy? Sylvia. Well what can I say? I received your resignation and this is just to let you know we will not be requiring you to

work your notice. Oh, and since you owe me for a Dior top, which I found in next door's bin, I will be keeping your holiday pay. Goodbye.' Click.

We look around each other. Purple-faced. Nick is the first to laugh. My sides ache. Guess I should have listened to my instincts after all, and just told her to piss off. Kind of did, I guess.

The upside is that Nick and I can head to Edinburgh the very next day without me taking any sick time. Nick has two days off. He works as a carer with disabled adults and often works weekends. We arrive in Edinburgh and I breathe in the Scottish air.

'Put hairs on your chest this will,' I announce.

'Bloody Hell! It's cold,' shivers Nick.

It's possibly only one degree colder in Scotland than in England, but so may English people expect it to be like the Antarctic that they find it colder than it actually is. We take the bus up to the Care Home where I have to meet Maisie's solicitor. As we sit in the interview room, Ellie and I reminisce about Maisie. She elbows me, and leans in to whisper:

'Remember that student Social Care Officer we had?'

'Don't,' I hiss. 'Do not make me laugh. This is supposed to be solemn. He will think I'm disrespecting the dead.' I nod in the direction of the solicitor, pulling up outside in his Mercedes.

Ellie continues to Nick, as if I'm not there, in hushed tones.

'Lucy was supervising the student, assisting Maisie with her bath.' She glances at me for confirmation.

"Och, Maisie," says the student, "you have letters on your sponges, now let's see. Is B for body?"

"No," says Maisie. "B is for boobs."

So, then the student picks up one with A, on it.

"Well, what can A be for?" she asks.

"What do they teach you young 'uns in college these days?' Maisie sighed, "A is for me arse, dearie."'

Nick and Ellie chortle. I can't help but join in. I wipe tears of mirth from my eyes, just in time for the Centre Manager to open the door and announce,

'Mr. White, the solicitor, is here,' before shaking her head in confusion and walking out.

So all is done and dusted. My cheque from Maisie is banked, but I have yet to open a letter they found addressed to me. I want to do that without Nick around. It's personal. I know he would just irritate me by looking over my shoulder to read along. We head up to the crematorium to place flowers on Maisie's little plot, where her ashes are buried. I unscrew a bottle of sherry and tip half on.

'A toast! Maisie – to you! Cheers, hen! For all the good times, the memories and, of course, the money. You really shouldn't have, but I appreciate it. I promise to spend it on booze, shoes and gorgeous young men. I won't waste a penny of it.'

I swig from the sherry and pass the bottle to Nick for a swig. He makes a disgusted face and hands it back to me. I tip the rest out onto Maisie's plot.

'Come see me sometime on the big psychic telephone,' I say. 'Love and miss you lots!'

Nick and I walk through the drizzle and head to Prince's Street for an impromptu, and very belated, wake. Nick heads to the bar. There are many people waiting to be served.

'Luce, I'm just going to pop to the cash point, back in a mo,' he tells me. Perfect, I think, reaching into my bag for Maisie's letter. I have been itching to read it for hours now. I look at her familiar scrawl on the envelope and feel a pang of loss. Much as I adored working with older people, it takes a certain kind of person to have the ability to detach themselves when the inevitable for us all happens. Looking back, I wonder at why I ever thought I could do this job. As Ellie put it when I handed in my notice:

'It's not for the chicken-hearted among us.'

I ended up doing my bereavement counselling course, anyway. Very kind of them, I thought. Ellie informed me that even though I was leaving, they still felt it would be of benefit to me. It was and it wasn't. Much of it was about distancing yourself in the first place. That didn't make sense to me. Many of these people have no family who visit. Where's the harm in a little hug here and there? Or sitting and having a chat, which I often did while I ate my lunch, in either Harry, Bessie or Maisie's rooms? Maisie actually told me once that she couldn't remember the last time someone had hugged her before I arrived. Probably her husband, who had died twenty years ago. Many of the care staff found my approach slightly unprofessional, but I didn't care; distancing myself never was an option. The part of the course that did help me a bit was the philosophical approach they encouraged you to have. How the quality of care they received had enhanced their wellbeing, how they had been fortunate to have long, healthy and mostly happy lives... blah de blah. I open Maisie's letter as carefully as I can, and begin to read.

My Darling Lucy,
If you are reading this it means I've popped my clogs! Excellent news for your Bank Manager, not so great for me. Obviously I have got fed up sitting in my own pish and dribble and, let's face it, the hubby has got off lightly with twenty odd years peace and quiet from me, it's about time I made up for it. Anyway, I thought I'd drop you a wee note to say why I've left you all my worldlies. This includes any incontinence pads left over, you'll need them one day, ducky, don't think you won't. Oh, and the crocheted loo roll cover I know you so admire, hahaha. Back to the point. I wanted to leave you a little something because you may not have realised it, but you really made the last couple of years of my life very happy. When you left, I thought that'd be the end of it, but I really enjoyed your letters about your life in London. They really made me laugh. I wish I'd done it

myself. I guess what I'm saying, Lucy, is that I thought of you as the daughter I never had. You did so much for all us wrinklies, but expected nothing in return. Don't get me wrong, the staff in the home were all lovely, but with you, we could tell you weren't being PAID to care. You really did. So raise a toast for me and know I'll be around, haunting you. What fun that'll be! I'll come and dance at your wedding for you. IF you ever bloody well get married!
Love and hugs (thanks for all of yours),
Maisie Munroe
xxx

I stare into space as Nick walks back in, covered in a layer of drizzle. He gives me a big hug and I smile. I hand him the letter to read and head over to the bar. It's definitely Maisie's round.

Chapter Thirteen

Nick and I catch the train up to Arbroath. He hasn't met any of the family yet, and I want to spend as much time as I can with them since we will soon be in Tenerife. We'll be too busy, I'm assuming, to have a holiday back home. Nick nervously looks out of the window at the sea rushing past us.
'Gorgeous scenery,' he mumbles.
'Don't be nervous,' I say, picking up on his tension. 'They will love you. More importantly, you're probably the most normal boyfriend I have ever had. So far.' I give him a suspicious once over. I call Mary from Dundee and she says she will be at the station. Nick fidgets uncomfortably in his seat.
'She's the least of your worries,' I mutter under my breath.

Mum has organised a big family meal out. We've been here for an hour and, so far, Nick has met Mum, Mary and, of course, Poopsy. So far, so painless – even if Poops did decide to use Nick's leg as a scratching post. Mum has loved the newby in the house and has taken advantage of the fact he's too polite to say no to her endless food offerings. I eventually point out that he is not a foie gras goose and she reluctantly agrees that enough is enough. I haven't actually mentioned the money yet, but I'm aiming to give my Mum and sister a small share. After what Gran, via Brenda the medium, has said, Mary will need every penny. I choose my moment carefully and then casually mention to Mum about Maisie's inheritance. She gives a loud whoop and says how kind Maisie was. She goes quiet when I mention we are heading off to Tenerife, but I reason with her that it takes less time to fly there than it takes to travel to London by train. She seems a bit happier with this. That and the fact that it means Nick and I must be reasonably serious about each other; there's a possibility of the daughter not being a maiden. She has, however, accepted that she will only have grand-kittens and not grandchildren from me.

An hour and a half later and we have all congregated in our favourite restaurant near the harbour. It does all traditional Scottish dishes and I'm attempting to force Nick to try some haggis. He eventually gives in, turns a touch green and then announces he loves it.

'It's the idea of knowing what it is, I think,' says Nick. 'The taste is actually really nice, though. What is offal anyway? I've always been scared to ask, but I know it can't be good.'

'Sheep's arsehole,' Craig informs him. Nick coughs and spits his third forkful into a napkin, much to the hilarity of the rest of us. I'm pleased to see Nick is managing to hold his own with some of the more sarcastic family members.

We head back to Mum's house and, of course, the family albums are pulled out. No new boyfriend escapes the initiation of: Seeing how fat I was as a baby.

'We called her football face,' Betty helpfully provides.

The naked in the bath photo, aged five, with my fingers covering my teeny nipples.

The 'toilet surprise' picture from last year, when my Mum's bathroom lock was busted. At some point we have pictures of all of us staring like rabbits in headlights as the entire family attempted to cram into the doorway and shout, 'surprise!'

The subject turns to the car crash that is my love life – and it is discussed in great detail yet again. Something I hadn't intended to tell Nick about so early on, but it's pointed out by Mum that he'd best know what he's up against before we leave for Spain. My family love nothing better than fresh blood to spill all to about one of us. I do it myself. As a young family member, it's a rite of passage to be allowed to join in the humiliating stories about the others. Mum ponders for a moment. I try to read what she could possibly come up with next. I watch carefully as it clicks into place in her mind. She remembers the other album in the divan, and heads off to find it. I thought I'd got away with it. It is, unfortunately, the worst. The teenage years. Yes, the dodgy perm photo, of course, accompanied by fetching electric blue eyeliner and mascara, Twilight Teaser lilac lipstick and shoulder pads. I look like a quarterback in drag.

'I think I may have to dump you,' laughs Nick as he takes a second look, unable to quite believe what he's seen first time around.

'You wouldn't be the first,' declares my cousin, Claire. Nick laughs uproariously and then notices no one else is joining in.

'Joe never dumped me because of the pictures,' I smirk, 'the whole family moved to Portugal.'

'Yes, to a *safe* house,' whispers Mary, 'such was their fear you would breed with their son, they went into witness protection. He was the only other normal one until Nick came along, too.'

The evening continues in a similar fashion, with as many disastrous stories about me as they can remember. Luckily, it doesn't seem to have put Nick off. In fact, he gives me a squeeze in the kitchen when we make up yet more sandwiches and tells me he loves me even more now. I throw him a look that says, are you mad? I seem more *real* now, apparently.

The time comes, with my reputation now in shreds, to head back to London. You'd think we were leaving forever, the carry on there is. Many promises to visit; even some of the younger ones offering their services to do a summer's work experience. I assume that means get drunk every night and cop off with tourists without the beady eye of a parent nearby. Nick enthuses about the trip almost all the way back, recounting stories and anecdotes from the past few days. I have yet to find a boyfriend who doesn't love them. In fact, some 'exes' have even asked if I'd mind if they kept in touch with them all when we've broken up. We arrive back to mine at late that night, and decide to have an early one before we fly off to Tenerife in the morning. I make a couple of hot chocolates and fall asleep practically the second my head hits the pillow.

We arrive in Tenerife the next morning, after a turbulent white-knuckle ride of a flight that saw me spending twenty minutes breathing into a paper bag to calm a panic attack. Not sure what's worse, the indignity of being such a wimp on flights or that people think I'm a glue sniffer. The others joke that they will have to Mr. T. me in future. I retort that they're all crazy fools. After we land, I feel unbelievable relief overwhelm me. I glance back at our plane as I race down the steps. I'm checking for L- plates. I swear that a seventeen year-old boy-racer hijacked that flight. We make our way to the hotel, taking a more detailed interest in our surroundings than most of the tourists.
'What is "To Let" in Spanish?' I ask.
Becky shrugs: 'To Letto?' Now that we have arrived and it's all so real, I suddenly feel we are out of our depth. Nick and Mike have decided between them that they will take control of the negotiations. Nick speaks pretty good Spanish and Mike is a complete control freak – and we would never do it to his standards anyway. To be honest, Becky and I can't be arsed with the details and would probably completely muck it all up anyhow, ending up in a complete shack surrounded by cattle. I'd much prefer to be in charge of how my kitchen will run, the menu and the activities for the evening. If they want to take charge of the boring stuff then great. Suits me.
We find an 'Estato Agento'. Becky and I are cracking each other up with simply adding Os to things. Much to the annoyance of the boys.
'Not a difficult language to pick up,' Becky cackles. I join in.
'Oh my God. Shut up!' yells Mike.
It only makes us giggle like schoolgirls even more. I can tell

Mike is wondering what he has let himself in for. Perhaps a nursery would have been a more appropriate venture?

We arrange three properties to view tomorrow and as our flight isn't until 10pm on Sunday, we have three to see then too. We have dinner out and a few drinks in a Taverna.
'Taverno,' Becky whispers, and giggles mischievously to me. It's a warm evening, despite the locals being wrapped up in jumpers and coats. It's only March but feels like mid-summer to us.
'What is that?' Becky points to a flying insect buzzing around near her head. 'Is it a … mosquito?' she raises an eyebrow at Mike. I stifle a smile. He can't tell her off for adding a 'O' to something that should have one anyway.
'Too early for them, I'd say at a guess,' Mike sulks.
'Bore,' Becky pokes her tongue out at him. We head along the beach to a few bars. Everywhere we turn, free sickly drinks are thrust into our hands and British accents enquire:
'Y'all right love? Fancy a free cocktail?'
Mike shudders: 'This is so what I do not want for our place,' he says vehemently.
'No, tacky,' I agree, watching a Scouse girl shove her cleavage in some bloke's face. Turns out, there was a shot of tequila in there. She wouldn't even look at him back home. We jump in a taxi and ask the driver to take us somewhere quiet. He laughs, a little too hard actually.
'Ahh, you is all so old,' he smiles.

We find a nice wine bar on the sea front. Peace. The soothing sounds of the waves crashing on the beach eclipses the very distant thud, thud of bass coming from the clubs further along the coast.
'Now, somewhere like this would be perfect,' Mike indicates our surroundings, and we all take in a panoramic view. 'Classy, not over-priced and most importantly, away from

that lot,' He points along the beach to a sea of flashing, florescent lighting.

'You are looking to rent place?' The bar tender has been eavesdropping on our conversation since we arrived.

'Yes,' I smile, 'somewhere like this, but with a kitchen and preferably some living accommodation too.'

'I have brother on other side of island. I call.' He disappears behind the bar and begins chatting animatedly in Spanish. He returns five minutes later and introduces himself as George, the owner of the bar. He has arranged for us to see his brother's place on the other side of the island tomorrow. Living quarters upstairs, large kitchen, and a bar and dining area. Quiet, with only a few hotels nearby, but rarely anyone under twenty-five – unless they've booked without realising it's so far from the main drag.

'Like here,' George tells us. Right enough, as we look around, there are mainly people in the thirty to fifty age bracket.

The next morning we are up early for breakfast. We pile into our hire car and Mike drives us to the first viewing. It has taken us over an hour, as Becky is navigating and has been holding the map upside down for the first twenty minutes. She then complains that it's all in Spanish. After a bit of a fracas between Becky and Mike, Nick takes over the directions. I don't bother offering – would probably do a worse job than Becky and am prone to barf when I read anything on any kind of transport. I don't want to make Mike's foul mood any worse. It's a pretty disappointing lot. The first two are complete dives. It would take a good month of refurbishing and decorating before they were even halfway ready to move in to. Something we have neither the time nor the money to do. The third is so far off the beaten track that we wouldn't have any trade. In the back yard there are two goats tied up. The smell did not help matters.

We head on to George's brother's place. It's gorgeous! Right on the edge of a low cliff, the waves crash on to the rocks below us. The garden is large and shaded with huge parasols and overlooks the Atlantic. The décor is perfect, shades of deep blue, terracotta and sunshine yellow. It's everything I imagined. I walk into the kitchen and run my hand along the marble work surface. This will cost a bomb, but it's perfect. We won't have to touch a single thing.

Mike and Nick get down to business with George's brother, Roberto. Becky and I take an interest, but it's blatantly obvious we are dealing with a man's man here. Any questions from me, such as about the passing trade, nearby resorts and annual turnovers, are met with a steely glare. I am then coolly ignored. Yet when Nick or Mike reiterate my enquiries, Roberto (Becky wants to take it based solely on his name ending in an O. Business woman, she ain't) beams at them as if they were so clever to think of it. At one point he pinches Nick's cheek and says:

'Good boy! Nothing will get past you. But your waitress, she ask too much that is none of her business.' He shakes his head at Nick as a warning. I'm biding my time.

The summer figures for the past two years have been great, but before that it was a dive. Roberto had taken it over, redecorated and turned it around with his speciality paella and Spanish-themed nights. He now felt he was too old for a busy restaurant and wanted to work only part time in one of his quieter places. He was happy to let the premises and living area upstairs so he could continue making money on rent for his retirement fund.

There are two nearby resorts and private villas along the sea front; a good combination of business from tourism and ex-pats in the surrounding area. Between the two, the restaurant was pretty much packed out for breakfast, lunch and dinner times. It certainly was filling up quickly as we sat. Roberto was so confident that we would do well that he was willing to offer us the lease for six months, instead of one year. It would go quiet after September, but there was also a big Christmas and New Year crowd. He generally closed the place down in October and November, January and February. We would, however, have to continue to pay rent for these times – open or closed – if we decided to continue with the lease. He seemed very fair and honest for a misogynistic old git.

Then the good bit. Nick and Mike turned to me. Roberto looks confused.

'What do you think, Lucy? Can you see us being happy here?

'Why you ask her?' Roberto shrugs.

'Lucy is the major shareholder in the business, I'm the other one. Becky and Nick will be working as staff members. The profit sharing will be between Lucy and I; one third to me, two thirds to Lucy,' explains Mike. Realising that he has just dissed the deciding factor, Roberto smiles at me uncertainly and asks what I think of his restaurant? Ah, so *now* he cares about my opinion. I look around and sigh deeply.

'Well, it is very nice, good décor, prime location. And I am impressed with your turnover and negotiation over the rental agreement, Roberto.'

He looks at me curiously. Like I'm a creature he's never seen before. Not used to women talking and him actually listening, I'm sure.

'We do have three other places to see.' I look around at the others. They are pleading with me with their eyes.

'What do you guys think?' Nodding furiously, the lot of them. I hold my hand out to Roberto.

'OK, Roberto, I think we have a deal.'

He beams proudly. I sign a cheque for three month's rent and a deposit and we head out into the sunshine.

'Great! We now have the rest of Saturday and Sunday all to ourselves,' announces Becky, linking arms with Mike and

Nick.

We have a great evening of tapas and wine. In a frivolous moment, we take a cab back out to Roberto's to see what the night-time shift is like. Very atmospheric, very busy. Doesn't get much better than that. We sit in a quiet corner and I have a sudden attack of panic about not being able to cope with the kitchen side of things. What do I really know about catering? I voice my concerns to the others, who insist I will cope, no problem. I will have waitresses, kitchen staff and a dishwasher. I won't actually be doing the job of five people in there, like I would be if I were hosting a dinner party at home. Bolstered by the surge of wine and adrenaline in my bloodstream, I decide that it'll be fine – and start looking forward to the challenge. If I have any problems, we can always hire a chef and I can take on the *commis* role. This has been my dream for years. I can do it.

Chapter Fourteen

We head back to London the next day and prepare to hand in our notices to jobs and landlords. Well, except for me, who has already done the spectacular job notice bit. We have two weeks until we move. Mike may have to do a month's notice, but he is confident they can wangle it down to two weeks. Our rent begins the second week in April at Roberto's. Becky has only to give one week's notice as she temps for an office agency. So, we will head out a week before the boys to clean, shop for our own personal touches and get a feel for the place. I start a course on food hygiene and enrol on a week-long catering class next week. I am already quite a confident cook, but I want to add a few skills before we go. Every night I cook for all four of us. Different dishes that I think would be great on our menu. Almost everything is met with enthusiasm. We have decided to do a mixture of traditional British food and a few Spanish specialities, such as paella and tortilla. Chuck in a bit of Mexican (still kind of Spanish) and Italian, as pasta is definitely my *forte*. We have printed up fifty glossy menus. All things I can cook confidently, and we will add a different daily special, starter and main.

The night of our leaving party comes around. We are having it at home, so I can show off our menu and have feedback from friends. I have spent all day in the kitchen and have prepared four of our dishes for friends to try. Everyone seems very positive about the menu and we have a bittersweet night; sad to be leaving London and all our friends, but very excited about the future. It's unbelievable how quickly things have turned around for Becky and I since Christmas.

'Can you believe it was only a few months ago that we were both single, hated our jobs and where we live, moaning about the weather and how crap London is?' she asks.

It's not that London is crap, of course. A very fun place to live if the truth be known. The downside is that, by the time you have paid your rent, council tax and bills (Water! In England you pay for water. That was a shock to me. Never heard the like) you really don't have a lot of cash left with which to enjoy London. Friends from back home think we live a very glamorous lifestyle of non-stop shows, clubs and fancy restaurants. The reality is that, the week before pay day, Becky and I rummage through the dregs of our purses together and head to our local supermarket to stretch our funds as far as possible on 'Buy One Get One Free' items. I do find what has happened in the past few months very hard to believe. I'm taking a huge risk pooling finances, but I trust Mike. He was willing to invest in all of us with the money he had, expecting little in return. We would have really struggled without Maisie's inheritance. I'm not sure Roberto would have taken us seriously if we didn't have as much money as we do.

Saturday arrives. Becky and I head to the airport with Nick and Mike. Becky is worried about coping with me on the flight without back-up. I will try to be brave this time, as it isn't fair to put all that on her. My mobile rings. Amy's name flashes up on caller I.D. 'Hi Lucy,' she says uncomfortably, 'I need to talk to you about something before you go. Emily and I weren't going to tell you, but Jill said we should. Look, we've all been really ill. Taking it in turns to throw up all night. We're thinking it's something we ate.' Pause. 'It must have been at yours. We all had lunch at different places. I think we have food poisoning!'

I have an attack of the horrors. This can't be. How can I possibly run a kitchen if I can't even cook four dishes for my friends without half killing them?

'Oh my God,' I bluster, 'are you serious? I am so sorry. I was very careful and I passed my course with a hundred percent...'

'Joke!' laughs Amy. 'Becks just texted me and asked me to take your mind off the flight. Did it work? Did it?'

'Yes, you absolute cow! Valuable lesson learned in how things could be worse – now bugger off,' I laugh.

'OK, but just wanted to say thanks for an amazing night. I'm sure you'll all do very well. We'll be over to see you in June. Make sure you keep in touch, now.'

'Will do. Miss you all lots already.'

I hang up. Becky smirks and asks if I hate her?

'Yes', I announce, 'but since I have to live and work with you, I suppose I will have to forgive and forget.' After the food poisoning shock, I am surprisingly good on the flight. Of course, two double vodkas helped.

We land and take a taxi out to the restaurant. It has been closed for the past week, awaiting our arrival. Roberto and his staff have cleaned until it gleams. We start by making a list of all we need to do, starting by finding a list of suppliers. Roberto has thoughtfully left us a list of the people he uses, and says to contact him for anything we need to have imported. He has lots of contacts and is proving to be a great help. He also had offered to sell us tables, chairs, crockery, glasses – basically any kitchen equipment we want – at a very reasonable price. We said we would take them. Everything seemed in good condition last time we were here, and we can always replace things as we go along. Becky has made up fliers for our launch on her laptop. We decided on buffet style for the party. Let them try a little bit of everything in the hope they'll love it all and come back regularly. We plan to stand on the beach and hand out the fliers over the next few days. We settle into our accommodation upstairs and set about making it homely. It's only a two-bedroom flat, but we are all so used to sharing that I'm sure there will be no problem.

The next day we are up bright and early to visit the suppliers. We arrange the deliveries for the day before opening and head down to the beach to promote our launch night. It is already absolutely sweltering in the April sun. Many people body swerve us, insisting that they are not interested in a time-share. I'm not surprised. I'd do exactly the same. It takes some convincing to get people to take a flier. Five Euros off their meal if they bring the voucher on the night and a sound promise that it won't turn into a surprise time-share meeting. Luckily, we won't be suffering from this heat in the restaurant, as it has air conditioning. By 6pm Becky and I are practically walking blisters and so we head off to a 'Taverno' for tea. As we clink glasses and toast our new venture, neither of us can quite hide our excitement.

'Mike has been talking about us getting married,' squeaks Becky.

'Bloody hell! It's only been a few months,' I reply, incredulously.

'I know, I know,' she replies, 'but you can't deny things have moved really fast for us all. It just feels... well, right, I suppose.'

'Well go for it,' I reply. 'Good for you! I mean, OK it's fast, but then so is all this.' I indicate our surroundings. 'I just hope Nick doesn't go getting any funny ideas. I'm not ready for all that yet. So, Bob? Is he firmly in the past, where he belongs then?' I ask.

'I would say so,' Becky shrugs. 'I'm hardly likely to bump into him out here now, am I?'

'Becks, you need to be sure you are completely over him before you make that kind of commitment with Mike,' I anxiously explain. 'It's not fair on him if you feel you are "settling" for what he can give you.'

'Luce, chill! Of course I love Mike, he's adorable and gorgeous. What girl wouldn't want to be with him?'

I watch Becky suspiciously. I'm not convinced she does want

marriage and kids with Mike. She loves him, definitely, but he's not Bob. God knows what she saw in Bob, but each to their own. Becky interrupts my thoughts.

'Stop scowling,' she scolds. 'You'll make your wrinkles worse.'

    The day of the boy's arrival is upon us. Becky is beside herself with excitement. I am looking forward to seeing Nick, but seem strangely detached in this relationship. I have no idea why. Probably, it's nothing more sinister than the fact that he has been unlucky enough to come along at the tail end of a bunch of losers. I'm kind of over men. Same kind of thing with kids. Well, not all of them, obviously. I know lots of lovely little ankle-biters, but the last lot certainly poisoned any remaining maternal instincts I possessed. I could practically feel my ovaries shrivel to raisins every time I came into contact with one of them. I expect I'd be desperate for my own by now if I hadn't spent years looking after other people's kids. I think back to my last week as a nanny, and shudder. What possessed me? I would have been deliriously happy cleaning toilets compared to that. Funny how we do things we hate on a daily basis just to prevent a change to our routine. I was constantly running around in those days. I was late for everything, and not once actually my fault. The second last day, I had to apologise to Katie's teacher for my tardiness, the third time that week. I swear Georgie repeatedly chose that precise moment to fill his pants. I dashed into school, tipping the buggy dangerously round a sharp bend and through a muddy puddle. Mrs Gray towered over a bored-looking Katie, looking tiny in her hat, coat and scarf.

'Mrs Gray, I am so sorry, again!' I breathlessly explained.

'What's the excuse today, Lucy?' she glanced at her watch and sighed dramatically. Is it just me or do teachers retain the power to terrorise the crap out of you, even in your thirties? It's like when you see a policeman. You automatically feel guilty despite doing nothing wrong. Teachers always manage to make me feel naughty and ashamed.

'Last minute poo,' I announced.

She looks at me with undisguised disgust.

'Oh no! not me!' I stutter. 'Georgie! I never, you know, well rarely...' Oh Christ! Shut up! Now! She looks at me with pity, as I point lamely at Georgie.

'If it happens again I will have no choice but to inform Katie's parents,' she informs me, turning away. I laugh and look at Katie.

'If it happens again...' I mimic quietly. Katie giggles.

'Something you'd like to share with me, perhaps? Lucy, hmmm?'

Bloody hell! She's back. She hands me Katie's forgotten reading book.

'No, nothing.' I mutter, and turn the buggy around, quick smart.

The night of our launch has arrived. Becky and I have sweated our arses off all day in the kitchen. We have pre-cooked everything that we can, ready to go at a moment's notice. We have wheeled out a couple of Bain Maries to serve from as people queue. The place is filling up slowly but surely; a combination of curiosity at the newbys and the promise of a discounted 'all you can eat' meal have proven a strong temptation. We have kept on a waiter, Gino, and a waitress, Maria, from Roberto's old staff. They are ridiculously fast and efficient compared to us.

We fire out the buffet platters as fast as we can. The atmosphere is great fun out in the restaurant, but it's a different story behind the scenes. Becky and I are screaming at each other across the kitchen, dropping food, pots boiling over. I've burned myself twice already. Maria and Gino do nothing to help. They simply look on with a disapproving, stony glare. That's the thanks we get for saving their jobs, is it?

A Spanish band plays out front and are actively encouraging the tourists to get up and sing, karaoke style. At the moment some florid-faced, large English guy, with a peeling sunburnt nose and Hawaiian shirt stretched over his beer gut, is murdering *Viva, Espana*.

Amazingly, we receive no complaints. Lots of praise, however, and promises of,

'We'll be back tomorrow night!' We'll see.

Closing time, and the boys take an unnecessarily long time saying goodbye to our new clientele. I am desperate for bed. Finally, they see off the stragglers at the door and begin to scrub down the bar. They definitely have the best end of the deal. Both are hammered, having drunk loads of shots with the punters. Becky and I have managed one cup of espresso each, and even then it was thrown down our throats in an attempt to liven up our reserves.

'Mike, lock the door,' I shout, 'It's never a good idea to cash up in an empty pub with an open door.'

'Yes, in a minute,' he is leaning against Nick and laughing loudly about one of the customers. The bell rings, signalling someone coming in.

'Sorry, we're closed,' Mike shouts cheerfully.

Silence. Even from the kitchen I can tell it's an uncomfortable silence. A look of concern flashes between Becky and me. I walk out from the kitchen, Becky closely following, and almost trip over Gino and Maria hiding behind the counter.

'What the... get up! What are you doing?' I ask.

'Sssshh!' Gino pulls me down. 'It is Pablo. He want money. Roberto, he no pay.' I stand and walk round to the bar, looking back to see Maria and Gino disappear through the kitchen doors. Becky looks from me to them and back again, uncertain what to do.

'Call the police,' I hiss. Becky shrugs. Shit! I don't know the number either. I gathered that much from one shrug. I gesture to the kitchen. She nods, understanding that I am telling her to ask the Spanish ones. She reappears and shrugs again. From the sea breeze blowing through, I realise they have done a bunk through the back door.

This can't be good. I walk round to the bar, bravado taking over. Bravado – Becky would be proud that something ending in an 'O' was my dying thought. Shame she won't know since, in five minutes, I'll probably have a bullet through my skull. Bravado aka foolishness. I see Mike shoved against the back of the bar. A huge man is dwarfing him and menacingly informing Mike that he owes him. Eyes bulging and swallowing repeatedly, Nick looks like he's swallowed a frog.

'We owe you nothing.' Is that really my voice? 'Take it up with Roberto. We took this place over. Now get out of my restaurant!' He walks towards me, leering and swaggering.

'I like a woman with spirit,' he says in a thick Spanish accent.

'Yeh? Well, you've come to the right place,' I inform him, regaining a little bit of courage. Four of us and one of him. I reckon we could take him. Of course, I'm absolutely terrified, but someone has to do something. Mike and Frog Boy are paralysed with fear, and none of us know the number for the Policio but I refuse to let this idiot away with our night's takings. I can tell from his skin-tight vest and jeans that he doesn't have a weapon on him.

'We have no business with you. I will show you our rental agreement.'

'Well, if you work for Roberto, then *you* owe me.' He is inches from my face. I can smell his rancid tequila and cigarette breath.

'Oh, your Mother must be so proud, you bloody bully!' I look at him with disgust.

'I am no bully,' he looks wounded. 'My Mama, she was proud of me. She tell me all time, Pablo, I proud of you, you good boy.'

I'm seeing an opening here.

'Well, maybe I should pay her a visit. I would love to let her know how you came shoving your way into *my* restaurant and terrifying innocent people.' Pablo crosses himself.

'She is with the angels.' He raises his eyes to the ceiling. 'I frighten you? I'm sorry, I not mean to, I just want my money,' he looks at the floor ashamed. I frantically indicate to Mike for the tequila bottle and a shot glass. He stumbles over, losing grip momentarily on the bottle before catching it again. I roll my eyes at him.

'Sorry', he mouths back.

'Look, have a drink. Roberto seems like a decent guy. If he owes you, then I'm sure we can do something about it.'

Pablo nods, and sits heavily on a bar stool, shoulders hunched.

'Service!' I shout. Mike and Nick trip over themselves to get to us.

'Wine please,' I sigh. Nick passes a bottle and two glasses. Becky appears from the kitchen at the sound of the cork.

Thank God for my combined years of bar work and nannying.

Drunk men, kids.

Kids, drunk men.

Much of a muchness.

Turns out Pablo was 'security' for Roberto. Oh, how the irony pains me. He owed him one month's wages and had buggered off to goodness knows where, without paying him. Pablo was desperate. He needed food for his wife and children and was behind on his rent. Not worried enough to actually go and buy food instead of fags and booze, however. But hey-ho, takes all sorts. I ask him how much Roberto was paying him; not a lot. I inform him that if he works on the door for us, I will double that. It will do us no harm to have a meathead – albeit it a Mammy's boy one – on the door. We leave the evening on a good note. I will get in touch with Roberto and insist on Pablo's wages, or we won't sign the lease for any longer than six months. He seems happy with this. Well, if the fact he practically snogged all four of us was anything to go by.

'No harm, no harm,' he insists to Mike.

'No!' Mike laughs nervously. 'Just havin' a laugh, aye?'

'Aye,' confirms Pablo, mimicking Mike's Scottish accent. 'Just havin' a laugh.'

Mike and Nick later relay the story as if they were moments away from whacking him over the head with a bottle, forgetting that I was actually present the whole time.

'*You*, Lucy, have just embroiled us in a protection racket,' Mike announces.

'Oh away and shite, Mike. I had to take him on because if we rely on you two pussies for security our establishment will be a target for any dodgy type on a daily basis. And, for your information, I was torn between lamping him one with an optic bottle and putting him on the naughty step. So, get over yourselves.'

And with that, I storm angrily upstairs to bed. Idiots – the both of them. We could have lost an entire day's takings because of them. I don't have the energy to take care of all this by myself. Thank goodness we have Pablo on board. He was our wake-up call. Better to have him with us than against us.

Chapter Fifteen

The next month passes in a blur. Who would have thought I would have given up a fifty-hour week, which feels like a part time job now, for a one hundred and twenty hour one catering for over a hundred people per day? The upside being, we are raking in an absolute fortune. We see the same faces for one or two weeks, and then they are replaced by new faces for another one or two weeks. Anyone who happens upon us seems to spread the word. Our profits are more than we ever imagined. We all seem to be getting along well too. Bonded by the non-stop rush of our new lives. Well, when I say *we* are getting along fine, I mean Mike, Becky and me; and also the combination of Becky, Mike and Nick. Nick and I seem somewhat fraught. Probably the long hours, I think, and dismiss it to the back of my head.

Pablo is working out wonderfully. He hugs me every time he sees me and informs me: 'Mama sent you Lucia. You! My gift from Mama! She was just like you.' Not such a compliment as it appears, as he later told us everyone in the area was shit scared of her and she was as mad as a box of frogs. But, she could cook like no-one else he knew.
We have doubled his wages – they were horrendously low in the first place – we send home a share of leftovers every night for his family. I know there is not a single person on the island that will give us any trouble; his family are so well-known and many of the locals either feel they have to befriend them or give them a wide berth. The extra money we pay out to him is worth every penny. Maria and Gino get no leftovers and a basic wage plus tips. As a result of their cowardice on opening night, I now view them with suspicion. Not that I expected them to be have-a-go heroes, but they could have at least called the police before they scarpered. We could all now be

dead, thanks to them.

Two months on, and we decide to take on cover staff so we can all have two days off a week. Probably a Monday and Tuesday, but who cares? At this point, an hour off would seem like bliss. Another four months of this before things even halfway begin to calm down. Don't get me wrong, I'm not complaining. I'd much rather be doing this than spend another second at Sylvia's. We are making thousands of Euros in profit each month, and two thirds of that is mine. One night after closing, we are all sitting around the bar. Nick has just cashed up.

'Wow, Luce, we're rich!' he exclaims. We are? We, I think? Since when was this *our* money? I tell him as much. Nicer than I had said in my head, though.

'What, you mean you don't see this as ours?' he asks, looking visibly shocked and more than a little pissed off.

'Nick,' I lean forward, 'look, no offence meant here, but I have known you only a few months. I, via Maisie, have taken the biggest gamble on this place. If it had failed, do you assume you would be liable for a share of the debt?'

'Well, no,' he manages to get out, 'but I just thought...'

'Well no, Nick. Just un-think that. We are not married. Mike and I pay you the same hourly rate as you were making in London, which means, on the hours you are working, you are raking it in. I am not about to hand over half my profits to someone I have known five minutes and may not be a permanent fixture in my life.'

'Fuck, Lucy. You never used to be so bitter and money-grabbing,' he sneers. 'I work my ass off for you every day and for what? Nothing!'

'Nick, I never had any money to grab. I was only crap with money because I had more money going out than coming in. This is the first time, ever, that I have had a chance to make something of myself. I'm not saying there is no "us", but when

I was on five hundred pounds per week in London, do you think I had rights to the fact you earned six hundred? And besides, you are not obligated to me. You're a free man and if you wish to quit and go back to London, then you hand in your notice like any other job.'

'Point taken,' he smiles sarcastically, and heads up to bed. There seems to be a lot of that with us these days.

The following week again passes in a blur. Our week is punctuated by:

Monday: Karaoke.

Tuesday: Spanish night. Food, drink, dancers and band.

Wednesday: Quiz night.

Thursday: Family night. Kiddies disco.

Urgh! That's what I would have said a few months ago, but they are now strangely cute again.

Friday: Party night for grown-ups only. Though it doesn't start until ten. We know a lot of our business comes from family meals.

Saturday: Another party night, but for the leaving/arriving crew. Spanish-themed and much like a Tuesday, but with extra Sangria.

Sunday: UK day. Traditional roast with football and rugby on the big screens.

Monday comes around again. Thanks to the fact we finally have staff to take over on a Monday and Tuesday, we are all very excited at the prospect of two days off. We plan a morning on the beach near the restaurant, so we can be close at hand to help with any problem that may occur. Nick rolls his eyes at this suggestion. I ignore it, but Mike notices.

'Everything all right, mate?' Becky gives a concerned look. Nick nods seriously.

Oh, Purrleeeease! The only thing wrong with him is having the hump over the fact he can't get his mitts on my cash. Funny, you never know someone until money is involved.

Becky and Nick disappear to the beach bar for more drinks. My first in over a week; I haven't had the energy. Fell asleep with a glass of wine in my hand last night – the shame! I grab the opportunity to ask Mike if he thinks I am being unreasonable. He thinks for a moment, looking into the distance at a palm blowing in the breeze.

'Depends, Lucy. I mean, Becky and I, well, we want to get married. I see what's mine as hers. It's fast for us, though and may be too fast for you and Nick's speed. What do you see for your future together?'

I think about this. Nothing. I see nothing for us as a couple. Where do you go when you're not fussed about marriage and kids? In a way it punctuates everything and speeds things along. There's no rush if your biological clock seems to have run out of batteries years before. I remember having these marriage and baby instincts. But now, it just seems to complicate everything. I see so many bedraggled women, very unhappy and desperate to get out. It's like a life sentence. This man, who wined and dined you, indulged your desire for a huge wedding in a Scottish castle, listened intently to your tales of woe from work. Then, a year into marriage and a new-born baby later, this same man suddenly develops selective hearing to the constant squalling through the night – and any tales of woe become nagging. No, it's not for me.

But what *do* I want? For me? The freedom of choice to take off around the world at a moment's notice? The choice to be with a man because we want to be together and not because we're bound by a mortgage or child? Mike is looking at me intently.

'I guess, I'm not sure, Mike. I don't need a man, I just want to have security. With money for me and my family, travel and a nice house. And a cat, oh yes, a cat, a Jack Russell and a herb garden. To be able to do my weekly shop in Marks and Spencer without worrying about having an overdraft on my overdraft,' I smile wistfully.

'You just answered your own question then, Luce.'
'How so?'
'Nick didn't feature in any of your dream.'

Chapter Sixteen

And so it was out there. I didn't see Nick as part of my future. Now for the hard part, why? Did I not want Nick because of a spate of idiots in my past? Did I not love him? Did I detect something in him that raised the hackles? Is it a disaster waiting to happen? I have no idea. I decided I'd ask him what he wanted, keeping in mind that I was getting wealthier by the day. Would I believe him regardless of what he said? OK, not me. Someone though. Who was this a job for?
Mike? No.
Becky? Yes!
I gave her the low-down. She was great at this kind of thing. Becky was an undiscovered treasure. She should have worked for the Secret Service. With her inquisition techniques, she could leave a grown man crying within ten minutes. She was similarly good with females. Within five minutes she knew all about their first crush and which guy in the room they fancied. Mike and I did the next bar run, leaving Nick and Becky alone. I could almost feel the tension from across the five-minute stretch of beach. I see Nick, leaning forward, talking urgently. Becky laid back in a relaxed pose, luring him in like a silent spider on the outskirts of her web.
'What are they saying? I hiss to Mike. He looks incredulous.
'Lucy! How the fuck would I possibly know that?'
'It was a rhetorical question, Mike,' I tut. I watch anxiously. I can almost see a trickle of sweat run down the side of Nick's face. We return to the beach.
'Oh Lucy, I need to cool down with a paddle. Come with me?' says Becky. Nick throws her a suspicious look. 'Coming too Nick?' He shakes his head and relaxes a bit, not realising it's a ploy to make him think that by inviting him, she won't be talking about their conversation.
'So? I demand, the second our ankles are wet with sea water.

'OK, he doesn't see a future as he senses you don't. He's worried that you don't see each other as a couple – and it's not just about the money, it's about the sentiment behind it. Also, Mike and I talking about kids and marriage has made him think he maybe wants that. But you don't.'

'Do you believe him?' I ask.

'Do I bollocks! I know he doesn't want kids. Marriage, maybe, I can see. I think he's scared. You scare him, Lucy. It's OK to be cautious, given your past, but be careful it doesn't turn you into a ball breaker!'

'I no longer consider any man in my future,' I reply, with a superior sniff, hitching up my white gypsy skirt and tucking the hem into my knickers. 'Fine if I ever actually meet someone decent and they want to stick around, so long as it's all on my terms. And definitely separate finances, all straight down the middle. I can't be arsed with the whole complicated thing. It's never long term.'

Becky looks at me sadly for a moment. I know what she's thinking. I haven't found what she

has. Well, I had. Or so I thought. If it all can fall through with Alfie, then it can happen again. For Becky's sake, I hope I'm wrong. I do hope she does have her fairytale. I don't believe them anymore. The Brothers Grimm are more my style these days. No romantic illusions these days. They're dead in the water, all of them.

So what do I do? Break it off, but continue with him working for us? Keep things going so he doesn't feel he has to go back to London?

'What does he want then?' I ask Becky.

'I suppose just for things to be better than they are at the moment, at a guess.'

'That's fine. I will leave things how they are then and try to be a bit more of a proper couple. Maybe a few date nights. I'm not unhappy, just not going to hand over half my profits to someone who could take off at any moment and shag some seventeen-year-old Senorita.'

Our two days off pass without a hitch. True professionals, the Spanish. They don't moan about long hours, the heat or lugging crates around like the Brits would. They just get on with it. We start to discuss what we will do with our time off in October and November. We have listened to Roberto and his comments that it's not worth opening; we'd probably spend more on air con and wasted food than we'd take in. And God knows we all need a break. A simple 'Back in November' note on the door seems to suffice in Spain, But in London a

'Gone for lunch, back in half an hour' note would be met with a tirade of expletives on your return. Anyway, I'm with Becky's suggestion on this one. A week at home then fly off to Australia for seven weeks, back here for the Christmas rush, and take it from there. I'd love to see Australia. We can go on a holiday visa for up to three months.

Nick is very quiet through this conversation. These days, he seems to be either very hyperactive and enthusiastic or low and moody. When he's up, he's great. Like the Old Nick. When he's low, he is snappy and glowers into space. Mike can't get to the bottom of it, and neither can I.

'Nick? Australia?' I urge.

He shrugs,'dunno.'

It's like living with a teenager. Even down to the breakouts on his face. He is regressing.

'Well,' I breeze to Mike and Becky, 'I'm in. Let's book the flights and if Nick decides to come along then he can book his own and catch us up.' I'm certainly not massaging his ego and pleading with him to come along. A break from him would be just as welcome as a break from work. Becky and Mike glance at each other cautiously.

'OK,' Mike shrugs, 'I'll book tomorrow. Let me know if you change your mind before then, mate.' Nick says nothing, just stares grumpily into space.

The next few weeks pass at the same frenetic pace. I love it. I love the whole thing, actually. Money aside, I am having a ball. We have started a new chef two evenings a week, so I can be 'front of shop.' The atmosphere is amazing. The air almost buzzes. Mike and I are a double act behind the bar; the punters love us, our sarcastic remarks to each other and mock flirtatious behaviour.

'You two should be together!' shouts Wilma, of Wilma and John from Southall, over the music. 'We will be back next summer to see.' I shake my head at her over the pint I'm pouring.

'No, Wilma, I'm with Nick and Mike is with Becky.'

'I sense sexuaaaaaal chemistry.' Wilma shakes her booty.

'Get her,' I laugh, nudging Mike and thrusting a thumb in Wilma's direction. Mike leans conspiratorially over the bar. Wilma leans in, dramatically.

'The interest Luce and I have in each other...' he smiles, seductively, 'is financial.'

He booms with laughter and Wilma slaps his arm.

'Don't give me that!' she raises her eyebrows, 'like I said, I'll be back and I bet you fifty quid...' Mike and Wilma shake on it and seal the deal. I glance over at Nick. He isn't even paying attention. Distracted and looking around for someone. Probably fancies one of the tourists. He takes a hell of a lot of toilet breaks these days. I'm sure he's working the room.

'He always does that,' shrugs Mike, when I ask. 'You just don't see it because you're always in the back shop.' I decide it's time for a chat. The last thing I want is to be with someone who doesn't want to be with me. Or doesn't want to be here at all.

The next morning I tentatively approach the subject with Nick.

'Are you happy here, Nick? I mean us, work?'

'I'm fine.' He rolls over in bed, facing away from me.

'You do know that if you want out of work, or us, that I won't hold you back. Don't you? I do want you to be happy, even if it's not with me. There is always a job here for you if you want it. We can set up the front room as an extra bedroom. Or you can find somewhere else if you'd prefer?'

'Mmmmhmmm.'

'Please, Nick. Listen. If you're not happy, either with me or the job, I really don't mind if you want to go.'

'Yes! Lucy. For fuck's sake, I hear you,' he snaps.

I decide to speak to Pablo. He will know what's going on or if the same woman comes here every night. I'm guessing now but I really have no clue.

'Not woman, same man,' announces Pablo, chewing on a piece of gum and closely watching some drunken teens heading our way. He turns away anyone he feels will lower the tone of our establishment. It works. Many of our regulars say part of the reason they come along to ours is the lack of young drunkards.

'What are you saying? That Nick is gay? Pablo?'

'No!' he looks at me shocked. 'It is the snaw.'

'Snaw?'

He places one finger on the right side of his nose and sniffs. Such is his friendship with Mike, he is proudly cultivating a Scottish accent.

'OK, Pablo, by snaw, do we mean snow?'

'Well, we... I don't know... but me, yes I mean... snow.' He says the word as if it's alien to him.

'As in Charlie? Coke? Cocaine? Pablo, are we talking about cocaine?'

'Yes,' he says slowly, as if I am a tad simple.

'Mike say to me: "If I didn'ae ken any better I'd say wur wee man was on the snaw." But I know the signs. My own brother is waste of space. I not let dealer in, but cannot stop Nick from going out. He says is nothing, just mate he chat to.'

Fine! I know what I'm dealing with here. Ha! Ironic, but no pun intended. That's exactly what

Nick has been looking around for, his dealer.

He did tell me he'd messed around with drugs in the past. No biggie, lots of people have. Personally, I once had a couple of puffs on a joint, aged eighteen. I then chucked my ringer up for the next three hours, the beginning and end of my drug history.

Nick has a drug problem. OK. It explains a lot. The spots, the mood swings, the manic behaviour. I have coped with worse.

I approach the subject that night, very gently and tactfully.

'Nick, I think you're on drugs.' OK, fail on the tact!

'What? Lucy, no! Why …Why would you think that?'

'Nick,' I say gently. 'I don't think, I know. Your behaviour is so erratic and, well you know, you have mood swings and…erm… bad skin and…I know you've had a dealer coming here, waiting outside for you, unless you've suddenly taken an interest in sharing a toilet cubicle with men… I know you and some of the guys have been disappearing in there a couple of times a night.'

'Fine! Yes Lucy, I take drugs occasionally. You knew that I sometimes did, so what?'

'You told me you dabbled a long time ago. That you hadn't had any for years,' I reply.

'Oh for Christ's sake, Lucy! What I do with my money and my body is up to me, and nothing to do with you.'

'Fine, well, I'm not sharing my living space with someone as erratic as you. You can sleep in the front room for a few days but I want you to make other plans for accommodation and you will *not* be taking drugs on shift in future.

'Don't be ridiculous,' Nick spits the words at me, 'a little pick-me-up to get me through all those God forsaken hours you make me work. I bloody deserve it.'

I head downstairs to the bar. Mike is surrounded by till receipts, the cashing up book and bank book. He looks up guiltily as I approach.

'What's wrong, Mike?' Instinctively I think I already know.

'Lucy,' he sighs, 'now, don't take this the wrong way but...'

I'll save him the embarrassment.

'How much are we down?'

Mike exhales with relief. 'We are missing around a couple of hundred Euros.'

'Not as bad as I thought, at least,' I sigh resignedly.

'Per day!' Mike looks serious.

I storm up to the flat, Mike following closely behind.

'Where is it?' I scream, bursting into the bedroom. Nick looks startled and sits up in bed.

'Where's what? He has an attempt at nonchalance, but doesn't even convince himself. I start throwing things out of the wardrobe and drawers. I find a bag of white powder at the back of his sock drawer.

'Is our fucking money up your nose?' I yell. 'Is it?'

I storm to the bathroom with the bag, in an attempt to tip the whole lot down the toilet. My head is suddenly pulled backwards as Nick grabs my hair. I whack my head on the wall as I try to pull away. My head spins, there's a ringing in my ears. I stagger and then fall against the cistern. Mike pulls Nick off me in one easy move. He forces him down the stairs and through the back door. Becky joins us outside, looking puzzled as she dries her hands on a tea towel. In the distance we can hear sirens, thanks to Pablo. Finally! Someone knows the phone number for the police. Nick is arrested. Charged with possession of an illegal substance, theft and assault, Pablo tells us later. It was in Spanish. I head to hospital with Mike for stitches. Becky stays behind to hold the fort and call in the part time staff to cover the evening shift.

Over the next few days Mike and Becky couldn't be nicer to

me, bringing me cups of tea and setting up a bed on the sofa. But, by day three, I'm bored and insist on going back for some of the quieter shifts. Mike looked through all Nick's things, which had been strewn over the room after the police had searched for narcotics. He finds a bundle of rolled-up notes in a hidden pocket in Nick's rucksack. Mike has the same rucksack in black – you would never realise the pocket was there unless you knew. Mike finds 6,753 Euros. Nick's been cleaning us out for a long time. This infuriates us. We paid him so well and he still felt the need to steal. I guess he was angrier than we all thought about my insistence on us having separate finances. He had always insisted on cashing up every night – I didn't think much of it. Perhaps seeing what he was missing out on and how lucrative sticking with me could be, but never did I suspect theft. I could never be bothered cashing up; too exhausted after the kitchen shifts and usually a bit tipsy after the bar ones. I was happy to leave it to the boys. When Nick did do the money, he counted it right in front of us while we sat at the bar. How dodgy could it be? But how clever, doing it right under our noses. The till receipt nightly totals did not match with the amount in the cashing-in book, and sometimes even the amount banked differed from both the till receipt and the cash-in book. Mike and I decide that, from now on, only we do the cashing up. No matter how tired we are. Now that we have a lot of our money back from the rucksack, it seems that a fairly small amount of our profit has disappeared up Nick's nose. However, it turned out a huge price for Nick. In time, that is. Receiving somewhere in the region of three years, or so we heard from some insiders Pablo knows. That's it. I am officially done with men. I am so sick of this constant cycle of users and losers. From now on it's me, my friends and family – and no room for anyone else. The male species have finally got on my last nerve. I reiterate this to Becky, Mike and Pablo. From now on I have no interest in a relationship. I want no attempts to be made at matchmaking. I will run my business and forget about men altogether. There's only so much I can take and every time it goes wrong. It's fine for Becky and Mike and other people, but for me, I'm taking early retirement from men.

Chapter Seventeen

And so the season ends. To say that it's been eventful would be putting it mildly. I receive a letter from Nick in prison, asking if I'd visit him since he is so far from home and knows nobody here. The nerve of him! After all he has done. I don't even bother replying. I tell Becky and Mike that I won't bother going on the Australia trip. We are several weeks later than planned as it was still busy. We didn't want to close up while our trade was still there. We won't be earning anything over the quiet times, but still paying our huge rent. Mike put our flights back by three weeks. Luckily, it had occurred to him to take out insurance, which covered the cost of the change. We now have one week at home and only three weeks in Australia. Mike and Becky won't hear of me bailing out and I insist I won't be a gooseberry.

We pack up the restaurant until the end of November, and ask Pablo to keep an eye on the place a few times a week. He and his family are moving to another house, but will be renovating it in the meantime. He can do better than keeping an eye on the place; they can all move in to keep it extra safe. Sneaky, but very true. And it makes us happier about leaving the restaurant. Even if we will spend months afterwards cleaning crayon off the walls. He is astounded that we are paying him to not work. Roberto never did. I tell him that this way we make sure he comes back to us. He nods seriously and seems genuinely upset when we leave. I give him a hug and tell him it's only for a month.

'I will miss you, but is not why I am sad. My wife say I must look after the children while not working as she has to supervise builders.'

He drives us to the airport and waves us off. After that, a white-knuckle ride of a journey, I am no longer scared to get on the plane.

We arrive back in Edinburgh and walk out into the freezing cold evening.
'Bloody hell! Was it always this cold?' asks Mike, 'and do we usually have Christmas lights up in October?' He glances around in confusion. We all head to Waverley station to catch the train home. Edinburgh looks even more beautiful than usual. Prince's Street twinkles with fairy lights. People hold hands and skate around on the manmade ice rink in the park. Everything is covered in a soft haze of frost. Beautiful. Then a nut seller on the corner breaks the spell.
'Hot chestnuuuuts. Get your nuts here!'
'Welcome back to Scotland,' I laugh.

We fall asleep on the journey home, soothed by the gentle rocking and the repetitive sound of the train on the tracks. I waken at Dundee station as some drunk revellers alight. I yawn widely and stretch, nudging Becky so I can say goodbye. Time to phone home. I gather up my bags and three stuffed donkeys with sombreros. Yes, I have taken home tacky gifts, but it's intentional. I know full well that no-one will throw out anything I give them. I like the thought of annoying my family when I'm not there. As they open a cupboard and a large stuffed donkey with a hat on falls out every time. I can imagine them kicking it with frustration for several months, before guiltily wrapping it in bin bags and shoving it up the loft. I chortle to myself, I've missed my family. Annoying them is long overdue.
 I hug Becky and Mike goodbye, telling them I'll see them in a week's time and clamber out of the carriage in as dignified a way as I can, and make my usual trip up the staircase and down the other. There's Mary, in her usual parking spot, usual pose. But she's not smoking any more. Happy with her Bill-free life now, she gave up. She still enjoys a drink or two.

Well, when the kids are away for the weekend, as they are on this particular one. They've seen enough debauchery in their short lives thanks to their father. The new Mary wants to show her children how they should live, in a happy and healthy way. She feels and actually looks like a teenager again; I'm sure that's due to being much happier. I'm desperate to catch up on gossip.

'So how did Bill take it?' I ask, as we reverse, narrowly missing a man with a suitcase.

'Stupid cow!' he shouts.

'Up yours!' shouts Mary jovially.

Mary told Bill to sling his hook a few months ago. He was extremely shocked. Even more surprised was his father, Bill senior, who shortly afterwards was booted out by his wife. Inspired by Mary, Joan was happier than she had ever been, and was currently causing havoc on the speed-dating circuit.

'Not good at first,' admits Mary. 'Seems OK now, if having a nineteen-year-old Polish girlfriend named Kasia is anything to go by. She bugs me so much, she's actually teaching the kids Polish and now they won't speak to each other in English. I don't have a clue what they are saying, but I know they're probably plotting against me.'

'That's not good. Why don't you insist they speak English at home?' I ask.

'Nah. They would do it even more if they knew it annoyed me. Besides, I thought it'd be funnier if I beat them at their own game,' Mary gives a mischievous laugh and revs up her engine at the pensioner in front of us, who has stalled at a green light.

'Shift your arse, Grandpa! Anyway, I've enrolled in an evening class twice a week, learning Polish. They think it's a pottery class. Can't wait 'til I learn enough to play them at their own game. Also means I get to find out what the little buggers are saying about me. I'm not too bad at it, actually.'

We head up to Uncle Robert's house, where the whole family is gathered. The racket coming from the house is immense, with everyone talking over each other and at least five different conversations going on at one time. It makes my restaurant on Spanish karaoke night sound tame. I arrive to lots of hugs and several,

'Ooh, you're not as fat as you were' comments. They can't just be nice and say I've lost weight. It has to be the worst possible way of giving a compliment. We all do it to each other. It's not mean. Rather, it's character building. Made me who I am today.

'So, I hear you excelled yourself with the latest boyfriend then?' Auntie Betty takes the first shot of open season.

'Yeh, what would you know! A violent, junkie thief,' I reply.

'With a dead wife?' asks Uncle Jim.

'No. No dead wife that he told me about.'

'How long did he get?' Craig, this time.

'Seven years.'

'Lucky bastard. Got off lightly compared to a lifetime with you.'

'Stop. Bloody. Swearing.' Slaps from Betty punctuate each word.

'Oww! Yeh right, ma. No idea where I get it from! The apple didn't fall too far from the tree, did it?'

'So how's the business?' Auntie Sarah, the sensible, normal one. Probably because she married into our lot instead of being born in. Same with Uncle Jim – they are the only two semi-normal ones. Even then, years of corruption are apparent.

'Great,' I enthuse, 'we are making an absolute fortune. It's so much fun too. You must come over next summer.'

'We all are,' says Mum. 'Booking up for two weeks in July. Make sure you get time off.'

'Ma, I'm the boss, I can do what I like,' I laugh. It still hasn't sunk in yet with Mum that I have my own restaurant. An entire resort subjected to the Ramseys. God help us.

It's so good being at home. Being cooked for again is a novelty. My sister seems infinitely happier without Bill. So do the kids. She thinks that's what they said anyway. It was in Polish. Her flat is gorgeous – airy and bright, with an amazing colour scheme and classic furniture. She always has had good taste, well, except for in men, and she's gone back to work, but as a window dresser this time. She couldn't be happier. A guy from my year at school, working in white goods, has been flirting with her non-stop. She is lapping up the attention after years of being starved of it. I give her an early Christmas present: three tickets to Tenerife for New Year. Thanks to Bill's various addictions, they have never had a family holiday. She is over the moon and phones up to tell the kids. It could wait, but I'm guessing it has the added bonus of annoying Bill. I give Mum her Christmas present too: a ticket to fly out with Mary and the kids. She beams at me and tells me how proud she is of what I'm doing.

On Sunday afternoon Mary arrives to pick me up to go to her place. Josh and Jess are arriving home this afternoon and I can't wait to see them. Before they get back, and she's not allowed to swear, she gives me a lot of abuse over the stuffed donkey. Halfway through the *Eastenders* omnibus, two coffees and half a packet of chocolate biscuits later, there is a loud, irate beep from a car in the street. Mary stands up to look out of the window. Immediately, there's another louder and more insistent beep.

'For Christ's sake, I'm going as fast as I can,' Mary snaps. 'Oh, I might have known. Kasia! Why that idiot wouldn't want to spend every moment he can with his children is beyond me.' She makes a face at me, steps into her trainers and heads down the stairs to street level. Determined not to miss out on getting a glimpse of Bill's new girlfriend, I shove on Mary's slippers and follow her downstairs. Kasia is unloading the kids' bags from the boot of her car. She straightens up and I take in her tall, slim form. With her enormous chest, she looks as if she could topple over at any given moment. 'Those can't be real,' I stare at Mary in shock. 'Probably not, I guess it's the reason he's taken on a second job as a taxi driver. To pay for that rack,' Mary coughs back a laugh. Kasia is talking quickly in Polish as she helps Jess from the back seat. I'm awestruck to hear my small niece babble away in her new found language. If it wasn't disloyal to Mary, I'd be seriously impressed. Kasia loads up the kids with their bags and crosses her arm across her chest – with difficulty, I must say – and aims an attitude-laden glare at my sister. I snort with laughter. The nerve of the woman! Sorry, adolescent. Mary shoots me a look of amusement. '*Tam jest twoja Mama, idz do niej,*' Kasia says to Josh and Jess. '*Idz do niej.*' She ushers them towards Mary. I watch as my sister frantically tries to translate her words. 'There is your Mother, go to her,' Mary covers her mouth and says just loud enough for me to hear.

'*Pamietaj mow, po Polsku w domu,*' continues Kasia. I see Mary's hackles rise.

'*Mamus sie to nie podoba!*' shouts my sister. I can't decide who is most shocked. Jess looks at Josh open-mouthed, Josh drops his bag and Kasia's chin drops to the ground, well almost, her boobs were in the way.
'*Mow po Angielsku do moich dzieci, krowo!*' Mary coolly informs her. Of what, I'm not sure at this stage. Josh laughs and Jess, seeing this is an obviously acceptable thing to do if Josh does, joins in.
'Come on, where are my hugs?' calls Mary. The children run towards her.
'No you don't,' I stop Jessica mid-run and scoop her up, 'I'm

long overdue for a hug, Mummy can wait.'

Mary and I walk back towards the flat with Josh and Jess, when she suddenly remembers something and turns back towards the car:

'Oh, Kasia, can you hold on just one moment please? I've got some toys for the kids to take to their Dad's house. I know they don't have many there.' Kasia rolls her eyes and looks at her watch with a dramatic sigh. Mary runs upstairs and arrives back moments later with a large stuffed donkey under each arm (I can bring another for Mum next time.) We walk back to the flat holding on to each other through our mirth. The slam of a car door and a screech of tyres indicates Kasia's pissed off departure.

'So, what did you say to her?' I ask Mary, when the children are settled with juice and crisps in front of *Ballamory*. 'I just politely asked her to speak English to my kids,' is her reply.

'So what's a *krowo* then?'

'A cow,' replies Josh. Oops, I didn't think he was listening.

Chapter Eighteen

All too soon, the time comes to head off to Manchester airport for the Australian leg of the trip. With my fear of flying this is, undoubtedly, the ultimate test for me. Actually, I don't have a fear of flying. I have a fear of crashing! Why do people say that it is flying they fear? That's the easy bit. I work myself into a complete state of anxiety; I feel physically sick. Mike and Becky try their best to reassure me. I hate feeling like this. It's so unfair to the others, but completely out of my control. Armed with my panic attack brown paper, I'm sitting in the aisle seat. That way I am free to bolt to the loo to throw up if need be – and it also lessens the fear of claustrophobia. The only thing worse than having to take a flight, is being penned in at the window seat. Urgh! I attempt some deep breathing exercises, resisting the urge to hyperventilate. I've never flown on a Jumbo before. It looks clumsy and lumbering – and incapable of taking off. Mike assures me that the bigger the plane, the less turbulence – and lets me squeeze his hand on take-off. He doesn't complain once, even though I notice that his fingers have turned purple. Becky is quiet and subdued. Like something is on her mind.

'Is she OK? I nudge Mike, when Becky falls asleep.

'Call from Bob,' he whispers. 'It's unsettled her, she's been quiet all week. I don't know if he's hoping to get back together with her. I can't see why else he'd call.'

'She won't seriously be thinking of getting back with him, Mike. No way, she loves you too much. You're going to get married, and he was a total shit to her,' I whisper back.

'I know,' he sighs, 'she reckons he's heard from her Mum how well she's doing in Tenerife. He wants her to be pining for him. Her life must seem so exciting to him now. That's all,' he says with finality. Subject closed.

I glance over at Becky and her eyelids flicker. I reckon she's awake and has been listening.

No, Becky, I try to tell her telepathically. Don't even be considering it. I ponder on this thought; what if she and Bob did get back together? Becky would have to leave. I would miss her so much. I don't know if I'd want to continue with it, she makes it so much fun. It would be down to just Mike and me to keep the business going. I just can't imagine it without Becky. And if they did break up, I would lose faith completely in love. I shake my head in an attempt to physically remove the thoughts. It won't happen, so why worry?

After what seems like an eternity, I wake to hear the announcement that we will be shortly be arriving at Sydney airport. I shift in my seat, no longer able to feel my bottom. I'm numb all over and desperate to stretch out horizontally.

'I'd like to take this opportunity to welcome all our passengers to Australia. The temperature in Sydney today is thirty-six degrees and sunny. Please fasten your seatbelts as we begin our descent,' the Australian pilot says chirpily. Easy for him, he does this every day.

'Nooo,' I mumble. This is the worst bit. Actually, just before take-off I say that was the worst bit; on coming into land, I declare that's the bit I hate most. Mike smiles reassuringly and offers his hand. I grip on tight, gratefully. The liar Mike is! Less turbulence in a Jumbo, my arse! He also forgot to mention there would be a four-hour stop off in Abu Dhabi to refuel. Said it was better I didn't know there were two take-offs and two landings to worry about. He was right. It meant they got a bit of respite from my stressing. It's actually impossible to stress constantly on such a long flight. It's far too exhausting. I had actually calmed down around two hours into the journey. About the same time the fourth vodka kicked in, come to think of it.

With shaking legs, I make my way to the baggage claim. We

collect our cases and head off to find a cab to take us to our hotel. Mike is exhausted with jetlag and heads off for a sleep. Becky seems a bit cheerier, so I suggest heading out into Sydney for lunch. We walk through Hyde Park to Oxford Street and find a café bar with an outside seating area. I now have a chance to grill Becky about Bob. We sit down under the shade of a tree and eat our lunch of Thai noodles and two glasses of Australian white wine. The sun is glorious after the chill of Scotland. Australian summertime: how strange and un-Christmassy. On the way to the bar Becky and I had laughed at the Christmas cards with snow and robins, that we saw in shop windows. Why would Australians choose to send those to each other? We decided to ask a passing Aussie. He had no idea, but said they always had done.

I wait until after we have finished lunch and then tentatively approach the subject of Bob.
'So, Mike says you had a random caller the other day.'
Becky screws her face up.
'Yes, Bob called. Wanted to see how I was.'
'And how did Mike take it?'
'Oh, fine, I guess. Bob was a bit weird though. He wants to come out to Tenerife to visit us soon, maybe in January.'
'And do you think that's a good idea?' I enquire.
'God, I don't know,' Becky shakes her head sadly, putting down her chopsticks, 'I mean, I thought I was totally over him, but after hearing his voice again, I'm not so sure any more.'
'You're not thinking of taking him back, are you?'
The very thought leaves me aghast, and not just because it will end in tears, I feel really bad for poor Mike. Dumped by Sam, and now possibly by Becky too. He deserves better.
'I really don't know, Lucy,' Becky looks pained. 'I honestly can't say I don't want to. That would be a lie.' She looks down at her hands in her lap. 'It would kill me to leave Mike, but I

don't know if I want to be with him anymore.'
Good God no! It's the worst-case scenario.

So, until Becky makes her decision, I am left stuck between a rock and a hard place. I care about both of them. I don't want to worry Mike in case this is just a blip and things settle down when we get back to Tenerife. I do my best to constantly remind Becky what a shit Bob was to her, and how he didn't care about her feelings when he broke it off. His work fling didn't last. He wanted a bit of excitement as he had felt he and Becky were stagnating. He quickly realised he had nothing in common with this other girl, out- with the sheets, and woke up to the terrible mistake he'd made.

'He will do it again,' I reiterated over and over. Hoping some of it may stick in her brain. I try my best to have a good time. Becky cheers up and Mike is seemingly oblivious to the dilemma in her head. We visit Circular Quay, Coogee, Bondi, Manly and Palm beaches. We climb the Sydney Harbour Bridge and explore the markets around the Rocks area of the city.

'We have definitely got to come here again,' Mike says to both of us. Becky and I exchange a look. Will there be a next time? I know it's what we are both thinking. I decide to head off to Adelaide for the last week and let them have some space. Maybe without me around, Becky will rediscover what she loves about Mike and we can all live happily ever after.

I have the most amazing time in Adelaide. I love Australia, the climate, the laid back people, the food, everything. I will definitely be back. The space Becky and Mike had seemed to have helped their cause a bit. I notice this when I meet up with them for the flight back to Tenerife. This was just what I needed – proper time off without worrying about anyone else. I'm sure that once we get back Becky will be fine. She'll be too busy even to think of Bob. I had stayed with Emily's sister in Adelaide for the week I left the other two. It was hard to imagine someone louder and more over the top than Em, but Kate surpassed her by far. We had a great week of going to bars, eating out and, for the last night, a traditional Aussie Barbie. I even managed to get some interest from a cute surfer called Jude.

'Jude the dude,' I laughed, when he introduced himself.

'Hey! I never thought of that, man,' he snorts with laughter. Hmm, perhaps he's been caught in a few too many rip tides. Jude is heading off to backpack around the world in three months and is looking for a bit of bar work over next summer. So, it wasn't my dazzling good looks he was interested in after all. Not that I'm interested. I'm off men. I give him my email address and hope he doesn't contact me. One Manuel-type per restaurant is quite enough, thank you. Poor Gino, bless him. Still hasn't quite got used to the combination of Scottish and Irish accents, and no longer has Nick to translate. He spends most of his time looking blankly at us when we ask him to do something.

We arrive back at Sydney airport, running late due to traffic. I head towards the bar. I have never once flown without at least two drinks in me. Becky grabs my arm and drags me towards check-in. We make it. In fact, there were actually a spare two minutes. It was a horrible journey, just horrible. The most horrendous turbulence I have ever encountered. I used the panic bag twice and several times I asked,

'What's that noise?' and 'should that wing be wobbling like that?' or similar. But I didn't throw up at all. By the time we land on mainland Spain for our connecting flight, I was a nervous wreck.

After what feels like forever, we are making our way back to our restaurant. Bliss! Tomorrow we have a day off. Pablo and his wife have been in to clean and have placed the food and drinks orders. Wonderful people they are. I may have to give Pablo a hefty Christmas bonus. We get ready to go out for dinner. Mike heads off for a shower. I wander past Becky and Mike's bedroom on my way to the kitchen to make myself a coffee. I pause outside, about to knock and ask Becky if she would like one. I can hear her muffled voice through the door, arguing with someone on the phone. I would never normally listen, but when I hear,

'No, Bob, please listen,' I feel I have no choice. I'm sure she's not telling me everything. 'Look Bob, I can't come home before Christmas, It's going to be so busy. I owe it to Mike and Lucy to help out. Yes, of course I'll be sleeping in the spare room now. I told you I'd ended things with Mike. You just need to wait until January and I'll be home. I've already booked the flight. You know that, you were with me.'

A few short sentences, but already I've heard enough to know exactly what's going on. When? She was in Aberdeen with Mike before Australia – she didn't even go home to Ireland. How could he have been with her when she booked the flight home? I turn to walk away.

'She went to spend a night with her "Great Aunt" in Stonehaven.'

I turn to see a dejected-looking Mike, towel round his waist and hair sticking up at funny angles. A small puddle of shower water is collecting at his feet. He has been listening too.

'You read my mind,' I say sadly, shaking my head. 'I'm so sorry Mike. What are you going to do?'

'Let her go,' he shrugs, 'just let her go.' He gives me a sad little smile, walks into the bedroom and closes the door.

Two hours on and there's quite a bit of shouting from Mike and Becky's room. Actually, it's from Becky and, surprisingly, not Mike. He seems to have resigned himself to it all. I try hard not to listen and even turn the TV up as loud as I can bear it, but still the unmistakable, panic-stricken voice of Becky is all I can hear. She is persuading Mike to let her stay; she can't let me down. I don't hear what Mike says but Becky's hysterical reply of:

'Yes, Mike. I'm sorry, but it is what I want, I just don't want to let you and Lucy down at a busy time of the year,' gives me an inkling that he had asked if she really wanted them to be over. Eventually, Mike helps a very tearful-looking Becky down the stairs with her bags. She looks at me, ashamed. I walk over and give her a hug. The floodgates open.

'I'm so sorry, Lucy,' she bawls tears and snot onto my shoulder.

'Shh-shh,' I soothe. 'Look, you keep in touch, OK? I want to know how you're doing. I do hope it works out Becks, but I'm always here for you no matter what. We're friends first, OK? We just happen to work together. That's not what binds us together.'

She nods, sniffs and glances over at Mike, pleading forgiveness with her eyes. He looks away, resting his chin on his hand and swirling the remains of a pint around his glass. What did she expect really? I walk Becky to the taxi to wave her off.

'I mean it,' I tell her, 'keep in touch. Don't forget, you and I were friends before Mike. I'm not going to hold this against you.'

'But the restaurant, I'm really letting you down.'

'It's fine, Becky,' I reassure her, 'people leave jobs all the time. It makes no difference to our friendship.' Becky sniffs and pulls me to her. There is desperation in the hug.

'Stay safe,' I give her a squeeze. 'Let me know how it goes.'

She shuts the cab door and waves tearfully. I see her pull out her phone and hold it to her ear before she even rounds the corner. I wave, but she doesn't see. I have lost her already. I walk back towards the restaurant – and Mike.

And then there were two.

Chapter Nineteen

With Becky gone, Mike sets about the task of finding us new staff. I leave him to it. He's really not been himself since she left. Gone are his cheeky smile and the sparkle in his eyes. His work behind the bar is fulfilled in a purely perfunctory fashion. The punter asks for a drink, the punter receives a drink. Mike isn't being rude, but the banter is gone. He is polite enough to ask the usual questions: Are you enjoying your holiday? Which resort are you in? Just the basic niceties. Even Pablo can't make him smile with his 'Scotticisms'. He told Mike he had a face on him like a cat's arse – not even a flicker of a smile. Poor Pablo stands on the door all night and then disappears home at closing time with just a dejected wave goodbye. Gone are the late-night drinking sessions with him and Mike and the card games on the bar during the afternoon slump. I leave Mike to handle all the new staff's interviews and induction. The distraction is good for him.

I receive a text a month later from Becky saying she had moved in with Bob and things are going well. Fast work, I think, but good for her. I mean that. I really do hope she'll be happy. I just wish it wasn't to Mike's detriment, but she would only make him unhappier in the long term by stringing him along. I suspected she wasn't over Bob. Maybe he has changed, but I have my doubts. I have always assumed, once a cheater always a cheater, leopards can't change their spots and various other clichés. It's almost like she's condoning his past behaviour by taking him back. But, in spite of my true feelings towards Bob, I text back to tell her that I'm glad things are going well, that we are all fine and I miss having her around. She thanks me and says she'll leave it up to me how much I tell Mike about her life. After giving it some thought, I decide to tell him she got back safely and leave it at that. There's no point in embellishing the tale, it's not going to make him feel better, nor will he really be interested. He acknowledges my information with a grim nod and we say no more on the subject.

Mike has taken on two new waitresses to help with the workload. They are fast and efficient, flirty enough to keep the lads happy, but not in an inappropriate way that would upset the oldies. It has cooled down dramatically since we left Tenerife for our trip home. Still T-shirt weather, but gone is the intense heat. This temperature is so much nicer to work in, for us at least. The Spaniards complain about the weather and wrap up warm. I've even seen a few in hats and gloves.

'Fucking freezing,' declares Pablo.

'Try living in Scotland,' I retort. He shudders.

'I will come see you, after Christmas. I need to see this Scotland. Feel what cold really is.'

'Oh, you'll feel it, mate. Our summer is like your winter most of the time,' I reply.

The Christmas and New Year season takes us by shock. It's almost as busy as the summer months. I decide Pablo's bonus will be a trip to Scotland for him, his wife and three kids. They have enough money to get by on now and live a very comfortable lifestyle. I'd like to give him something with more thought put into it than money. Mike agrees, but says we must keep it quiet from the other staff because they are receiving a much lesser amount. As Pablo does a completely different job to the rest, I don't feel bad that he's on much more. He is security after all. Where is the risk in carrying plates to and from a table? Besides, Pablo is a friend to us. He stays late and comes in early, often sitting around on his days off just to keep an eye on things over the more busy periods. He also found us an equally reliable doorman for when he is off. Pablo most definitely goes the extra mile.

The hectic atmosphere has speeded Mike's recovery from

Becky leaving. Daily, he slowly but surely gets back towards his usual self. It starts with him cracking a joke at my expense, teasing me about the fact I had muddled orders for the third time that day and sent them out to the wrong tables. It's nothing major, but enough to turn mine and Pablo's heads. In fairness to me, it wasn't entirely my fault as the new staff hadn't quite got the hang of writing in English yet. Popping in the odd Spanish word for things if they had forgotten the English translation. In order to decipher it all, I had to ask them to point to the menu at what they were trying to describe, occasionally incorporating an impromptu game of charades.

I knew Mike was definitely on his way to recovery when I discovered him loitering in the doorway, cracking up at me trying to explain that we did not have Sophia's customer's request for 'chicken's legs' in a cream and tarragon sauce, only chicken breast. I strutted around doing my best impression of a chicken, then pointed to my right boob, before blushing furiously as I noticed Mike watching me with great amusement. He said nothing, just laughed, shook his head and walked away. Then, the day after, he asked

Pablo for a game of cards. Pablo smiled affectionately at him, like a proud father.

'Wur wee boy's coming back to us,' he told me later.

Within another two weeks, he was back to goofing around with me and the other staff – just like the old days. It also appears that he has a bit of an eye for the ladies. I've never known him as a singleton, since he was with Sam on our train home when we met, then immediately after with Becky. I know so much more about him since Becky left. We spent a lot of our off time together, chatting and eating restaurant leftovers, or on the beach on our days off. Of course, I still miss Becky, but the old dynamic seems to still work; from four of us, to two.

One Friday evening, at the end of the lull between

lunch and dinner, I was sitting tallying up our lunchtime takings. Things are good for the time of year. We knew Christmas would be reasonable for takings, but it seems we're on a par with last year's Easter break. Not bad, not bad at all. Mike has looked out the box of Christmas decorations that Roberto had left in the cellar. We planned to go through it this afternoon to check they were tasteful and not tacky; then, we could either put them up or head into town for some new ones tomorrow. I look up as the door swings open. I thought the place would be empty for at least another hour. We're off the main drag, so rarely get the passers-by popping in for a drink like many places do. Also, being more a restaurant type, people will be more inclined to come into eat than to drink. But, nevertheless, we have a customer. In walks a pretty girl with long, white blonde hair and the kind of perfectly honed look of someone who has a lot of beauty treatments. I run my finger self-consciously over my eyebrows and smooth down my hair. I'm aware I could do with some urgent attention in the personal grooming department, but I just don't have the time and, if I'm being honest, the inclination. She walks confidently to the bar, swinging what looks like this season's most lusted-after Balenciaga bag from her finger. Up close she is stunning, if a little over-manicured. Too perfect and too intimidating. Trailing behind her is a thirty-something man several notches down her league. He must have a large appendage of some sort – be it his wallet or otherwise, I think unreasonably.

'Can I help you?' I smile, attempting to match the confidence she exudes.

'I'm not sure.' She casts a critical eye around the bar before giving me a quick once over.

'Is your boss Michael Johnston?'

'Well, we are both the boss, but yes, he's here. Would you like to speak to him?'

She attempts to furrow her brow in confusion. Botox. OK, so

she may not have a wrinkle on her pretty little face, but give me them, any day, over looking like a constipated gerbil every time you try to pull a facial expression. A few of our regulars – well about as regular customers as you can get on a two-week holiday – look on with interest. Jean, of Jean and Phil from Stockton, raises her eyebrows questioningly at me. I shrug in reply.

'Obviously,' she gives me a sarcastic half-smile. 'I didn't come all this way for nothing.'

'I'll go get him for you,' I reply, with just a hint of the irritation that I feel at her attempt at superior behaviour.

'Cool,' she drawls. 'Just tell him it's Sammy-babes.'

Terrific!

'Mike,' I yell down to the cellar. 'Visitor.'

He appears at the bottom of the steps, wiping his hands on his jeans.

'We need to order more Bud. Only twenty crates down there and it seems to be our biggest seller at the moment.'

'Never mind that,' I hiss. 'Sam's here – or should I say Sammy-babes?'

'What does *she* want?' He easily takes the steps two at a time and pulls me to the side, as an impatient-looking Sam tries to peer through the door to the back.

'No, in fact, I know what she wants. Sammy-babes is the name she gives whenever it means she wants something. Usually money for some must-have Jimmy Choos if I remember correctly. Shit, what's she playing at?'

'Well, go and see,' I reply impatiently, giving him a shove.

Mike walks through the door and nods nonchalantly at Sam.

'Oh darling, look at you, all grown up with your own restaurant,' she baby voices, coming around to his side of the bar and slinking her arms around his neck.

'Sorry, going to have to move you out of here,' I say officiously. 'No customers behind the bar – Health and Safety regs,' I smile a sarcastic apology.

Jean from Stockton makes an impressed O with her mouth and bites back a smile.

'What can I do for you, Sam?' Mike is straight down to business. 'We have a large selection of cocktails: Sex on the Beach; a Slow Comfortable Screw; or a Screaming Orgasm.' I choke back a laugh. I hope he's trying to imply that she meant nothing to him, just a conquest, but maybe that's just my claws coming out.

'Our Specials on the menu today are Toad in the Hole or battered sausage,' Mike continues. Oh, stop already! I laugh out loud, that is so not our Specials! Credit me with a bit of class. Sam shoots me a look that would curdle milk, while her boyfriend shifts uncomfortably and squints at the TV, taking a sudden interest in a tampon advert, before realising what it's for and staring safely at his feet. Sam bristles with indignation.

'Actually, Michael, I only popped by to say that I accidentally packed some of your CDs when I left. I just wondered if you wanted them back. I called your Mum, she said you were out here, so I thought I'd pay you a personal visit,' she beams widely as if this makes Mike the most honoured man in Spain.

'Yeah, sure. You got them in there?' he indicates to Sam's over-sized bag. 'I'm impressed you felt the urge to come all the way out to Tenerife just to give me a few CDs, but cheers.'

'Oh no, silly,' Sam laughs, 'I don't have them in here. I need room to take back all my purchases. But I'll send them on to you.'

'Natch, when would you ever come on holiday and go home without at least a grand's worth of presents for yourself? Anyway, will that be all?' Mike asks.

'We were thinking of having an early supper,' she casts a critical eye over our menu.

'Fine, I'll send the waitress over for your order. I have work to do in the cellar. Enjoy your meal, and your trip.' Mike nods an acknowledgement to Sam's boyfriend, then heads off back towards the stairs.

Sam fumes silently in her seat and stares after Mike's retreating back.

'I cannot believe I did not notice before,' declares Jean. Phil rolls his eyes in a 'here we go' manner to me.

'Notice what?' I say distractedly, watching Sam and her still nameless boyfriend bicker amongst themselves. Sam slams her bag down on the seat next to her and folds her arms defiantly.

'You and Mike,' says Jean, in wonderment.

'What about us?' I look at her in confusion.

'You were *jealous*. Your face when she hugged Mike was a picture. I take it that's the ex then?'

'Yes, and no way was I jealous,' I retort. Phil smiles and nods slowly.

'For once, she's right Lucy.' Jean kicks him on the shin with her flip flop.

'And what's more,' continues Jean, 'he was searching around for you to save him like a little lost puppy.'

'Oh whisht,' I dismiss them with a toss of my head, 'remind me, when is your flight home?'

'A week on Thursday,' laughs Jean. 'But we'll be checking out your website for news once we get back. This is better than *Coronation Street.*'

The waitress carries over lunch for Sam and her boyfriend. Sam glowers over at me and nibbles daintily on a salad leaf. Tenacity of a Jack Russell in season, that one. I can spot the type. She'll be going nowhere after lunch. She straightens in her seat as Mike walks back into the bar and peers at him coyly under eyelashes heavy with mascara. She whispers something to her boyfriend and then makes her way over, sidling up to Mike.

'I need a private word,' she demands.

'Oh, now what could this be? You're not going to tell me you're pregnant are you?' Mike asks.

'Good God no!' She runs a hand over her concave stomach

and looks at him aghast.

'Why, do I *look* pregnant?' she fusses. Mike tuts and rolls his eyes.

'Look, not here,' she whispers, looking pointedly at me. 'Too many eavesdroppers.'

'Like Lucy said, Sam, you are not allowed around this side of the bar, so whatever you have to say, say it here.'

'Or, we could take a walk on the beach? Sam suggests hopefully.

'No Sam, I already told you, I have work to do. The evening crowd will be in soon and…'

'Fine!' she snaps, a flash of annoyance crosses her face before she quickly gathers herself. She perches on the edge of a bar stool and turns her body away from the rest of us; we're all trying desperately to hear what's being said whilst making it appear like we're not interested. Sam begins her tale of woe.

'Things with my ex didn't work out. He'd lost his job and…'

'… couldn't afford to fund your lifestyle,' Mike finishes.

'No! Will you let me speak?' she spits, like the spoilt Madam that she is. 'Well, anyway, I've been with Oscar now for almost three weeks, but I'm bored already,' she sighs dramatically. 'So,' a confident pause and smile, 'I've decided to give us another try.'

'Oh, you have, have you?' Mike replies in amazement, his booming laugh carries through the entire bar, startling some men sitting in the corner watching football on the big screen.

'Yes,' she replies with a wide smile. 'We were so happy in Chiswick, but here would be even better. I may even do a few shifts for you,' she trails a finger down the side of his face.

Mike looks lost in thought for a moment. He looks down at Sam, his eyes rest on her cleavage. Sam smiles slowly, thinking she's got him at last.

Phil, Jean and I look at each other in disbelief. Jean nods furiously at me to do something. I'm about to declare that the lager's gone off when Mike looks into Sam's eyes.

She flutters prettily.

'Are your implants sagging?' he enquires.

Sam gives a shriek and clutches her bosom.

'No! They are not! Are they?' her voice wavers.

'Looks like it to me,' Mike replies seriously. 'You should have stuck to your original Harley Street plan. Those backstreet plastic surgeons are a false economy. Look Sam,' his voice is low and angry, 'don't waste my time. I have all I could ask for in a woman now.' He gives a nod in my direction, as I look on in amusement and surprise, 'So, leave me alone.'

'Ha! I'd be happy to leave you *alone*. It's leaving you with her, that's the problem,' Sam announces with disgust. 'She doesn't even do her eyebrows! God only knows what her bikini line is like!'

Bitch! Just fine, thanks, I smart indignantly.

'Sam, you are being offensive to the landlady. I'm going to have to ask you to leave.'

'Fine,' she hisses, 'I was only trying to do you a favour anyway. I don't need you. Oscar's a lawyer,' she adds childishly, before stropping over to her table, still holding on to her chest.

'Come on Oscar, we're leaving,' she announces. Oscar reluctantly puts down his fork, which is halfway to his mouth and loaded with fish and chips. Sam snatches up her bag and turns hopefully as Mike calls out her name.

'And you can keep the CDs if it means I never have to hear from you again. Besides, I know how much you secretly love S-Club Seven – I wouldn't take them away from you.' Phil high fives Mike. With a final flounce, Sam is gone, Oscar trailing obediently behind – no doubt with several whoops and a round of applause ringing in their ears.

Chapter twenty

Mike's little speech about how I'm all he'd ask for in a woman has caused quite a stir in the restaurant. It changes the dynamic between us a bit, too. Largely due to Jean, Phil and a few of the others declaring that he must have meant it, even if it was subconsciously. I'm of the opinion that I was the first person he spotted whilst looking for an escape route. And besides, I am all he would look for in a woman: financially independent, hardworking, don't nag him and quite happy to spend my days off doing what he enjoys – in other words, trailing around the island, eating somewhere other than the place where we spend most of our time, and drinking copious amounts of wine. What's not to like? But that does not mean he sees me in the way they mean. I analyse the statement:
'Lucy is all I want in a woman.' What? A woman friend – that's what! I come back to it time and time again. I inform the others that they need to get out more.

Mike notes my slight discomfort over the next few days. I make my excuses for going to bed straight after shifts and take myself off on daytrips around the island on days' off. I do feel bad, leaving him staring after me, like a hurt bunny. Even if he did fancy me, which of course he doesn't, he's a no-go area because he is Becky's ex. No way would she do that to me. I wouldn't even consider doing it to her. I feel slightly uncomfortable about the whole situation. I want to make it crystal clear that I am not interested. I love Mike, just not in that way. I'm not actually interested in a relationship, full stop!

Sunday's busy lunch shift comes around. We are backed up with stock and waiting for a lull in the rush to have time to put it in the fridges. I feel even more awkward than usual today because last night Pablo, Mike, Jean, Phil and a couple of this week's other regulars had a bit of a lock-in. Jean had dragged me off to the loo and had insisted that it was more obvious than ever that there was something between us. Mike had kissed me on the top of my head, and said how wonderful his life was now because of what we had. Yes, I'd insisted to Jean, what we have. That being, the restaurant, warm weather, all the food we can eat and all the alcohol we can drink. What more could a man want? OK, apart from the obvious. But we aren't involved like that. Jean shrugs and gives me a smile that says, you'll see. I'm beginning to get more than a little tired of the speculation.

So, Sunday lunchtime. Mike squeezes past me behind the bar, through the minute space left to work in. He places his hands on my waist to manoeuvre through. I give a little squeal and promptly spill the pint I am pouring all over the bar. Several customers dash out of the way.

'What is *wrong* with you?' Mike asks exasperatedly. 'Are you due on or something?'

'No!' I say, horrified, looking around at the smirking faces of the male punters. 'But you'll be due a kick in the knackers if you say anything like that again.' The men surrounding the bar laugh loudly. I watch as Phil beckons Mike over. He leans over the bar so Phil can whisper into his ear. Mike nods, looks confused, then shakes his head and whispers something back to Phil. Phil whispers some more, this time with hand gestures to emphasise his point. Mike looks shocked, before glancing back over at me as realisation seems to dawn, and makes his way across the bar towards me. I may as well get this out of the way.

'Look Mike,' I begin, 'I don't think you fancy me, despite what everyone else thinks, and I'm sorry, but I don't fancy you. I couldn't anyway because of Becky, even if I did, which, of course, I already mentioned, I don't.' I am aware that I'm babbling, but continue anyway. 'You are an extremely good looking bloke and we are very compatible, but if we broke up it would be very awkward around here and... why... why is Phil gurning at me like that?'

'I dunno.' Mike throws a glance at Phil. 'Probably because all he said was he thinks you need a holiday. But thanks for sharing,' and he walks away.

I cringe. Not to worry, that cleared that little issue up once and for all.

Christmas passes in a blur and no days off. One day blends into the next. No time to feel awkward around Mike, so all is good once again. We barely have enough energy to crawl into our respective beds at the end of an evening. Our customers are having an absolute ball and we are raking in the cash. There will be plenty of time for rest in the New Year. The downside of the very busy times is that we don't get to know our customers as well as in the quiet times. Still, they seem to be OK with that. They don't know any different, as we haven't been here long enough to have returning custom. So, I don't feel too bad about it.

Hogmanay comes around again. Hard to believe this time last year we didn't even know all this was to happen. Mike and Becky, Nick and I had only just met. Such a lot has changed, and then changed again. Still, it has been far from dull.

Mum, Mary and the kids are in a cab from the airport on their way for their Hogmanay holiday. I can't wait to see them. I rush around wiping imaginary dust from everything and fuss over the menu. Mike laughs at me. The place is immaculate; I cleaned just after the cleaners left. And now I have a whole glorious week off. A loud clatter as the door swings open and hits the wall, accompanied by lots of excited chat, announces the arrival of my family. Josh and Jess immediately begin to investigate their surroundings, pulling on the beer taps and squirming away from my attempts of a hug.

'This is gorgeous, Lucy,' my Mum twirls around, smiling broadly at me. 'Well done you.'

'Yes, you're not useless after all,' says Mary in a surprised tone. Mike walks over to greet them all.

'Woah!' Mary looks at me in amazement and whispers, 'you never told me Mike was fit! Have you… you know… yet?'

'No!' I reply, a little too loudly. I manage to attract the attention of Mum, Mike and half of the restaurant. 'We're not like that,' I hiss.

'You were so busted there,' she laughs, and walks off to stop Jess from using our curtain as a Tarzan swing. 'You should though… seriously,' she throws over her shoulder.

'Should what?' enquires Mike, from behind me.

'Oh… nothing, think you may have a fan, that's all,' I reply, a blush creeping up from my neck.

The plan for this evening is for us all to have dinner and drinks together in the restaurant. Mike will be working with three bar staff and will float between there and kitchen, where another three are on. I'll be on hand to pull a few pints if necessary, but we should have more than enough cover. We have dinner, the Specials today being my Mum and sister's favourite meals and the usual kiddy, junk food favourites. The karaoke party kicks off and Mary and I murder a few tunes. Several glasses of wine down and I forget that I'm making a complete idiot of myself. Well, I'm off home in a week, who cares? I won't see any of these people again. I look around and marvel at our surroundings, it's great to be on this side of the bar, looking objectively as a customer. Mike laughs at Mary and me, shaking his head in mock disapproval. Josh and Jess get up and sing Bon Jovi. They share my sister's 1980s rock music fixation. To their delight, people start to throw Euros onto the stage. My sister mutters something about being entitled to twenty percent as their agent.

At the end of the evening, after dancing and singing ourselves out, we head off to put the kids to bed. We find Jess, bum in the air, fast asleep on a pile of coats. Jean's coat is on top, now complete with dribble mark. Josh is enthusiastically throwing some shapes on the dance floor with Mike and has to be carried, yelling all the way upstairs to bed by Mary and I.

'I'm not even tired,' Mary sighs and shakes her head as we tuck the kids up in bed. 'Best night I've had in ages. Shame it has to end.'

'That's where this comes in handy then,' I smile and wave a baby monitor at Mary. 'I bought it specially.' We kiddy-proof the entire apartment, pulling out every plug socket and securing all the windows, and head back downstairs for a lock-in. Mike has assured Mary that he won't drink more than a couple, having been flat out all night and only on his first sip of a pint. Mike is a serial insomniac. I regularly hear him creeping around in the night, not in a weird way, just making a hot chocolate at three in the morning kind of thing. I trust him completely with my niece and nephew. Seriously, even in a deep sleep, he'd hear a mouse fart in the next room. Mary relaxes and enjoys the evening, slurring to Mike that she's going to marry him and drag him off back to Scotland. He leans in to Mary and whispers something. She looks at him in surprise, and laughs uproariously. Good, they're getting on, I think. I feel a tiny pang; happiness, that's what it is, and that's what I want for my sister. She deserves it. I watch them giggle and feel nostalgic for that feeling. Maybe soon it will be down to one from the original crew? Well, I will have Pablo, if he doesn't love Scotland too much.

The week flies by far too quickly, as time off always does. Everyone has had a great time and the kids have taken to their first overseas holiday like ducks to water. My sister looks happier than she's been in years, and attracted lots of attention from the Spaniards. She has a list of phone numbers from men hoping to take her out on a date when she comes back in July. She's still flirting lots with Mike, he won't be back here, I can feel it. Well, I'll be fine on my own. I can do it. Maybe Pablo's wife would help in the kitchen? I can try and arrange some childcare for the baby and after-school care for the other kids. Anyway, we'll see. Tomorrow, I'm flying back with Mike and my family. This is our break until Easter. It feels really weird to be going home. I won't be living with Mike. We are so used to each other; it feels like I'm missing a limb when he's not around. Like an old, married couple, we even finish each other's sentences. Nothing has been mentioned about travel plans this time. I want to suggest something, but don't want Mike to get the wrong idea. But he will probably be down from Aberdeen to see Mary, so I will get to catch up on all his gossip. I decide I'll head over to Dublin to see Becky. Just jump on a flight from Edinburgh airport. It will be a nightmare flying alone, but at least no-one will have to put up with my constant worrying. If it wasn't for the fact that my sea sickness is worse than my fear of flying, I'd take the ferry. After all, I can swim but I cannot fly. Mike is hugely impressed that I'll do it alone, but a flicker of worry crosses his face. I miss Becky and I want to catch up with her. I also feel like having a little chilled-out holiday before I go back to the craziness of home. It will also give Mary and Mike a chance to chat without me being around as a spare part on the train journey.

I text Becky from the airport and she says of course its fine to come over and she can't wait to see me. We all arrive back in Edinburgh and I head to the desk to see if I can book a last-minute flight. There is a flight to Dublin in just under two hours. I have to wait to see if it will be full. Probably not, they reckon; it's common for short flights to have one or two people not turn up as they're often on business trips, and therefore don't care too much if they miss it and the company is paying the cost. I walk Mike and my family to the door of the airport. They will take the train home together and Mike will stay on until Aberdeen. I hug Mum, Mary and the kids and tell them I will see them in a few days. Mike hovers self-consciously, before leaning in for a hug. We share an awkward embrace and Mike goes to kiss my cheek at the same time as I go to kiss his, resulting in what is an embarrassing full-on smacker. I blush furiously and Mike fakes a coughing fit to cover his red face. Mary smiles slyly and gives me a sidelong glance.

'Well, if you two are finished molesting each other, we'd best be off,' Mum declares.

'Good old Ma, always says what I want to,' Mary giggles.

After an awkward goodbye, I head back to the check-in desk. They have a seat on this flight. Great! I couldn't be bothered waiting around three hours for the next one. I head to the bar; this was the stupidest of stupid ideas, flying alone. My phone beeps.

Becky: 'Hi babes will be at airport to pick you up at 5. See ya then.'

I put my phone away. It beeps again.

Mike: 'You OK? Worried 'bout ya!'

Me: 'Cos I'm best snog you ever had? You after more?'

Mike: 'Your Ma just asked what I'm laughing at. I'm gonna tell her.'

Me: 'NO!'

Mike: 'Yes!'

Me: 'NOOOOO!'

Mike: Yes! Oops! Too late.'

Me: Git! I shall never snog you again.'

Mike: 'Bet you wanna tho! Stay safe Hun. Text when you get there. Miss ya.'

I press Mike's message to save. Why did I do that? I order a drink. Oh well, by the time he gets back he'll have arranged a date with Mary. Fair play to him – she's a real catch, even if she doesn't think so. Another beep from my phone:

Mary: 'Chatting shit to the fox that is Michael. Seriously there's sumat wrong wi' you if you don't fancy him!'

Me: 'He fancies you!'

Then nothing, I switch off my phone, down my drink and head to the departure gate.

Chapter Twenty-One

I arrive in Dublin just before teatime. I have never been to Ireland before. It reminds me a lot of Scotland. Very green, very lush and, if you're listening with the ear of an outsider, you'd not have a clue what anyone is saying. I collect my case and head off to find Becky, pausing briefly to switch on my phone to text Mike, then Mary, to say I've arrived safely. No point in texting Mum, I'd only get a reply three months later asking where I have arrived safely to. Her phone is stuck on Caps Lock too. She never has been able to work it – and that was even before Josh messed about and put it all in French. She doesn't do technology.

It wasn't too painful a flight. Barely in the air and then we were landing again. I was sat next to a grumpy-looking businessman who didn't look like he'd take too kindly to any 'what's that noise?' conversations. I had no choice but to get on with it and suffer through my pain. My phone beeps twice before I can even retrieve it from my bag.

Mary: 'Glad you are safe. Mike is such a shag. If you don't, I will!'

Mike: 'Glad you're ok. Weird without you. Fancy a wknd in Aberdeen soon?'

I beam, and quickly type back that I'd love to. I feel a nice buzz. Mike does seem to fancy Mary, but she appears to be oblivious. It's only natural that Mike would miss me as we spend all our time together. It's nice to be missed, parting and sweet sorrows and the like. I walk through arrivals and hear an excited scream. I follow the noise with my eyes and see an ecstatic-looking Becky, waving frantically at me. I make my way towards her and she squeezes me like she'll never let go.

'I have so missed you,' she announces, linking arms with me. 'How are you? How's the business?'

'Better than ever – me and the business, that is,' I smile. I feel a slight pang of guilt that she is no longer part of it, but she looks so happy. She definitely made the best decision for her, with the added bonus of no longer stinking of chip fat. We walk out towards her car. I stare in amazement as Becky points her key fob and unlocks a flashy red sporty number that Bob has bought her to apologise for shagging the girl from work.

'Almost worth it,' announces Becky. I laugh an attempt of agreement. I must admit that's it's a great gift to say sorry with. Though still not convinced it was worth it. Almost or otherwise. We drive to her house, chatting and laughing all the way. I'm relieved to see there's no awkwardness between us. I think Mike being around would have affected things, but the old Becky and Lucy dynamic is still there.

We arrive at Becky's house and unload my case. I turn to take in the view.

'Wow! Look at this place Becks, it's gorgeous!' And it is, even if I have only seen the outside so far. It screams wealthy, all leafy and suburban with imposing, grand homes surrounding us.

'I know,' she squeaks, and squeezes my arm. We walk into Becky's gorgeous red brick three-storey town house. I take in the split-level front room with a deep, plush white rug over the polished original floorboards. Two squashy, red sofas dominate the room and there, in the corner, is a state-of-the-art sound system that I wouldn't even attempt to work out. The front room is massive, with a bay window that looks onto the private garden and duck pond. Up some spiral stairs, leading to nowhere, is a gallery. How frivolous to spend all that money on a staircase to nowhere. It overlooks the living room. Real paintings, not prints, each illuminated by individual lights, but low enough not to damage the paintings. It looks like something out of a London riverside show home. I am insanely jealous. I wander in awe into the kitchen. There is a huge Aga stove with a large wooden chopping block in the middle of the kitchen. Pots and pans hang from the beams. The worktops are marble and stainless steel fixtures gleam under the spotlights. I quickly move on to the bathroom, needing to drink it all in. There is a sunken Jacuzzi bath surrounded by Jo Malone candles, gorgeous terracotta tiled floor and a massive wet room with power shower that could knock you off your feet if you weren't expecting the force. There are five bedrooms, all in varying colour schemes, and a huge dining room with a twelve-seater table. Basically, everything I would ever dream of in a home.

'Who did you let him shag to get this?' I look around in wonder. 'Angelina Jolie?'

Becky giggles:

'It is gorgeous, isn't it? I am so happy this time around. Bob says it made him realise what he could have lost, and he'll do anything to make me happy.' She twirls around in joy, like a little girl.

'I am so pleased for you, Becky,' I say, slipping my arm around her waist. 'And so bloody jealous, you cow.' She laughs delightedly and pulls out a bottle of wine from a well-stocked rack in the wine cellar.

Two bottles later and Bob arrives home. He looks like a different person from when I saw him last. He kisses me hello on each cheek, and smacks Becky playfully on the bottom. She squeals and throws me an apologetic look.

'Did you tell Lucy yet?' he asks.

'Tell me what?' I eye them both suspiciously in turn.

Becky coyly holds out her left hand. A rock that would feed starving millions, if ever sold, glistens on Becky's finger. How could I have missed it?

'Oh my God! You never told me you were engaged,' I shout. 'When is the wedding?'

'In March,' she smiles indulgently at Bob, 'we wanted to make sure it was off season so you can be my bridesmaid… Will you?'

'Of course! It would be an honour. Congratulations.' I give them both a hug, attempting to mask the fact that I do feel a tiny bit uneasy at this news. It's extremely fast.

After an amazing home cooked meal by Becky, we sit around the crackling log fire and chat about the restaurant. Bob pays a particular interest in the business side of things and Becky enjoys the stories about Pablo, the other staff and the customers. She's very much a people person and tires easily of business talk.

'How is Mike?' Becky eventually asks.

I glance at Bob. He doesn't appear to show even an ounce of jealousy, just smiles contently as he swirls his wine. I have intentionally left any information on Mike out, in case it causes awkwardness.

'He's good,' I reply. 'Sam turned up out of the blue, new man in tow.'

'No,' laughs Becky 'did he tell her to get lost?'

'He did, it was hilarious. Her face was a picture. He told her that her implants had sagged. She ran screaming for the hills. It was her man I felt sorry for, though. She dragged the poor bloke out in the middle of his lunch. Humiliating enough that she was so blatantly coming on to her ex in front of him, without making him look like a lapdog.' I shake my head at the memory. 'But Mike was cool as anything, He pretended we were together. She was fuming.'

'Maybe you should be,' Becky smiles slyly.

'Oh, don't you start,' I laugh, and shake my head, 'I hear that all the time.'

'Well, I always thought you two would make a great couple,' Becky continues, 'I always thought he had a thing for you when we were together. A kind of admiration.'

Oh no, not another one! And I certainly don't feel comfortable discussing this with Becky, Bob or no Bob.

'Yes, but only because I managed to pull together a lot of funds at the last minute and not even to my credit – it was an inheritance. Nothing more,' I say hurriedly. But I flush, and Becky notices with a smile.

'Well, just so you know, I'd be absolutely fine with it if you did get together. He's a great guy. I just had someone greater, to me.' She smiles over at Bob. He smiles sleepily and sighs gently. He must be putting in all the hours God sends to have come up with a place like this.

'Well, I best get "Sleeping Beauty" off to bed. Let's do lunch tomorrow. Just me and you, like the old times.'

'That sounds great,' I reply, yawning and stretching. It's been a long day. We all head upstairs. My room is the main guest room with *en suite*. The purple room, Becky and Bob call it. I slip between the Egyptian cotton sheets and fall immediately into a deep, dreamless sleep.

I awaken to almost complete silence. Bliss. No traffic, no tourists and no goats – just an occasional bird twittering. I check my phone. It's 11am. How could I have slept so long? I pad downstairs to find Becky humming happily to herself in the kitchen as she unloads the dishwasher of last night's dishes. She was so right to come home. I've never seen her so content. She was right to follow her heart. She wouldn't have been this happy with Mike. As the saying goes, you have to break a few eggs to make an omelette.

'Morning babe,' she gives me a quick hug before heading to the coffee percolator.

She knows me so well. I can barely muster up a grunt before my first cup of coffee.

Becky busies herself around the kitchen, grilling some bacon for breakfast and letting the cat out. I sip away, feeling more human again. I remember last night's sleepy, drunken conversation. I feel ready to chat now. So I tell Becky how I could never imagine being with Mike, how my sister is so much better suited to him. I'm ever so practical and boring, Mike needs a flirtatious, girly type. Someone who would never neglect their fluffy upper lip in need of a wax or their legs covered in stubble. I run a finger over my upper lip to check just how bad it is. Not too fluffy and, fortunately, it's blonde.

'You know, Mike really isn't into all that stuff. You're comparing yourself too much with Sam,' Becky replies. 'I mean, look at me, I'm not exactly Kate Moss, am I?'

'I know what you mean,' I reply, 'but it's just, well, I'm so dull, so ordinary.'

Becky walks across the kitchen, pulling me gently down from my stool at the breakfast bar and into the bathroom. She places me gently in front of the mirror.

'How long is it since you had a really good look at yourself?' she asks me, peering questionably at my reflection.

Ages, at a guess. I have a good look. OK: eyes slightly puffy from sleep and too much wine, but OK complexion. Hair like a birds nest, but white blond and tousled from the sun and sea air. I seem to be missing the extra chin I had before, though. Probably down to the running around behind the bar and in the sweatbox of a kitchen in Tenerife. If I had to categorise myself, I'd say bohemian. Natural, tanned, tousled. Not as bad as I'd expected, actually.

'Still could do with losing a stone though, Becks.'

'From where?' she stares at me incredulous, peeling back the top of my T-shirt.

'Size ten and it hangs off you,' she dismisses my comment with sweep of her hand. 'How much do you weigh?' she demands.

'I dunno. Ten... Ten and a half stone?'

She marches me over to the scales. The digital display informs me that I am, in fact, eight stone eleven pounds.

'Shit!' I exclaim, rushing back to the mirror for a second

opinion.

'Exactly,' Becky proclaims smugly. 'Now let's go shopping.'

We hit Dublin city centre and have a great time trailing armfuls of clothes to the changing rooms. How could I have not noticed such a massive weight loss? OK, so everyone has been telling me I'm getting far too skinny – well, Mum has – but then she always does. Armed with an entirely new spring wardrobe, we head to the bridal shops. Becky runs her hand dreamily over the fabric of a gorgeous ivory gown sparkling with crystals under the bright lights of the shop that are no doubt designed for that purpose.

'Try it,' I urge. She looks abashed, and then glances over to the sales assistant, who is already heading our way. Becky tries on the gown. She looks beautiful – there is no other word for it. We squeal with excitement, and despite doing this day in, day out, the sales girl squeals along with us. Just to be safe, Becky tries on several more but her first choice was the one. She grins at the sales assistant and tells her she'll put a deposit on it today. She never even checked the price. How I would love to have such a *laissez faire* attitude with money.

'Now you, Lucy,' she announces. I try on various coloured gowns, all size eight I am delighted to notice. We settle on a pale lilac empire line with a line of crystals under the bust. I feel like a princess. After settling on shoes and a tasteful and simple hairpiece for Becky (the dress doesn't need any upstaging) we decide that I'll be having a single white orchid. Becky wants her wedding to be understated and tasteful. She knows exactly what she wants, right down to the napkin rings and favours. Bob is giving her free rein and, to a point, unlimited finances. If it wasn't for having to sleep with Bob, I'd almost wish I was Becky. It's so good to see her happy. She has done nothing but smile since I arrived. Eventually, we head out into the pale mid-afternoon sunshine and practically dance to the nearest pub.

Chapter Twenty-Two

I'm coming to the end of my stay with Becky and Bob. I have had a great time in their amazing home; I am suitably jealous and reassured all at the same time. Becky is fine and Bob is treating her to my standards. I don't need to worry any more. There was enough time for him to slip his guard, enough moments where I guiltily hovered just outside their room to see if he really spoke to her respectfully, or if it was all pretence for my benefit. The plan is to head back to Arbroath until Becky's wedding in March and return to Tenerife in April for the beginning of the summer season. Two blissful months off stretch before me and I can't wait. Becky drives me back to the airport. I'm flying into Glasgow, where I will take the train home. I text Mary to let her know I'll be arriving back soon. Mary messages back,

'Thank God Mum being nightmare! You know she had new man? Just found out 2 days ago! Name is Bert!'

I stare at my phone in puzzlement. Mum has never to my knowledge had any man – new or otherwise – since my Dad. This warrants a phone call. I flick expertly through my phone's contact list and click on Mary's name.

'You what?' I practically shout at my sister when she answers.

'I am not joking, Luce. He's an Environmental Health Officer. I popped down to hers at lunchtime, when she wasn't expecting me. I let myself in with the spare key under the flowerpot and there they were...'

'La la la la,' I sing loudly, receiving strange looks from a couple passing by with a buggy. They alter their direction and walk a few paces away.

'Shut up!' Mary yells over my tuneless singing. 'There they were, sitting on the sofa with a pot of tea and scones. Mum even had the good teacups out. It's serious!'

I don't know what to say.

'It gets worse,' Mary's tone is low. 'I stayed for tea after I picked the kids up from school, well, I couldn't not, she would have thought I was pissed off with her. I put on some chicken dippers for the kids. Mum, being Health and Safety, commented on the fact that they were due to be eaten yesterday – was it safe? *Him*, being Environmental Health, then had a ten-minute discussion about this with Mum, while I had two squalling, hungry kids around my ankles kicking off.'

'But... when? Where?' I begin, and am immediately cut off. Mary, it appears, is still in full flow and was merely pausing for breath.

'But worse than that, when they finally allowed me to cook dinner for my children, which let's face it, I have been doing for nearly seven years without poisoning any of them – well, except that one time, but in my defence it was a takeaway. He reached over my shoulder, stuck a temperature probe into a nugget and informed me it could do with another minute and a half. He asked Mum what she thought, and she reckoned two, to be safe. Arrrrgh!' shouts my sister in frustration. Silence. Finally, I can speak.

'So where did she meet him?' I enquire.

'He gave a talk on some changes to Section 2.1 in the NHS Health and Safety legislation, *apparently*,' she spits out bitterly. 'They're doing my fucking head in. He's there *every* time I go down to Mum's. Them getting together is like a risk assessment made in hell!' I sigh. My boarding has just been announced.

'Look, I'll call you back from Glasgow,' I tell Mary, 'and try to chill.'

I walk down the tunnel, not appearing to notice I'm about to board a plane. My Mum has a man. I smile to myself; fair play to her, about bloody time. I've no idea what Mary's problem is yet, but I'll get to the bottom of it.

I land in Glasgow airport to a text from Mike. How was

Dublin? Hmm, how do I deal with this? I text back that it was a great trip, Becky looks well. No reply. Oh dear, well it was a no-win situation that one. What was I supposed to say? Mary collects me from the station yet again. She wants to go for a cruise in the car. We drive down the familiarly comforting streets. Down the West port, turning right along Millgate Loan, out past Tuttie's Neuk pub, the Plege indoor fairground, Bally's nightclub and finally come to a stop in front of the blue-black North Sea. Pitch dark other than the white foam of the crashing waves and the occasional flash of the Bell Rock lighthouse. The sea is always soothing to me. It always seemed to reflect my mood as a child: bright blue and playful, with seagulls diving over it, when I was in a good mood; moody and turbulent with waves crashing over the barriers if things weren't going good that day. Today, the bonnet of the car is soaked with the overspill from the high tide waves. Mary seems not to notice. I can taste the salt as I bite my lip, waiting for her latest outpouring and trying not to find the deafening silence so amusing. She steps out from the car and walks straight into a wave, soaking her from over the barrier. It pushes her almost off her feet. She stands so still after, in shock. Shit! I think, snorting with laughter, that's not going to help her mood. She stares at me aghast for a moment, sea water dripping from her hair. I stare back, unsure what to say and scared to move. Eventually, I grab the blanket from the back seat and open the passenger door, nervously waiting for the next wave to hit. I place the blanket around her shoulders. Mary laughs, a small chortle to begin with, growing louder and with a hysterical edge. I join in and before we know it, we are both unable to catch a breath.

'Ah, come on home,' she says when we eventually calm down.

We head back to the car. I instinctively know what's up now. Being in my sister's company I can almost read her mind. Sometimes we will argue when one of us relates a story that happened years ago, over whether it happened to me or her. Sometimes I forget where I end and my sister begins, so close are we. She never met Dad and I did. I know she finds this new man hard to take. An impostor. Even though I don't actually remember Dad, I used to relay to her stories told to me by Mum. I guess they seemed real to Mary, like I had some inside knowledge or memories. We used to tell stories, late at night, about how there was a mix-up at the hospital. Dad hadn't really died and turned up at school one day to take us to the Inverpark Hotel for fish and chips and a lime soda. Of course, we knew deep down it was fantasy, but I think it helped with a lot of unresolved grief that we felt we had no right to have. How can you grieve for someone you never met or don't remember?

'Let's at least give him a chance, for Mum's sake,' I break the silence. Without a word, Mary starts up the engine and points the car towards the harbour – and Mum's house.

It's so strange to see what Mum's taste in men is, having never experienced it from memory. OK, she has quite a broad taste in celebrity men. Mel Gibson, Morgan Freeman, the guy who plays Rebus, the cute Asian guy from the corner shop, well he's famous round our bit anyway, for being rather easy on the eye. We used to laugh at Mum whenever anyone she fancied appeared on our screens.

'Oh, he'd get it!' To which Mary and I would pretend to gag. Parents and sex lives are too gross to even consider. But this man here, in the armchair with our Poopsy puss on his lap, is greying, slightly portly in the belly area, and has a warm, smiley red face and a glass of wine by his side.

'Don't get up,' I smile, 'Poops looks so comfy. I'm Lucy, daughter eldest.' I lean in to kiss Bert's soft, soapy-smelling cheek.

'And ugliest,' Mary adds. Bert chuckles.

'Lovely to meet you, Lucy, your Mum's told me lots about

you, our budding entrepreneur.'

I jolt a little at the 'our' mention, but it feels nice, comfortable and settled. It's so good to hear a unity of my mother and someone else for the first time. I glance at Mary. She looks warily at me. Bert misreads the situation.

'Of course, who could match our little earth mother?' he smiles, keen to play down my success and highlight Mary's. I like what he's doing. It's endearing rather than annoying.

'Did you know she's taking another language course, Lucy? Claims she can barely speak English, but you should hear her Polish!'

'Yes Bert, I've heard it,' I say seriously, before Mary and I laugh uncontrollably at the memory of the confrontation with Kasia. Bert looks confused. Bless him – he has two boys and his wife died years ago. He doesn't have a great deal of experience with girly ways. Mum bustles through, fussing around Bert like a mother hen. Pushing him forward to re-arrange his cushions – he has a bad back, apparently, and it's not good for his posture to slump like he is. She informs him that tea won't be long, does he need another glass of wine? This is the biggest shock. Mum having a boyfriend was nothing compared to this. My mother, feminist to the point of making Emmeline Pankhurst look like a Stepford Wife, is pandering over a man. Mary rolls her eyes, but I can tell already that me being back has made her see them in a new light. Mary and I appear never to have a real perspective on things until we have both discussed it; we're two sides of a brain working together. She's like a thirteen-month late identical twin.

And so a month flies by. I go to bed late, watching TV with Mum and Bert, hang out at Mary's and with other family members and generally have a very lazy and relaxed time. I get the chance to catch up with old school friends, something I never usually get a chance to do in my flying visits home. Walk over the footsteps of old childhood trails, along the beach, out to the cliffs and Auchmithie, a tiny, but beautiful fishing village. I trail for miles with Bobby, Bert's son's Jack Russell. It clears even the most stubborn cobwebs from the recesses of my head. Mike and I keep in touch, but the trip to Aberdeen never materialises. I don't mention it again and neither does he. Then just before March, I receive a phone call from him. He has received a wedding invite from Becky.

'Are you going to go?' I ask, waiting on edge for a barrage of abuse.

'I might do. Be nice to go with you though.'

'Why don't you ask Mary?' I play devil's advocate. Mary hasn't mentioned Mike again, but it won't end there. I'll keep trying.

'Mary? Your sister, Mary?'

'Yes. Why not? I thought there was a bit of a spark between you two,' I answer.

'Nah, she's sweet and all, but no, I don't really see her in that way.'

Oh. I'm quite surprised by this. My beautiful, bubbly sister is not fancied by Mike.

'OK, well I'll call you in a couple of days and we'll discuss flights and stuff then.'

Maybe Mike is planning to be the one at the wedding who stands up to challenge the vicar when he asks should there be any reason the couple shouldn't get married. I have waited with baited breath at every wedding I have ever attended for this bit. How exciting to have someone stand up and declare that, actually, he did have a problem, he wanted to marry the girl in question himself. But I guess that kind of stuff only happens in books or movies. It has no place in real life.

I walk back along the Vicky Park to Mum's. On the horizon I

see a frantically waving Mary, rushing towards me. She picks up speed as she gets closer. Bobby strains at his lead in recognition, ready for one of his renowned sniff-fests. Mary reaches me, panting and brushing off Bobby's attempts to slobber all over her.

'Bert's son is at Mum's. He is gorgeous!' she wheezes at me.

'No he's not,' I look at Mary in alarm. Jeez, is she that desperate for a man?'

'No-ooo,' she replies impatiently, 'not Jim, Bobby's Dad, the other one. You've got to see this.' Mary grabs me by the arm and pulls me along towards Mum's house, adopting a simpering manner before my eyes as we open the gate.

Bloody hell, she's right. What a fox! He's as pathetic over her as she is over him. I drag her to the kitchen on the pretext of helping me refill the wine glasses.

'You can't do anything, what if he becomes our stepbrother? That's sick,' I shake my head at her, the second we close the kitchen door.

'No, actually you're the weird one. We have no blood ties at all, and I will happily race Mum to the altar if it comes down to it.'

'But, Mike?' I raise an eyebrow questionably at her.

'Mike? What your Mike?' I nod. 'No, Euw! Don't want your sloppy seconds, thanks,' and with that, she flounces out of the kitchen with two glasses, back to Drew the screw, as she's named him.

A few days on, and I'm packing up my things for my flight to Ireland the next day. I have had a great time with my family and friends but feel quite content to be moving on. Mum is settled and happier than I've ever known. Drew seems to be reciprocating Mary's intentions for him. Well, if the fact I haven't seen them for a couple of days is anything to go by. Still, Kasia will be bringing the kids back tonight, that'll put a stop to it all. At least I'll get to see my niece and nephew before I head off again, even if it's just for a couple of hours. All the Ramseys will be congregating at Mary's in an hour for the big send off. Mum books a taxi and Bert helps her load all the drink and foodstuffs into a carrier bag. Well, all the non-perishables that is, the other things will be packed into freezer bags, military style as the taxi honks its horn outside. Contrary to what Mary said, Mum and Bert are in fact a risk assessment made in Heaven – and just adorable to watch. We arrive at Mary's flat to the usual noise. Many hugs and comments on how they can't wait until July for the grand Ramsey piss-up. I am so looking forward to it – it will see me through the first half of the summer season. The doorbell goes and I head down to answer. A very tearful-looking Kasia stands there. Josh and Jess shove around her, ignoring me in their quest to find Craig and hear his attempts to burp the alphabet. He made it to N last time, apparently.

'Kasia, are you OK?' I ask with concern. Mary appears behind me.

'He is dick! Mary, how you put up with him so long? I hate him and I leave tonight,' she nods her confirmation.

'Oh Kasia,' Mary gives her an awkward hug. 'What has he done?'

'Kasia sighs, 'I pay all rent, I loan him money for his sick mother.' Mary and I exchange a look; Joan has never been better, bedridden on occasion, but not in the way Kasia thinks. 'If it wasn't for these children, I would have gone, long ago!'

'Kasia, come in and have a drink,' Mary ushers her upstairs and into the flat. Craig looks up in awe, halting on L of the burp alphabet and smiles at the beautiful Kasia. She laughs delightedly, wiping her eyes.

'Continue, please! My Papa, he can do most of alphabet, but not all.'

Chapter Twenty-three

I arrive in Ireland for Becky's wedding. Mike has yet to decide whether he will attend or not. He has told Becky to keep his invite open until he can see if he can get a flight. Load of crap, of course, and she knows that, but can't really do anything else about it. So I arrive on my own. Becky picks me up from the airport, despite my insistence that I could take a taxi; she has enough to deal with. Becky looks gorgeous! She has lost around a stone since I saw her last – not that she needed to – and has had her dark blonde hair highlighted and cut into a face framing style. That alone makes a huge difference, and softens her pretty features even more. Part of me kind of hopes Mike won't turn up. It may just remind him of what he's missing.

Bob has gone to stay at his parent's house for the night so that Becky and I can have a girly evening, but also to avoid him seeing the bride before the ceremony. We kick off by ordering out for pizza, and then watching a movie aptly titled *My Best Friend's Wedding* with diet cokes and face packs on. This is followed by the arrival of a beautician friend of Becky's to give us both a French manicure. Both of us have our hair set in bendy rollers and are informed that hair always sits better the day after it's washed. Urg! I need to wash my hair every day. It feels like an oil slick if I don't. But Becky will follow the advice to the word. We eventually head to bed, unable to get comfortable due to a combination of rollers and excitement. We share the same King-size double bed, as we occasionally did when we lived together. It reminds us both of growing up, sharing a room with our sisters and giggling late into the night.

Morning comes. I don't actually remember falling asleep, simply finishing my hot chocolate, switching off the TV and listening to the gentle sound of Becky's snoring. I awaken around eight o'clock to the sound of an over-enthusiastic bird outside the window. Early spring, such a nice time of the year, with all the new baby things. Chicks, I hear at the moment. Mum always tells me it reminds her of me. I was a spring baby too, and woke her every morning with an internal kick. Her very own dawn chorus. Becky stirs and rolls over, slumping an arm across my chest. Nose inches from mine. I try not to laugh at her close proximity, but my shaking shoulders rouse her. She opens her eyes and, seeing me out of context, is momentarily disorientated. Then, gathering her senses, she smiles widely at me and announces:

'I'm getting married today!'

'You sure are honey, but best you do something about your breath first.'

The next few hours fly by in a flurry of appointments: first, the beautician to finish off the manicure polish and apply the make-up, then the hairdresser to style our hair and fix our hairpieces. I am separated from Becky for well over an hour while the stylist helps her to dress. I am just having the orchid placed in my new curls when Becky walks in.

She is stunning!

'Bob is the luckiest guy in the world,' I give her a proud smile. She hugs me and then holds me out at arm's length to view my *ensemble*.

'Gorgeous,' she exhales, and we crack open some champagne to celebrate. Becky's little nieces arrive in full flower girl regalia – how cute. Not at all what I would have said only a year ago when I was off kids. Becky anticipates motherhood greatly. She can't wait to have one and is already off the pill to try for a honeymoon baby. The little girls are in violet, a couple of shades deeper than my dress and, at Niamh's request, wearing floral head-dresses and fairy wings. Becky, ever indulgent, gave in. I love this look on me. Empire line really disguises the fact that my hips are a bit bigger than my chest. I make a mental note to make sure I buy similar styles in the future.

The cars arrive. Becky, her Mum, the little nieces, Emer and Niamh, and I, all pile in. As ladylike as we can, which isn't ladylike at all, really. Arms, legs and lopsided head-dresses everywhere. The little ones chat excitedly, but Becky looks nervous.

'You OK?' I ask her. She exhales loudly.

'I am so excited Lucy,' she shakes her head, looking dangerously tearful.

'Don't smudge!' shouts Emer. 'Mummy warned me not to let you,' and she pulls a fairy embroidered tissue from her little bag and shakes it towards Becky. This small gesture diffuses the situation and Becky laughs. Back to her usual self.

We arrive and walk to the door of the church. Becky's Mum is giving her away. I organise the small ones behind me and instruct them to keep a few paces back to prevent treading on the fishtail of my dress. We hear whispered chatter from inside the church. People are twisting round in their seats to get the first glimpse. The organ begins to play the opening bars of *Ave Maria* and we begin to walk down the aisle. I hear giggles as we pass by, and turn to see Emer cross-eyed and poking her tongue out as she passes everyone.

'No! *Emer*,' I hiss, trying hard not to laugh and turn back before I fall headfirst into Becky and cause a pile up. On the seventh aisle from the front I see Mike. He turns around to look at us and Becky reaches out to give his hand a squeeze on the way past, smiling broadly and mouthing 'thanks' to him. Mike catches my eye. He looks me up and down, raising his eyebrows in approval. I smile and give him a sidelong look. He's looking quite buff. Still a hint of a tan and has obviously been at the gym. Bob's face is one of rapt joy – he cannot believe his eyes. Two rows back I see a red-faced, slightly swaying, bald man. He leans out and smacks Becky on the bottom as she passes. She turns and glowers at him. He winks and clicks his tongue twice. His wife elbows him roughly. I accidentally kick his ankle on the way past. Oops, clumsy old me! He yelps and clutches his ankle, making Emer and Niamh giggle.

The ceremony is lovely. I don't attend church regularly but do enjoy a good Christmas Mass or wedding. Oh, and nativity plays of course. Jess was the cutest sheep ever at hers. I saw the video. Shame she wee'd on the stage, but I guess sheep do that sometimes. The time comes to take the vows and the priest asks if we know of any reason why this couple should not be joined in matrimony. A couple of years ago I could have written a speech on the subject, but not now. I hear a throat clearing behind me.
'Actually, yes, I do.'
No way! Mike? We all swing round in shock. Not Mike. Drunken bloke struggles to his feet.
'Yes?' The priest removes his bottle-end, thick glasses and looks stunned. I'm betting this has never happened to him before in his entire career, but he'll have to take it seriously.
'See, Father, she secretly fancies me, got the wrong brother didn't ye, love.'
Hushed whispers and quite a few shouts echo around the church.
'Oi, shurrup!'
'Drunken erse!'
'Sit down, ya fecking eedjit! Sorry Father.'
Bob laughs, Becky joins in and the brother is dragged by his collar out of the church by his rather large wife. Panic over, we continue and everything else, thankfully, goes without a hitch.

Outside, the sun is shining brightly. Becks has the best day for her wedding. We do the obligatory line-up for the photographs. Drunken George has been allowed back, on the condition that he shuts the feck up and has no more to drink 'til the dancing begins. The photographer, who appears to have a lifetime ambition to become the next Gok Wan, takes an age, fiddling with our dresses and trying to position us perfectly. Amazing how a foot at the wrong angle will ruin the picture. If I ever marry, (ha!) I would much prefer paparazzi-style shots. They're much more natural and spontaneous. Also means you don't spend hours blistering in the sun with Emer and Niamh, who are the world's biggest fidgets. We almost had a perfect shot till Gok-alike realised Niamh was scratching her bum in it. Her excuse, a leftover chicken pock from two weeks ago. Elderly relatives recoil to a safe distance from the threat of shingles. The photographer lines us up again for a final reel of film.

'Make me look thinner,' Becky shouts.

'It's a fecking camera, Becky, not a magic wand.' George could contain himself no more. When it is developed the photo shows four severely pissed-off faces and Emer picking her nose.

It isn't until after the speeches and meal that I finally get a chance to speak to Mike. He looks relieved to see me after the trauma of being seated next to Becky's elderly aunt. He has had to take her to the toilet three times already and, due to her incontinence problem and twice had to rummage through her bag to find clean drawers and a fresh pad. I drag him off to an empty table so we can have a catch up.

'You look good Lucy. Scrub up not too bad at all.'

'Thanks,' I brush off his compliment, 'so what made you decide to come to the wedding?' I have to know.

'Just decided that it was silly not to, really. I'm over Becky and wish her well. Besides, I have my eye on someone else now.'

'Oh, from Aberdeen?'

'No, not from Aberdeen,' he laughs and gives me a knowing look. Shit! Mary. I must have put the suggestion in his head. She's happily hooked up with Drew now.

'Oh Mike,' I cover his hand with mine. 'The object of your affections loves another. I'm sorry.'

'Oh!' Mike looks shocked. 'That was quick, she was single last I checked.'

'I know, it happened really unexpectedly, my Mum's boyfriend's son of all people.'

'I see,' Mike shrugs dismissively, but I can tell it's bothered him. 'Oh well, never mind. Fancy a dance?'

'Sure,' I smile, apologetically. I hate to be the bearer of bad news, but he needs to know. It couldn't work anyway, unless he was to move to Arbroath, and I really can't have him do that. I can't run the restaurant on my own. I know it crossed my mind before, but with hindsight, I doubt I could. From four of us to one in a year – I shudder at the thought.

The evening passes too quickly. George is being an arse and groping anything in a skirt – his poor wife, I really feel for her. Becky has a ball, but I barely get to speak to her. Everyone seems to have had a good day. And Becky is married. I can hardly believe that this sparkling, happy girl is the same one I knew a year ago. Mike and I head back to our hotel, preparing to turn in for the night. I can't stay at Becky's as it is all locked up for honeymoon. She did offer, but it was going to be complicated with keys and stuff. Also, the flight is for nine in the morning and her house is a fair bit away from the airport. On arriving back at the hotel, we notice the bar is still open. Great rules in Ireland and Scotland for opening times; if people still want to drink, the bars will stay open.

We order a couple of vodka and cokes, rather generously-sized ones, and flop onto a squashy sofa in front of the log fire, me still in my dress and Mike in his kilt. The change of drinks, from champagne to wine and then vodka makes me feel fuzzy-headed and there appears to be two Mikes. I put my hand out in front of Mike's face and grab thin air. Nope, not that one, I laugh. I reach for the other one, and catch his stubbly cheek. He smiles and covers my hand with his. Holding it against his face. I take a wobbly sip of my drink, peering curiously at him over the rim of my glass and snort an unattractive laugh.

'Michael Johnston, if I didn't know better I'd think you'd be flirting with me,' I say in a Dublin accent. It's hard to shake off after being surrounded by them for days.

'Maybe I am, to be sure,' he replies, with a lopsided smirk.

'Woah! I'm drunker than I thunk.' I lean away from him, slopping vodka down my pretty bodice. 'I mean, I'm sorry about Mary an' all, but I am not the consolation prize.'

Mike looks confused.

'It's got bugger all to do with Mary? But I'm not going there with *you*, dating a man who's practically your brother,' Mike laughs. 'Only you would dare do something so...out there. One of the many amazing things about you.'

My mind is fuddled by alcohol. Not Mary? Hmmm.

'Ha! I am so not wonderful. OK, go on then, tell me why I am so great.' I am at the drunken stage of attempting to be self-deprecating, but actually desperate to hear lovely things.

'OK, where do I start?' Mike places my hand down gently and leans back on the sofa, eyeing me like a specimen over his vodka glass. 'I like the fact that you stopped smoking, even though you loved it, 'cos you don't like anything being in control of you.'

'Booo-oooooring,' I announce, with a dramatic sigh, secretly feeling like Scarlett O'Hara. Must be the dress.

'Right... er... I like the way you have ambition, drive and aren't scared to go for what you want.'

'Mmmm-hmmm, better.'

'And how you would rather have no man than the wrong

man.'

'You know what, Michael, you are correct on that one. Fuck 'em! Fuck 'em all, I say. Here's to being single.' I toast myself. Mike doesn't seem to want to. 'More please.'

Ooh, Mike's getting closer, no longer two Mikes, but three, no wait, four. I can feel his breath on my face.

'But most of all, because you're beautiful and I love you.'

I feel the soft pressure of Mike's lips on mine. I can taste vodka and the chocolate pudding that he had earlier. Is Mike *kissing* me? This is wrong. This can't happen. It's the kiss of death. Any relationship I touch turns to shit. If Mike leaves, I'll have to go back to London, be a nanny again. Be a failure at my business as well as my love life. I stand up, tipping vodka onto my ivory satin shoes.

'Fuck!' Mike is close behind me.

'Keys!' I yell urgently to the barman-cum-receptionist. He tosses me Room 24's keys and I head for the stairs.

'Lucy, wait!' Mike shouts urgently behind me. I hook my fishtail train over my arm, probably flashing my satin clad arse, but who cares?

'Lucy!' Mike calls from the bottom of the stairs. I clumsily shove the key into the lock, dropping it twice and cursing. Finally, I'm in. I flop onto the bed and the ceiling rose swirls round and round. Mike kissed me. I ponder on this for a second or two and then, in true O'Hara style, decide that I will think of it tomorrow. I close my eyes, still wearing my dress, and fall into the dreamless sleep of the truly pissed.

Chapter Twenty-Four

My alarm call arrives at six o'clock in the morning in the form of Seamus, the multi-tasking hotelier. He raps loudly on the door.

'Miss Lucy, there's a full Irish for you here. Your taxi will be here in turty-five minutes! I have been shouting you for ages. Michael is waiting for you downstairs.'

'Mmmmphhhmm.'

'Miss Lucy, I don't want to have to come in there and see you in a state of undress...'

Seamus says this as if he can't imagine anything better. I stumble to the door, open it, and lean my head against the cool paintwork. Seamus visibly recoils and backs off slowly. He stops and places the full Irish and a black coffee on the floor. I wait until he's gone and stumble over to pick it up. Urg! Black pudding! Congealed pig's blood for breakfast. I pick up a piece of toast and stagger to the bathroom. As I view my reflection, I recoil myself. One barf up and a very quick shower later, I walk tentatively downstairs. I can't look at Mike. I apologetically hand my breakfast back to Seamus, complete but for one single bite mark out of the toast.

'Tis OK,' he smiles kindly and disappears with it. We loiter awkwardly in the doorway waiting for the taxi. The bright morning sun is streaming into my sun-glassed eyes. I notice I'm wearing odd trainers. Seamus reappears with two glasses of neat vodka.

'Hair of the dog that bit yer,' he announces.

'Not a chance!' I inform him.

Mike laughs for the first time since I saw him this morning. He looks slightly rough around the edges, but doesn't get the killer hangovers that I tend to.

'I will if you will,' he smiles. I groan inwardly and take the glass. I swoop it back in one, before I can change my mind.

My eyes water, as does my mouth, the water brash of the 'about-to-puke'.

'Please, Miss Lucy… not on the carpet.' Seamus directs me outside. The carpet is one of those red and orange swirly ones with splodges of brown through it that looks like it's actually been designed by someone throwing up on it. Doubt my contribution would even be noticed. I head for a bush and feel my wet hair being gently pulled off my face, my back being rubbed by a soothing hand. I slap backwards into the air and the hand stops. It makes me feel worse. The hair thing is handy though. When I finally finish, Seamus is beaming proudly at me, holding out a napkin and a shot of vodka. Mike had been the hair holder. I assumed it was Seamus. Mike laughs as Seamus thrusts the drink under my nose.

'The bad stuff is gone now, replenish your fluids.' I down the shot. Time stands still while we all wait with baited breath to see if there will be a rose bush encore. No, I'm good. I feel good. I give Seamus an enthusiastic hug as the taxi rolls up the drive.

'You know what I could just go for now?' I ask. Seamus holds one finger in the air and disappears back inside. He comes back out with two tin-foiled packages and two Styrofoam cups with lids balanced precariously on top of one another. I peer inside the foil.

'It's bacon sandwiches and black coffee. How did you..?'

'Ex-alcoholic Miss Lucy, I knows all the tricks.' He waves goodbye to us as we walk over to the taxi.

We land safely in Tenerife and wait outside in the hot March sunshine for Pablo to pick us up. There hasn't been too much awkwardness between us. We busied ourselves on the flight with stories about the wedding, how great Becky looked and how much Bob seems to have changed. The declaration of Mike's love for me goes unsaid. In fact, I remember it through such a fuzz - surreal almost - that I wonder if it happened at all. We have a couple more hairs of the dog, just to be on the safe side, and manage to piss off several passengers with our lairy laughter, later apologising shamefaced when the flight attendant gives us a heavily made-up scowl. No wonder they have weight restrictions on luggage, the make-up on each stewardesses must weigh a good few pounds. It all adds up. We cackle loudly at that too.

Pablo's old familiar wreck pulls up outside the arrival terminal. There's a new bash on the front red bumper to match the one at the back. All that money we pay him, and he won't buy a new car. An airport security guard walks over to Pablo's car, with the intention of telling him he can't park there. He's right in the zone where a tour bus is waiting to pull into. Pablo's large frame emerges from the car and towers over the guard. Words are exchanged and the security guy laughs, shakes Pablo's shovel hand, and shouts 'five minutes' in a thick Spanish accent to the tour bus driver, who rolls his eyes. He's the perfect choice of security, our Pablo. All the way back to the restaurant, he enlightens us with excited chatter about all the latest gossip: Maria won't be back, she is pregnant; and Pablo's wife is also expecting a new baby in August. He actually had a lovely time with his kids over the winter months. Taught his eldest son how to fish and even took his two daughters shopping. This next baby must be a boy, he informs us, to balance things out.

On our return we find a gleaming bar, kitchen and living area. Pablo and Rosa have obliterated any signs of an entire family packed into our living space over the past few months. They moved into their new place two weeks ago and are loving every second of it.
'My home is like a palace, I even have pool,' he tells us. 'My Rosa do great job. Builders were difficult, but Rosa kicked

ass.' He has reverted back to Spanish without Mike around. I smile and know that within a few days Pablo's Scottish accent will be back. He's like me that way – I'm very susceptible too. It's so good to be back. It's strange how you can have so many homes from home. Definitely one of them is here, but I also have the same feeling in London. I am very nomadic by nature, most uncharacteristic for a Taurean. But as we are the great homemakers of the zodiac, I figure that our ability to create a home makes us able to travel comfortably. Well, for me anyway. Mike and I sit up for a while with Pablo at the familiar bar with the familiar banter. Pablo is very excited about his gift of a trip to Scotland, but has said he will take it at the end of season so he is on hand to help us.

'Pablo, you do know you're welcome to take a break mid-season,' I tell him, 'You work so hard for us and we appreciate it. We will find someone to cover you.' He smiles:

'And miss all of this,' he holds out his hands to us. He is very sweet, for a hulk of a man. I know he loves us dearly.

Pablo heads home and Mike and I head up to bed. I slip between the cool, fresh sheets and think about new Specials for the menu when we open again in two days' time. I don't get very far. I'm so tired from the excitement of the past few days. Will Mike ever bring up the 'I love you' again? Who knows? But I doubt it. I think I made it very clear to him that I'm a no-go zone. I fail at all relationships. There's no point even trying anymore. Relationships are fine for Becky, Mary, Mum even – and for Mike when he meets the right one. But she isn't me, not by a long shot. I have too much to lose. My wonderful business, the best thing that has ever happened to me work-wise, and I won't jeopardise that for anything.

I wake up around ten thirty the next morning, enjoying a last lie-in while I can. The apartment is silent. Mike has obviously had the same idea. I pad down to the bathroom and have a long shower using all my lovely Christmas toiletries that smell of home. I close my eyes and I'm back in Mum's house. Smell is the most powerful sense for me. One whiff of Lulu perfume and I'm transported back to my twenty-first birthday party. Waitrose Angelica scented candles and I'm back in my old room in Islington, smoking a Marlboro Light and drinking red wine, with Keane on the CD player. I love the way smell can awaken the memory. I finish my shower and head back to my room. The smell of freshly brewed coffee tells me that Mike is up. I scurry along to get dressed and put on a bit of make-up. I have listened to Becky and how I should glam up a little now and then, boho is fine, hobo is not, apparently. I put on my long white skirt, black vest and a long love heart pendant. Fine, slightly dressy, but looks effortless. Why do I care, I wonder? Probably just have the urge, since I was so glammed up the other day. It is lovely to be back in summer clothes, though. I wander down to the living room to have some coffee with Mike. We've planned to have a holiday day today, before the mass shopathon tomorrow for all the new stock. Pablo, Rosa and the kids will be joining us for lunch at a small seaside café little known to the tourists. So good and authentically Spanish that the Spaniards want to keep it secret. We are seen as honorary Spaniards, not ex-pats. Thanks to Pablo.

Mike and I walk down to the beach and order Virgin cocktails from the beach bar. I stir my straw around my drink thoughtfully.

'I meant what I said, Lucy,' Mike says quietly. Oh, here we go, I thought we'd gone past this.

'Yes, me too,' I reply, without looking at him. I can feel the hurt vibes and I don't mean to hurt Mike. It would just be wrong. Mike sighs and jumps off his bar stool. He walks down to the water, and in spite of myself, I turn to look. Becky's voice, telling me not to become a ball breaker, echoes in my head. I'm just about to shout Mike back to explain, when I feel a soft thud by my side. Marina, Pablo's four-year-old beams up at me, before clambering onto my knee and helping herself to my drink.

'Hello, baby girl,' I kiss the top of her braided head.

'Marina, down!' orders Rosa.

'Oh leave her, she's fine,' I wave a dismissive hand at her. Mike heads back up the beach towards us, and the moment has gone.

We have a great day of paella, wine and laughter, chasing the children around the beach as they squeal in the sunshine. Pablo, Mike and the younger two kids make a huge sandcastle, while Marina plaits my hair, enjoying the grown-up girlie chat with Rosa and I. It's a perfect day. One of those, I realise, as the sun goes down and the children grow tired, that I'll always remember. They lean against us sleepily as we chat and drink the last of the wine. I am enjoying the quiet while it lasts, in so many ways that I would never have imagined.

Chapter Twenty-Five

The new season kicks off in the usual hectic style and we fall back into the flow straight away. Me back in the kitchen, whilst also attempting to be a temporary waitress in Maria's absence. All is going fine until mid-April. Strangely enough, I had a weird feeling about today when I woke. Right there, in the solar plexus. I looked out the window at eight this morning. All seemed calm, a few birds twittering, a couple of early beach bums taking a wander, even the sea seemed unusually calm. Flat, like a pond. I shrugged off my strange feeling and headed downstairs to the kitchen. I felt the hairs on the back of my neck stand up a couple of times throughout the morning. Like when you know someone is watching you, but you can't see them. The busy 11am period comes around and I forget my early morning creeps. It's around this time that Pablo bursts into the restaurant shouting angrily about needing the day off. I hear the kerfuffle from the kitchen and listen to Mike's attempts to find out what's happened. I place a hot tray of lasagne on the worktop and walk quickly through the swing doors to the restaurant area. Pablo is shouting and swearing in Spanish, unable to translate through sheer fury. Eventually he calms down enough to become coherent.

'OK, Pablo, that's fine, of course you can have the day off. Just tell me what's wrong, can we do anything?' I pull him round to the side bar while Mike opens him a beer.

'Fucking idiot builders!' he shouts. 'My children, in the bath, when the roof fall in. My children, my Rosa, could have been killed.'

'Oh my God, Pablo, I...'

'They did not put in... what you say?'

'A lintel?' Mike supplies. Pablo nods.

'My little Marco, in hospital, he be OK they say, but bruised and in for few days. My Rosa so *angry.*'

'Oh Pablo, but yes, you must take the day off, go and spend it with Rosa and Marco,' I begin.

'No, I go sort fucking builders!' he shouts angrily, and slams down his half-drunk beer. Pablo stands up and makes for the door. Mike moves quickly around the bar and runs outside after him. We watch, helplessly from the door as he speeds off in his rusty old car, and head back to the bar, what else can we do? We have no idea who he is going after or where. I raise my eyes up to the ceiling to offer up a quick prayer to his Mama to watch out for him.

After a fretful day we receive a call from Pablo to say all is OK. I couldn't get him out of my mind. He arrives into work the next day simmering with anger under the surface, but otherwise unscathed. Mike tries to find out what he's done. All Pablo tells him is that he didn't kill anyone, much as he was tempted, but they won't be doing it again to anyone else. I don't like the sound of this. Pablo is not a nasty person, but when his family are threatened, I know he'd at least give the person responsible a good warning off – if not a good hiding. But after a few days on tenterhooks, things settle down. I stop worrying. 'Pablo power' seems to carry a lot of weight on the island. It's not so big that people won't know who he is. The weekend after, we have the biggest downpour anyone local can ever remember. We have only five hardcore, drenched customers the whole day. Everyone else seems to have done a quick dash to the local shops and then stayed at home for the rest of the day. I stand at the door of the restaurant with Mike and gaze in wonder. I have never seen rain like it. Rivers of water rush by the door. By ten in the evening we decide to call it a night. Pablo heads off home after one drink and a quick game of cards. Mike and I sit and chat at the bar.

'Well, at least the garden tables will be getting a good clean up. I was going to pick up some industrial cleaner on the next supplies trip,' Mike muses, glancing out at the still falling rain. 'Oh, that reminds me, have you got the shopping list for tomorrow? Pablo has a new supplier he wants us to try. Fresh catches of fish that day, none of the two day-old stuff we get now.' I wander into the kitchen and hand Mike the list.

'Cheers. Are you turning in?' he asks. I nod wearily, glad for the opportunity of an early night. Yet when I go to bed, I can't sleep. My eyelids droop and I jolt awake straight after. I must cut down on the coffee during the day.

I don't remember falling asleep, but evidently I did. I awaken to hear the roar of a car engine outside and wander over to the window to have a look. Pablo's car revs and splutters like a forty-a-day old man. Mike wanders down the steps with my list in his hand. They're off to the suppliers. I throw on some clothes and head downstairs to start on a Spag Bol. I have a few dishes to make, so no point in having a shower now. I will be covered in grease and stinking of garlic within half an hour. I switch on the radio in the kitchen. I'm quite getting into Spanish music, though I don't understand the lyrics. I make the Bolognese and a paella rice and stock combo, ready to throw in the fresh seafood at the last minute. I prepare the *entrees* of soup and seafood cocktail (or *fruits de la mer* as Mike likes to call it. Posh git) and make a Banoffee Pie. I head back upstairs for a quick shower and a coffee – yes, my ban didn't last long, I know. Mike will be back by opening time to set up the bar.

I head back downstairs an hour later, still no sign of Mike. I call his mobile, but it rings out to voicemail. Great! Now the sun has come back out hungry mobs will be pounding at the door any minute. I set up the bar and pull the curtain to one side to view the car park. Where are they? The waiters arrive with the new waitress closely behind. I don't know what to do. None of them have ever worked the till, as Mike does the cash, but they have never done the cooking either. I silently curse myself for not making sure we have multi-tasking staff. Could do with Seamus here I think, with a giggle. I try Mike's mobile again. Still it rings out. I try Pablo's, but it's switched off. I grab Gina, the new waitress, from the kitchen and give her a crash course in working the till. Like a duck to water; I happily leave her there as I go back to the kitchen to prepare the first orders.

'Table fifteen away,' I yell, and glance again at the car park. I don't know if I should be angry or concerned. I leave Mike a message asking where the hell he is, and start another order that's appeared. By three in the afternoon, things slow down. Still no Mike! What if they've crashed? Pablo's crazy driving combined with that shit-tip excuse for a car, anything could have happened. I walk quickly back to the bar. Gina's English is perfect, so I will get her to call the police.

'Gina, I am worried about Mike and Pablo, please will you call the... erm, Policia? Yes? See if there have been any accidents.' Gina nods with concern and dials the number of the nearest Police Station. I listen intently as if I can understand every word. 'Si, si, gracias,' Gina hangs up and turns to me. 'They will come in to take description from you soon. Yes? Is OK?'

'Yes, thank you Gina,' I say wearily. 'Now you go get some rest before the evening shift.'

And then I am alone. Sitting on a barstool, absent-mindedly pouring brown sugar sachets into my coffee. At ten minutes past four the police arrive, breaking my reverie and shocking the life out of me.

'Sorry!' I jump, 'can I get you anything, coffee?'

'No thank you, we are fine. Now, you reported a missing person?'

'Well, two actually, but they've only been missing a few hours, but Mike definitely would have been back by now if everything was fine. He wouldn't leave me on my own.'

The policeman raises his hand to stop my babbling and says something in Spanish to the other officer. I curse myself for not learning Spanish. It's like grown-ups speaking in big words when you're small. You wish you could understand.

'Have you a photograph or description of your friends?' asks the first officer.

'Er, yes, I think so.' I rummage at the side of the till. What did Mike do with all the New Year snaps? I have no idea. I turn back to the men: 'Look, we do have some somewhere. Both men are tall, well-built, dark brown hair and eyes. Sorry, I know they sound identical but really, they could be brothers. And they left so early I didn't notice what they were wearing. Jeans, I think. Mike always wears them, it's a safe bet. They were in a red clapped-out old rust bucket car.' The officers exchange glances.

'You know registration?'

'I don't, but hang on.' I head into the kitchen to see if any of the waiters know. Men tend to remember these things better. Gino scrawls down Pablo's registration on the back of an old order, and I take it back through to the officers.

'This is the registration of the car your friends were in?' the eldest of the two officers, a greying man in his mid-forties, asks me. I nod dumbly, already fearing the worst. The officer talks into his walkie talkie for a few minutes, before turning back to me. My entire body tenses in anticipation.

'In that case Senorita, I will ask you to accompany us to the mortuary.'

I vomit into the nearest bin.

In my almost hysterical state, I am briefed about what to expect. The sympathetic female officer holds my shaking hand and tells me, as gently as she can, what happened. An eyewitness, there was just the one – around twenty-five others scarpered, not wanting any involvement in gunfire.

Gunfire!

'But I thought it was a car accident...'

The officer shakes her head slowly. In what appeared to be an unprovoked attack, Pablo's car had been showered in a hail of bullets before two men jumped into a van and took off. The witness was an elderly woman and couldn't give an accurate description of the men, other than they were definitely Spanish. Nor the van, other than it was blue. Her eyes weren't what they used to be. She had stayed at the scene because someone had to stand up for right and wrong around here. It was becoming ridiculous, people taking the law into their own hands. One of the men was seriously ill, having lost a lot of blood. The other was dead on arrival. From my description, they didn't know which was which, neither had any identification on them other than Pablo's license, which was in the glove compartment. Pablo would normally drive but, on occasion, if they stopped off for a pint, Mike would take over. He couldn't really deal with drinking in the day and working until the early hours. He preferred to stick to cokes. It really could be either one on the mortuary slab.

I'm clutching a paper bag in my trembling hands, either for the purpose of another panic attack or to vomit in, as the police woman escorts me to the door where I will find out which of my wonderful friends has gone. She opens the door and I see the sheet-covered perfectly still lumps and bumps of someone I love dearly. Neither is preferable. I know that sounds terribly sick, to even consider having a preference, I don't mean it the way it sounds. Mike, my smiley, happy Mike, wouldn't harm a fly. My best friend, I love him so much. Pablo, our funny, entertaining hulk of cuddles, our wannabe Scot, with his gorgeous family and adoring wife... I think of the day at the beach, Rosa slapping away Pablo's hands as he tries to hug her from behind. Her eyes and smile told the real truth, though. Grinning girlishly, her eyes seeking mine to show her pride, as if to say:

'Look, three kids and another on the way and still, he adores me.' I'd shaken my head and laughed, telling Pablo to get a room! I can't bear this. I cling to the doorframe as the policewoman gently holds onto my waist.

'Can't I please see the one in hospital? Rather than the one who died?' I plead with my eyes.

'Lucy, I know this is so hard for you, but you must identify your friend. Would you like Pablo's wife to have to do it? It would break her heart. Or do you want Michael's mama to have to fly from Scotland just to view her dead son? Please, be strong, for your friend.'

She's right. I swallow the bile rising in my throat and take a deep breath. I stumble towards the table. The officer holds me steady, mumbling comforting words in Spanish as we go. She places me gently at the edge of the table and I take a deep breath. She glances behind and nods. Strong arms reach around me and hold onto mine.

'Ready?' The woman officer smiles sympathetically. I give a tiny nod, and the cover is pulled back.

Chapter Twenty-Six

I slouch on my bed in my new room in Scotland. Mum has moved into Bert's house. I have Drew's old room, as he's moved in with Mary. Bert's promised to decorate it for me in a suitably girly style. He is currently trying to crack a smile onto my miserable face,

'Now Lucy, I was thinking of Victoria Plum or My Little Pony wallpaper, but I figure you're a bit old for that. So, I thought, how about Strawberry Shortcake?' I smile wanly.

'Bert that would be lovely, I did always like her.'

I watch Poopsy stretch out her back legs like a ballet dancer, warming up, and look back to see Bert, paint pot in hand, looking at me worriedly. His old brow furrowed in concern. Blink and you'd miss it though, and then he's back to his smiling self.

'Mum and I thought we'd take you out to the Brewhouse for tea. You fancy that?'

'Sure,' I attempt a smile. 'Thanks Bert, I really appreciate you taking me in like this. I mean, I'm not even your daughter, just some stray.'

'Don't talk nonsense!' He tuts. 'Always wanted girls, you know. And now I have two, with the added bonus of Joshy and Jessie.' I smile warmly at Bert. He's a good man. I've never seen Mum so happy. Well, she's not with me at the moment. I'm aware my weight has plummeted, but it's to be expected, so the doctor said. It'll come back on when I'm ready. Bert wanders downstairs and I hear him talk to Mum in hushed tones.

I sit for a moment, looking out of the window and watch a wisp of smoke curl out from a chimney, then reluctantly walk over to my laptop and open it up. Poopsy wanders over too and jumps onto my knees. She hasn't left me alone since I came home. Cats are intuitive that way, knowing when you need comfort. I click onto the restaurant's website. Best get this over with and tell our lovely past customers the sad news. They email regularly to say they view our blog and up-coming events. I've had a few emails asking what is going on. No updates for six weeks, we must be doing really well not to have found time to add new gossip. If only they knew. I click the familiar keys to add a new post. Taking a deep breath, I begin.

Hi all,
Sorry for the long hiatus. But at present I am back home in Scotland. I know you all regularly read our blog and I appreciate all the emails you send. It really is so good to hear how you're all getting on.
I'm so sad to be the bearer of bad news. I have come home to Scotland, because five weeks ago we sadly and very suddenly lost our wonderful friend…

'Lucy, are you nearly ready, sweetheart?' Mum shouts from the bottom of the stairs.
'OK, just a tick,' I reply, snapping closed the lid of my laptop. I'll have to finish it later. Another couple of hours won't fix anything that's happened. I slap on a bit of lip-gloss, Mum will only worry that I'm depressed otherwise. She watches me like a hawk for signs of not coping well. Be it, not eating, not showering or not applying make-up. It's a full-time job trying to appear like nothing is wrong. We go for a quick drink on the way to the restaurant. Mum and Bert exchange anxious looks. Mum keeps looking at her watch too. Maybe they've decided to invite the whole family along. I could do with a good lot of noise and laughter. Eventually, Bert takes out his mobile and calls Betty. How long will she be? Oh great, they are getting them all along. I did tell Mum from the start not to tell them to stay away. She said I'd suffered such a massive shock that everyone agreed that I needed time to recuperate. She had wanted to fly over with Bert to collect me, so I didn't

have to fly alone, but it seemed like such a horrendous waste of money to do that. As well as putting yet another two people I care about at risk, as I'm still not over the fear of flying. If anything, it's possibly a bit worse now. I see how someone can be laughing and joking, living and breathing one minute, then cruelly snatched away from you the next. And, of course, they were all right. For the first couple of weeks, I probably did need to have some space. I insisted on staying in Tenerife for a week after the horrible, heinous incident. I felt it was my duty to all concerned – and to see that my one remaining friend from our team was going to be all right. That done, I finally let the shock sink in. After the awful task of identification was over – and yet again throwing up in the nearest bin – I kicked into organising mode. I know it's common after bereavements – it's a distraction, I'm sure. Many people seem to cope perfectly well until after the funeral, then dissolve into helplessness.

I'm keen to get moving onto the Brewhouse. Drinking too much on an empty stomach is not a good idea. I haven't had a drink for five weeks; I've been too scared to. I can keep it together sober, but drunk, I think the grief would overwhelm me. That, and not eating, my weight has plummeted to unattractively skinny. A size zero, and not looking good. I'm weak as a kitten and feel breathless and panicky most of the time. I know I have to keep my strength up. So, tonight my family has decided it's time to move on. I like that, it gives me a sense of closure and peace. Much as they love to tease each other, not one of us would see a hair hurt on another's head. Fiercely tight knit, us lot. The door opens and in struts my sister's crew. Little Jess bounding as she walks up to me, hands behind her back. With a flourish, she produces a bunch of flowers with an Esso garage sticker on them. My sister rolls her eyes apologetically,
'Sorry, it was the only place open when she decided she

wanted to buy you some.'

'Jess, these are beautiful! Thank you, sweetie.' I take the drooping carnations from her. Some of the heads are missing; I can see them on the floor in the corner of the pub. She obviously caught them in the door on her way in. It endears her gesture all the more. I kiss her little brown head, which smells of Barbie perfume. Joshy's turn; he steps forward, chocolates this time.

'Cos Mum said you were too skinny and you're not allowed to be skinnier than her.'

Everyone laughs. I pull him onto my knee and give him a squeeze.

'I'm sorry your friend got shooted,' he says in a small voice, his big brown eyes full of concern. I kiss his soft cheek.

'Me too, Josh,' I whisper.

Bert's mobile rings, he smiles and answers.

'Yes, affirmative,' he says cryptically, and snaps it shut. 'Right you ugly bunch, drink up, our table's ready.'

The salty air is warm and balmy, with just the smallest hint of a sea breeze. It reminds me of happy childhood summer days, tearing along the sea front, Mary and I. Passing the paddling pool... passing the little train...passing the swings, leaving Mum and Gran dawdling and chatting behind. Feeling sick from running on a tummy full of ice cream but everything that's been bothering my young mind would disappear with the pound of plimsolls on tarmac. I feel that way tonight, but not sick, just excited. Like it's the start of something positive.

We walk into the restaurant and there they all are. Beaming, familiar faces, all talking at once, wandering towards me for a hug and a kiss. I'm handed a large glass of Pinot Grigio and ushered towards the table.

And it's then that I see him, crutches by his side, and the same old lopsided grin on his face – clouded by the occasional wince of pain – and tufty brown head that I know so well.

'Mike!'

I run towards him.

'No! Don't stand, I'll come to you.' I give him the biggest hug ever, and kiss his stubbly cheek. 'When did you get back? Why didn't you tell me you were coming home?'

'Sorry Luce, I wanted it to be a surprise. I flew back with Mum and Dad last night when the hospital finally let me go.'

'I'm sorry,' I smile apologetically. 'Your Mum and Dad sent me home, said I shouldn't be there on my own in case those idiots came back. I knew they were right. I wanted to stay to see you were OK though, and to stay with Rosa and the kids for a few days. And well, of course, to go to Pablo's funeral. Roberto said that he'll put some of his staff in to cover for us. He said he understands if we don't go back and not to worry about the lease.'

'Poor Pablo, he never did get his trip to Scotland,' Mike sighs, 'but Rosa brought the kids into hospital see me. She's so sad the new baby will never meet his father.' I glance over at Mary.

'It's sad when that happens, but I'm sure the older kids will have plenty of stories to tell, even if they are second hand from Rosa.' Mary smiles and nods knowingly.

Mike stays on in Arbroath for a few more days. Bert puts him up in the spare room. He's been so lucky. The doctor said it was amazing there wasn't more damage. A few inches up, and it could have been his spinal column; a few inches lower, his femoral artery. Mike said he'd never thought he'd be so glad to be shot in the arse. Pablo had apparently seen it coming, recognized the builders from his house and threw himself over Mike like a human shield. I felt awful for weeks. If we hadn't paid him so well, he wouldn't have been able to afford a bigger house; if he hadn't moved into the bigger house and had it renovated, he wouldn't have known the builders; if he hadn't met the builders, he wouldn't have threatened them and he wouldn't be dead now. Mike says I'll drive myself crazy like that. Rosa said the times with us were the happiest of all Pablo's working days. He was so proud to able to provide for his family. She certainly didn't blame us. How could we know? How strange that what you feel is the right path – the one that you think protects you most – may actually be the one to cause you harm. It's a lottery, a game of Russian roulette. Maybe it's best just to do what you want, when you want, so long as it doesn't hurt anyone. And don't be scared to love, to feel. Probably about time I take my own advice then.

Hi all,

Sorry for the long hiatus. But at present we are back home in Scotland. I know you all regularly read our blog and we appreciate all the emails you send. It really is so good to hear how you're all getting on.

I'm so sad to be the bearer of bad news. We have come home to Scotland because five weeks ago we sadly and very suddenly lost our wonderful friend Pablo in an unfortunate shooting incident. He was a loving and kind man, witty and a great friend to us. He is survived by his wife Rosa and their four gorgeous children – Marco, Marina, Sophia and new baby boy, Pablo junior. He will be always loved and sadly missed by all who knew him.

RIP our lovely Pablo.

We would like to give you some good news too. And for all the emails that will no doubt arrive after this – that's you, Wilma and John of Southall, Jean and Phil from Stockton and, actually, too many people to mention if we're being honest – let's hear one big chorus of:

"I told you so!"

Mike has decided that he's fed up of me being the Fairy Tale Princess destined to live Crappily ever after (a title for me which he pinched from my Uncle Robert on account of my unsuccessful love life). So anyway, I'll cut a long story short. Mike has asked me to marry him

– and I've said yes. We hope to see you all next summer (plenty of time to save up, so no excuses!) for our wedding. We will be back in Tenerife as soon as old 'Hop-Along' sitting here can walk properly again. I decided to stop pushing Mike away – he only keeps coming back. May as well marry the poor bugger and save his pride. Anyway, I've rambled long enough. Life is for living, enjoy.

Because I think I may finally be ready to embrace the possibility of living Happily Ever After!

Love, Lucy.

xxx

Louise Burness was born in 1971 and raised in the Scottish town of Arbroath. She spent several years living in Edinburgh and Fife, travelling around Australia and South East Asia and eight years living in West London. Louise has currently moved back home to be a full-time writer.

After many an entertaining conversation concerning Louise's latest love life disaster, her friends encouraged her to write her experiences down. What began as a humourous, cathartic exercise gained the approval of family and friends and 'Crappily Ever After' was born. The novel is therefore loosely based on truth and gives you some insight into the more dramatic relationships of her life so far. Louise has also written a second chick-lit, 'Ivy Eff,' and two children's books, 'Under the Sun,' and 'Rock upon a time.'

Printed in Great Britain
by Amazon.co.uk, Ltd.,
Marston Gate.